P. G. Wodehouse

Lord Emsworth
and Others

Penguin Books

PENGUIN BOOKS

Published by the Penguin Group
Penguin Books Ltd, 27 Wrights Lane, London W8 5TZ, England
Penguin Books USA Inc., 375 Hudson Street, New York, New York 10014, USA
Penguin Books Australia Ltd, Ringwood, Victoria, Australia
Penguin Books Canada Ltd, 10 Alcorn Avenue, Toronto, Ontario, Canada M4V 3B2
Penguin Books (NZ) Ltd, 182–190 Wairau Road, Auckland 10, New Zealand

Penguin Books Ltd, Registered Offices: Harmondsworth, Middlesex, England

First published in Great Britain by Herbert Jenkins 1937
Published in Penguin Books in the United States of America
by arrangement with Scott Meredith Literary Agency, Inc.
Published in Penguin Books 1966
20 19 18 17 16

Printed in England by Clays Ltd, St Ives plc
Set in Times Roman

PENGUIN BOOKS

LORD EMSWORTH AND OTHERS

P. G. Wodehouse was born in Guildford in 1881 and educated at Dulwich College. After working for the Hong Kong and Shangb Bank for two years, he left to earn his living as a journalist and storywriter, writing the 'By the Way' column in the old *Globe*. He also contributed a series of school stories the *Captain*, in one of which Psmith made his first appearance. Going to America before the First World War, he sold a serial to the *Saturday Evening Post*, and for the next twenty-five years almost all his books appeared first in this magazine. He was part author and writer of the lyrics of eighteen musical comedies, including *Kissing Time*. He married in 1914 and in 1955 took American citizenship. He wrote over ninety books, and his work has won worldwide acclaim, having been translated into many languages. *The Times* hailed him as a 'comic genius recognized in his lifetime as a classic and an old master of farce'.

P. G. Wodehouse said, 'I believe there are two ways of writing novels. One is mine, making a sort of musical comedy without music and ignoring real life altogether; the other is going right deep down into life and not caring a damn . . .' He was created a Knight of the British Empire in the New Year's Honours List in 1975. In a BBC interview he said that he had no ambition left now that he had been knighted and there was a waxwork of him in Madame Tussaud's. He died on St Valentine's Day in 1975 at the age of ninety-three.

Contents

1   The Crime Wave at Blandings   7

2   Buried Treasure   57

3   The Letter of the Law   77

4   Farewell to Legs   98

5   There's Always Golf   117

6   The Masked Troubadour   136

7   Ukridge and the Home from Home   159

8   The Come-back of Battling Billson   180

9   The Level Business Head   200

Chapter One
The Crime Wave at Blandings

The day on which Lawlessness reared its ugly head at Bland-ings Castle was one of singular beauty. The sun shone down from a sky of cornflower blue, and what one would really like would be to describe in leisurely detail the ancient battlements, the smooth green lawns, the rolling parkland, the majestic trees, the well-bred bees and the gentlemanly birds on which it shone.

But those who read thrillers are an impatient race. They chafe at scenic rhapsodies and want to get on to the rough stuff. When, they ask, did the dirty work start? Who were mixed up in it? Was there blood, and, if so, how much? And – most particularly – where was everybody and what was every-body doing at whatever time it was? The chronicler who wishes to grip must supply this information at the earliest possible moment.

The wave of crime, then, which was to rock one of Shrop-shire's stateliest homes to its foundations broke out towards the middle of a fine summer afternoon, and the persons in-volved in it were disposed as follows:

Clarence, ninth Earl of Emsworth, the castle's owner and overlord, was down in the potting-shed, in conference with Angus McAllister, his head gardener, on the subject of sweet peas.

His sister, Lady Constance, was strolling on the terrace with a swarthy young man in spectacles, whose name was Rupert Baxter and who had at one time been Lord Emsworth's private secretary.

Beach, the butler, was in a deck-chair outside the back prem-ises of the house, smoking a cigar and reading Chapter Sixteen of *The Man With The Missing Toe*.

George, Lord Emsworth's grandson, was prowling through

the shrubbery with the airgun which was his constant companion.

Jane, his lordship's niece, was in the summer-house by the lake.

And the sun shone serenely down – on, as we say, the lawns, the battlements, the trees, the bees, the best type of bird and the rolling parkland.

Presently Lord Emsworth left the potting-shed and started to wander towards the house. He had never felt happier. All day his mood had been one of perfect contentment and tranquillity, and for once in a way Angus McAllister had done nothing to disturb it. Too often, when you tried to reason with that human mule, he had a way of saying 'Mphm' and looking Scotch and then saying 'Grmph' and looking Scotch again, and after that just fingering his beard and looking Scotch without speaking, which was intensely irritating to a sensitive employer. But this afternoon Hollywood yes-men could have taken his correspondence course, and Lord Emsworth had none of that uneasy feeling, which usually came to him on these occasions, that the moment his back was turned his own sound, statesmanlike policies would be shelved and some sort of sweet pea New Deal put into practice as if he had never spoken a word.

He was humming as he approached the terrace. He had his programme all mapped out. For perhaps an hour, till the day had cooled off a little, he would read a Pig book in the library. After that he would go and take a sniff at a rose or two and possibly do a bit of snailing. These mild pleasures were all his simple soul demanded. He wanted nothing more. Just the quiet life, with nobody to fuss him.

And now that Baxter had left, he reflected buoyantly, nobody did fuss him. There had, he dimly recalled, been some sort of trouble a week or so back – something about some man his niece Jane wanted to marry and his sister Constance didn't want her to marry – but that had apparently all blown over. And even when the thing had been at its height, even when the air had been shrill with women's voices and Connie had kept popping out at him and saying 'Do *listen*, Clarence!' he had always been able to reflect that, though all this was pretty unpleasant, there was nevertheless a bright side. He had ceased to be the employer of Rupert Baxter.

There is a breed of granite-faced, strong-jawed business man to whom Lord Emsworth's attitude towards Rupert Baxter would have seemed frankly inexplicable. To these Titans a private secretary is simply a Hey-you, a Hi-there, a mere puppet to be ordered hither and thither at will. The trouble with Lord Emsworth was that it was he and not his secretary who had been the puppet. Their respective relations had always been those of a mild reigning monarch and the pushing young devil who has taken on the dictatorship. For years, until he had mercifully tendered his resignation to join an American named Jevons, Baxter had worried Lord Emsworth, bossed him, bustled him, had always been after him to do things and remember things and sign things. Never a moment's peace. Yes, it was certainly delightful to think that Baxter had departed for ever. His going had relieved this Garden of Eden of its one resident snake.

Still humming, Lord Emsworth reached the terrace. A moment later, the melody had died on his lips and he was rocking back on his heels as if he had received a solid punch on the nose.

'God bless my soul!' he ejaculated, shaken to the core.

His pince-nez, as always happened when he was emotionally stirred, had leaped from their moorings. He recovered them and put them on again, hoping feebly that the ghastly sight he had seen would prove to have been an optical illusion. But no. However much he blinked, he could not blink away the fact that the man over there talking to his sister Constance was Rupert Baxter in person. He stood gaping at him with a horror which would have been almost excessive if the other had returned from the tomb.

Lady Constance was smiling brightly, as women so often do when they are in the process of slipping something raw over on their nearest and dearest.

'Here is Mr Baxter, Clarence.'

'Ah,' said Lord Emsworth.

'He is touring England on his motor-bicycle, and finding himself in these parts, of course, he looked us up.'

'Ah,' said Lord Emsworth.

He spoke dully, for his soul was heavy with foreboding. It was all very well for Connie to say that Baxter was touring England, thus giving the idea that in about five minutes the man would leap on his motor-bicycle and dash off to some spot a hundred miles away. He knew his sister. She was plotting. Always ardently pro-Baxter, she was going to try to get Blandings Castle's leading incubus back into office again. Lord Emsworth would have been prepared to lay the odds on this in the most liberal spirit. So he said 'Ah.'

The monosyllable, taken in conjunction with the sagging of her brother's jaw and the glare of agony behind his pince-nez, caused Lady Constance's lips to tighten. A disciplinary light came into her fine eyes. She looked like a female lion-tamer about to assert her personality with one of the troupe.

'Clarence!' she said sharply. She turned to her companion. 'Would you excuse me for a moment, Mr Baxter. There is something I want to talk to Lord Emsworth about.'

She drew the pallid peer aside, and spoke with sharp rebuke. 'Just like a stuck pig!'

'Eh?' said Lord Emsworth. His mind had been wandering, as it so often did. The magic word brought it back. 'Pigs? What about pigs?'

'I was saying that you were looking like a stuck pig. You might at least have asked Mr Baxter how he was.'

'I could see how he was. What's he doing here?'

'I told you what he was doing here.'

'But how does he come to be touring England on motor-bicycles? I thought he was working for an American fellow named something or other.'

'He has left Mr Jevons.'

'What!'

'Yes. Mr Jevons had to return to America, and Mr Baxter did not want to leave England.'

Lord Emsworth reeled. Jevons had been his sheet-anchor. He had never met that genial Chicagoan, but he had always thought kindly and gratefully of him, as one does of some great doctor who has succeeded in isolating and confining a disease germ.

'You mean the chap's out of a job?' he cried aghast.

'Yes. And it could not have happened at a more fortunate time, because something has got to be done about George.'

'Who's George?'

'You have a grandson of that name,' explained Lady Constance with the sweet, frozen patience which she so often used when conversing with her brother. 'Your heir, Bosham, if you recollect, has two sons, James and George. George, the younger, is spending his summer holidays here. You may have noticed him about. A boy of twelve with auburn hair and freckles.'

'Oh, George? You mean George? Yes, I know George. He's my grandson. What about him?'

'He is completely out of hand. Only yesterday he broke another window with that airgun of his.'

'He needs a mother's care?' Lord Emsworth was vague, but he had an idea that that was the right thing to say.

'He needs a tutor's care, and I am glad to say that Mr Baxter has very kindly consented to accept the position.'

'What!'

'Yes. It is all settled. His things are at the Emsworth Arms, and I am sending down for them.'

Lord Emsworth sought feverishly for arguments which would quash this frightful scheme.

'But he can't be a tutor if he's galumphing all over England on a motor-bicycle.'

'I had not overlooked that point. He will stop galumphing over England on a motor-bicycle.'

'But –'

'It will be a wonderful solution of a problem which was becoming more difficult every day. Mr Baxter will keep George in order. He is so firm.'

She turned away, and Lord Emsworth resumed his progress towards the library.

It was a black moment for the ninth Earl. His worst fears had been realized. He knew just what all this meant. On one of his rare visits to London he had once heard an extraordinarily vivid phrase which had made a deep impression upon him. He had been taking his after-luncheon coffee at the Senior

Conservative Club and some fellows in an adjoining nest of armchairs had started a political discussion, and one of them had said about something or other that, mark his words, it was the 'thin end of the wedge'. He recognized what was happening now as the thin end of the wedge. From Baxter as a temporary tutor to Baxter as a permanent secretary would, he felt, be so short a step that the contemplation of it chilled him to the bone.

A short-sighted man whose pince-nez have gone astray at the very moment when vultures are gnawing at his bosom seldom guides his steps carefully. Anyone watching Lord Emsworth totter blindly across the terrace would have foreseen that he would shortly collide with something, the only point open to speculation being with what he would collide. This proved to be a small boy with ginger hair and freckles who emerged abruptly from the shrubbery carrying an airgun.

'Coo!' said the small boy. 'Sorry, grandpapa.'

Lord Emsworth recovered his pince-nez and, having adjusted them on the old spot, glared balefully.

'George! Why the dooce don't you look where you're going?'

'Sorry, grandpapa.'

'You might have injured me severely.'

'Sorry, grandpapa.'

'Be more careful another time.'

'Okay, big boy.'

'And don't call me "big boy".'

'Right ho, grandpapa. I say,' said George, shelving the topic, 'who's the bird talking to Aunt Connie?'

He pointed – a vulgarism which a good tutor would have corrected – and Lord Emsworth, following the finger, winced as his eye rested once more upon Rupert Baxter. The secretary – already Lord Emsworth had mentally abandoned the qualifying 'ex' – was gazing out over the rolling parkland, and it seemed to his lordship that his gaze was proprietorial. Rupert Baxter, flashing his spectacles over the grounds of Blandings Castle, wore – or so it appeared to Lord Emsworth – the smug air of some ruthless monarch of old surveying conquered territory.

'That is Mr Baxter,' he replied.

'Looks a bit of a blister,' said George critically.

The expression was new to Lord Emsworth, but he recognized it at once as the ideal description of Rupert Baxter. His heart warmed to the little fellow, and he might quite easily at this moment have given him sixpence.

'Do you think so?' he said lovingly.

'What's he doing here?'

Lord Emsworth felt a pang. It seemed brutal to dash the sunshine from the life of this admirable boy. Yet somebody had got to tell him.

'He is going to be your tutor.'

'Tutor?'

The word was a cry of agony forced from the depths of the boy's soul. A stunned sense that all the fundamental decencies of life were being outraged had swept over George. His voice was thick with emotion.

'Tutor?' he cried. '*Tew*-tor? Ter-YEWtor? In the middle of the summer holidays? What have I got to have a tutor for in the middle of the summer holidays? I do call this a bit off. I mean, in the middle of the summer holidays. Why do I want a tutor? I mean to say, in the middle of ...'

He would have spoken at greater length, for he had much to say on the subject, but at this point Lady Constance's voice, musical but imperious, interrupted his flow of speech.

'Gee-orge.'

'Coo! Right in the middle –'

'Come here, George. I want you to meet Mr Baxter.'

'Coo!' muttered the stricken child again and, frowning darkly, slouched across the terrace. Lord Emsworth proceeded to the library, a tender pity in his heart for this boy who by his crisp summing-up of Rupert Baxter had revealed himself so kindred a spirit. He knew just how George felt. It was not always easy to get anything into Lord Emsworth's head, but he had grasped the substance of his grandson's complaint unerringly. George, about to have a tutor in the middle of the summer holidays, did not want one.

Sighing a little, Lord Emsworth reached the library and found his book.

There were not many books which at a time like this could have diverted Lord Emsworth's mind from what weighed upon it, but this one did. It was Whiffle on *The Care Of The Pig* and, buried in its pages, he forgot everything. The chapter he was reading was that noble one about swill and bran-mash, and it took him completely out of the world, so much so that when some twenty minutes later the door suddenly burst open it was as if a bomb had been exploded under his nose. He dropped Whiffle and sat panting. Then, although his pince-nez had followed routine by flying off, he was able by some subtle instinct to sense that the intruder was his sister Constance, and an observation beginning with the words 'Good God, Connie!' had begun to leave his lips, when she cut him short.

'Clarence,' she said, and it was plain that her nervous system, like his, was much shaken, 'the most dreadful thing has happened!'

'Eh?'

'That man is here.'

'What man?'

'That man of Jane's. The man I told you about.'

'What man did you tell me about?'

Lady Constance seated herself. She would have preferred to have been able to do without tedious explanations, but long association with her brother had taught her that his was a memory that had to be refreshed. She embarked, accordingly, on these explanations, speaking wearily, like a schoolmistress to one of the duller members of her class.

'The man I told you about — certainly not less than a hundred times — was a man Jane met in the spring, when she went to stay with her friends the Leighs in Devonshire. She had a silly flirtation with him, which, of course, she insisted in magnifying into a great romance. She kept saying they were engaged. And he hasn't a penny. Nor prospects. Nor, so I gathered from Jane, a position.'

Lord Emsworth interrupted at this point to put a question.

'Who,' he asked courteously, 'is Jane?'

Lady Constance quivered a little.

'Oh, Clarence! Your niece Jane.'

'Oh, my *niece* Jane? Ah! Yes. Yes, of course. My niece Jane. Yes, of course, to be sure. My –'

'Clarence, please! For pity's sake! Do stop doddering and listen to me. For once in your life I want you to be firm.'

'Be what?'

'Firm. Put your foot down.'

'How do you mean?'

'About Jane. I had been hoping that she had got over this ridiculous infatuation – she has seemed perfectly happy and contented all this time – but no. Apparently they have been corresponding regularly, and now the man is here.'

'Here?'

'Yes.'

'Where?' asked Lord Emsworth, gazing in an interested manner about the room.

'He arrived last night and is staying in the village. I found out by the merest accident. I happened to ask George if he had seen Jane, because I wanted Mr Baxter to meet her, and he said he had met her going towards the lake. So I went down to the lake, and there I discovered her with a young man in a tweed coat and flannel knickerbockers. They were kissing one another in the summer-house.'

Lord Emsworth clicked his tongue.

'Ought to have been out in the sunshine,' he said, disapprovingly.

Lady Constance raised her foot quickly, but instead of kicking her brother on the shin merely tapped the carpet with it. Blood will tell.

'Jane was defiant. I think she must be off her head. She insisted that she was going to marry this man. And, as I say, not only has he not a penny, but he is apparently out of work.'

'What sort of work does he do?'

'I gather that he has been a land-agent on an estate in Devonshire.'

'It all comes back to me,' said Lord Emsworth. 'I remember now. This must be the man Jane was speaking to me about yesterday. Of course, yes. She asked me to give him Simmons's job. Simmons is retiring next month. Good fellow,' said Lord Emsworth sentimentally. 'Been here for years and years. I shall be sorry to lose him. Bless my soul, it won't seem like the same place without old Simmons. Still,' he said, brightening, for he was a man who could make the best of things, 'no doubt this new chap will turn out all right. Jane seems to think highly of him.'

Lady Constance had risen slowly from her chair. There was incredulous horror on her face.

'Clarence! You are not telling me that you have promised this man Simmons's place?'

'Eh? Yes, I have. Why not?'

'Why not! Do you realize that directly he gets it he will marry Jane?'

'Well, why shouldn't he? Very nice girl. Probably make him a good wife.'

Lady Constance struggled with her feelings for a space.

'Clarence,' she said, 'I am going out now to find Jane. I shall tell her that you have thought it over and changed your mind.'

'What about?'

'Giving this man Simmons's place.'

'But I haven't.'

'Yes, you have.'

And so, Lord Emsworth discovered as he met her eye, he had. It often happened that way after he and Connie had talked a thing over. But he was not pleased about it.

'But, Connie, dash it all –'

'We will not discuss it any more, Clarence.'

Her eye played upon him. Then she moved to the door and was gone.

Alone at last, Lord Emsworth took up his Whiffle on *The Care Of The Pig* in the hope that it might, as had happened before, bring calm to the troubled spirit. It did, and he was absorbed in it when the door opened once more.

His niece Jane stood on the threshold.

Lord Emsworth's niece was the third prettiest girl in Shropshire. In her general appearance she resembled a dewy rose, and it might have been thought that Lord Emsworth, who yielded to none in his appreciation of roses, would have felt his heart leap up at the sight of her.

This was not the case. His heart did leap, but not up. He was a man with certain definite views about roses. He preferred them without quite such tight lips and determined chins. And he did not like them to look at him as if he were something slimy and horrible which they had found under a flat stone.

The wretched man was now fully conscious of his position. Under the magic spell of Whiffle he had been able to thrust from his mind for a while the thought of what Jane was going to say when she heard the bad news; but now, as she started to advance slowly into the room in that sinister, purposeful way characteristic of so many of his female relations, he realized what he was in for, and his soul shrank into itself like a salted snail.

Jane, he could not but remember, was the daughter of his sister Charlotte, and many good judges considered Lady Charlotte a tougher egg even than Lady Constance, or her younger sister, Lady Julia. He still quivered at some of the things Charlotte had said to him in her time; and, eyeing Jane apprehensively, he saw no reason for supposing that she had not inherited quite a good deal of the maternal fire.

The girl came straight to the point. Her mother, Lord Emsworth recalled, had always done the same.

'I should like an explanation, Uncle Clarence.'

Lord Emsworth cleared his throat unhappily.

'Explanation, my dear?'

'Explanation was what I said.'

'Oh, explanation? Ah, yes. Er – what about?'

'You know jolly well what about. That agent job. Aunt Constance says you've changed your mind. Have you?'

'Er . . . Ah . . . Well . . .'

'Have you?'

'Ah . . . Well . . . Er . . .'

'Have you?'

'Well . . . Er . . . Ah . . . Yes.'

'Worm!' said Jane. 'Miserable, crawling, cringing, gelatine-backboned worm!'

Lord Emsworth, though he had been expecting something along these lines, quivered as if he had been harpooned.

'That,' he said, attempting a dignity which he was far from feeling, 'is not a very nice thing to say . . .'

'If you only knew the things I would like to say! I'm holding myself in. So you've changed your mind, have you? Ha! Does a sacred promise mean nothing to you, Uncle Clarence? Does a girl's whole life's happiness mean nothing to you? I never would have believed that you could have been such a blighter.'

'I am not a blighter.'

'Yes, you are. You're a life-blighter. You're trying to blight my life. Well, you aren't going to do it. Whatever happens, I mean to marry George.'

Lord Emsworth was genuinely surprised.

'Marry George? But Connie told me you were in love with this fellow you met in Devonshire.'

'His name is George Abercrombie.'

'Oh, ah?' said Lord Emsworth, enlightened. 'Bless my soul, I thought you meant my grandson, George, and it puzzled me. Because you couldn't marry him, of course. He's your brother or cousin or something. Besides, he's too young for you. What would George be? Ten? Eleven?'

He broke off. A reproachful look had hit him like a shell.

'Uncle Clarence!'

'My dear?'

'Is this a time for drivelling?'

'My dear!'

'Well, is it? Look in your heart and ask yourself. Here I am, with everybody spitting on their hands and dashing about trying to ruin my life's whole happiness, and instead of being kind and understanding and sympathetic you start talking rot about young George.'

'I was only saying –'

'I heard what you were saying, and it made me sick. You really must be the most callous man that ever lived. I can't understand you of all people behaving like this, Uncle Clarence. I always thought you were fond of me.'

'I am fond of you.'

'It doesn't look like it. Flinging yourself into this foul conspiracy to wreck my life.'

Lord Emsworth remembered a good one.

18

'I have your best interests at heart, my dear.'

It did not go very well. A distinct sheet of flame shot from the girl's eyes.

'What do you mean, my best interests? The way Aunt Constance talks, and the way you are backing her up, anyone would think that George was someone in a straw hat and a scarlet cummerbund that I'd picked up on the pier at Blackpool. The Abercrombies are one of the oldest families in Devonshire. They date back to the Conquest, and they practically ran the Crusades. When your ancestors were staying at home on the plea of war work of national importance and wangling jobs at the base, the Abercrombies were out fighting the Paynim.'

'I was at school with a boy named Abercrombie,' said Lord Emsworth musingly.

'I hope he kicked you. No, no, I don't mean that. I'm sorry. The one thing I'm trying to do is to keep this little talk free of — what's the word?'

Lord Emsworth said he did not know.

'Acrimony. I want to be calm and cool and sensible. Honestly, Uncle Clarence, you would love George. You'll be a sap if you give him the bird without seeing him. He's the most wonderful man on earth. He got into the last eight at Wimbledon this year.'

'Did he, indeed? Last eight what?'

'And there isn't anything he doesn't know about running an estate. The very first thing he said when he came into the park was that a lot of the timber wanted seeing to badly.'

'Blast his impertinence,' said Lord Emsworth warmly. 'My timber is in excellent condition.'

'Not if George says it isn't. George knows timber.'

'So do I know timber.'

'Not so well as George does. But never mind about that. Let's get back to this loathsome plot to ruin my life's whole happiness. Why can't you be a sport, Uncle Clarence, and stand up for me? Can't you understand what this means to me? Weren't you ever in love?'

'Certainly I was in love. Dozens of times. I'll tell you a very funny story —'

'I don't want to hear funny stories.'

'No, no. Quite. Exactly.'

'All I want is to hear you saying that you will give George Mr Simmons's job, so that we can get married.'

'But your aunt seems to feel so strongly –'

'I know what she feels strongly. She wants me to marry that ass Roegate.'

'Does she?'

'Yes, and I'm not going to. You can tell her from me that I wouldn't marry Bertie Roegate if he were the only man in the world –'

'There's a song of that name,' said Lord Emsworth, interested. 'They sang it during the War. No, it wasn't "man". It was "girl". If you were the only . . ." How did it go? Ah, yes. "If you were the only girl in the world and I was the only boy . . ." '

'Uncle Clarence!'

'My dear?'

'Please don't sing. You're not in the tap-room of the Emsworth Arms now.'

'I have never been in the tap-room of the Emsworth Arms.'

'Or at a smoking-concert. Really, you seem to have the most extraordinary idea of the sort of attitude that's fitting when you're talking to a girl whose life's happiness everybody is sprinting about trying to ruin. First you talk about young George, then you start trying to tell funny stories, and now you sing comic songs.'

'It wasn't a comic song.'

'It was, the way you sang it. Well?'

'Eh?'

'Have you decided what you are going to do about this?'

'About what?'

The girl was silent for a moment, during which moment she looked so like her mother that Lord Emsworth shuddered.

'Uncle Clarence,' she said in a low, trembling voice, 'you are not going to pretend that you don't know what we've been talking about all this time? Are you or are you not going to give George that job?'

'Well –'

'Well?'

'Well —'

'We can't stay here for ever, saying "Well" at one another. Are you or are you not?'

'My dear, I don't see how I can. Your aunt seems to feel so very strongly . . .'

He spoke mumbling, avoiding his companion's eye, and he had paused, searching for words, when from the drive outside there arose a sudden babble of noise. Raised voices were proceeding from the great open spaces. He recognized his sister Constance's penetrating soprano, and mingling with it his grandson George's treble 'Coo'. Competing with both, there came the throaty baritone of Rupert Baxter. Delighted with the opportunity of changing the subject, he hurried to the window.

'Bless my soul! What's all that?'

The battle, whatever it may have been about, had apparently rolled away in some unknown direction, for he could see nothing from the window but Rupert Baxter, who was smoking a cigarette in what seemed a rather overwrought manner. He turned back, and with infinite relief discovered that he was alone. His niece had disappeared. He took up Whiffle on *The Care Of The Pig* and had just started to savour once more the perfect prose of that chapter about swill and bran-mash, when the door opened. Jane was back. She stood on the threshold, eyeing her uncle coldly.

'Reading, Uncle Clarence?'

'Eh? Oh, ah, yes. I was just glancing at Whiffle on *The Care Of The Pig*!'

'So you actually have the heart to read at a time like this? Well, well! Do you ever read Western novels, Uncle Clarence?'

'Eh? Western novels? No. No, never.'

'I'm sorry. I was reading one the other day, and I hoped that you might be able to explain something that puzzled me. What one cowboy said to another cowboy.'

'Oh, yes?'

'This cowboy – the first cowboy – said to the other cowboy – the second cowboy – "Gol dern ye, Hank Spivis, for a sneaking, ornery, low-down, double-crossing, hornswoggling skunk." Can you tell me what a sneaking, ornery, low-down, double-cross-ing, hornswoggling skunk is, Uncle Clarence?'

'I'm afraid I can't, my dear.'

'I thought you might know.'

'No.'

'Oh.'

She passed from the room, and Lord Emsworth resumed his Whiffle.

But it was not long before the volume was resting on his knee while he stared before him with a sombre gaze. He was re-viewing the recent scene and wishing that he had come better out of it. He was a vague man, but not so vague as to be un-aware that he might have shown up in a more heroic light.

How long. he sat brooding, he could not have said. Some little time, undoubtedly, for the shadows on the terrace had, he observed as he glanced out of the window, lengthened quite a good deal since he had seen them last. He was about to rise and seek consolation from a ramble among the flowers in the garden below, when the door opened – it seemed to Lord Ems-worth, who was now feeling a little morbid, that that blasted door had never stopped opening since he had come to the lib-rary to be alone – and Beach, the butler, entered.

He was carrying an airgun in one hand and in the other a silver salver with a box of ammunition on it.

Beach was a man who invested all his actions with something of the impressiveness of a high priest conducting an intricate service at some romantic altar. It is not easy to be impressive when you are carrying an airgun in one hand and a silver salver with a box of ammunition on it in the other, but Beach man-aged it. Many butlers in such a position would have looked like sportsmen setting out for a day with the birds, but Beach still looked like a high priest. He advanced to the table at Lord Emsworth's side and laid his cargo upon it as if the gun and the box of ammunition had been a smoked offering and his lord-ship a tribal god.

Lord Emsworth eyed his faithful servitor sourly. His manner was that of a tribal god who considers the smoked offering not up to sample.

'What the devil's all this?'

'It is an airgun, m'lord.'

'I can see that, dash it. What are you bringing it here for?'

'Her ladyship instructed me to convey it to your lordship – I gathered for safe keeping, m'lord. The weapon was until recently the property of Master George.'

'Why the dooce are they taking his airgun away from the poor boy?' demanded Lord Emsworth hotly. Ever since the lad had called Rupert Baxter a blister he had been feeling a strong affection for his grandson.

'Her ladyship did not confide in me on that point, m'lord. I was merely instructed to convey the weapon to your lordship.'

At this moment, Lady Constance came sailing in to throw light on the mystery.

'Ah, I see Beach has brought it to you. I want you to lock that gun up somewhere, Clarence. George is not to be allowed to have it any more.'

'Why not?'

'Because he is not to be trusted with it. Do you know what happened? He shot Mr Baxter!'

'What!'

'Yes. Out on the drive just now. I noticed that the boy's manner was sullen when I introduced him to Mr Baxter, and said that he was going to be his tutor. He disappeared into the shrubbery, and just now, as Mr Baxter was standing on the drive, George shot him from behind a bush.'

'Good!' cried Lord Emsworth, then prudently added the word 'gracious'.

There was a pause. Lord Emsworth took up the gun and handled it curiously.

'Bang!' he said, pointing it at a bust of Aristotle which stood on a bracket by the book-shelves.

'Please don't wave the thing about like that, Clarence. It may be loaded.'

'Not if George has just shot Baxter with it. No,' said Lord Emsworth, pulling the trigger, 'it's not loaded.' He mused awhile. An odd, nostalgic feeling was creeping over him. Far-off memories of his boyhood had begun to stir within him. 'Bless my soul,' he said. 'I haven't had one of these things in my hand since I was a child. Did you ever have one of these things, Beach?'

'Yes, m'lord, when a small lad.'

'Bless my soul, I remember my sister Julia borrowing mine to shoot her governess. You remember Julia shooting the governess, Connie?'

'Don't be absurd, Clarence.'

'It's not absurd. She did shoot her. Fortunately women wore bustles in those days. Beach, don't you remember my sister Julia shooting the governess?'

'The incident would, no doubt, have occurred before my arrival at the castle, m'lord.'

'That will do, Beach,' said Lady Constance. 'I do wish, Clarence,' she continued as the door closed, 'that you would not say that sort of thing in front of Beach.'

'Julia did shoot the governess.'

'If she did, there is no need to make your butler a confidant.'

'Now, what was that governess's name? I have an idea it began with –'

'Never mind what her name was or what it began with. Tell me about Jane. I saw her coming out of the library. Had you been speaking to her?'

'Yes. Oh, yes. I spoke to her.'

'I hope you were firm.'

'Oh, very firm. I said "Jane . . ." But listen, Connie, damn it, aren't we being a little hard on the girl? One doesn't want to ruin her whole life's happiness, dash it.'

'I knew she would get round you. But you are not to give way an inch.'

'But this fellow seems to be a most suitable fellow. One of the Abercrombies and all that. Did well in the Crusades.'

'I am not going to have my niece throwing herself away on a man without a penny.'

'She isn't going to marry Roegate, you know. Nothing will induce her. She said she wouldn't marry Roegate if she were the only girl in the world and he was the only boy.'

'I don't care what she said. And I don't want to discuss the matter any longer. I am now going to send George in, for you to give him a good talking-to.'

'I haven't time.'

'You have time.'

'I haven't. I'm going to look at my flowers.'

'You are not. You are going to talk to George. I want you to make him see quite clearly what a wicked thing he has done. Mr Baxter was furious.'

'It all comes back to me,' cried Lord Emsworth, 'Mapleton!'

'What *are* you talking about?'

'Her name was Mapleton. Julia's governess.'

'Do stop about Julia's governess. Will you talk to George?'

'Oh, all right, all right.'

'Good. I'll go and send him to you.'

And presently George entered. For a boy who had just stained the escutcheon of a proud family by shooting tutors with airguns, he seemed remarkably cheerful. His manner was that of one getting together with an old crony for a cosy chat.

'Hullo, grandpapa,' he said breezily.

'Hullo, my boy,' replied Lord Emsworth, with equal affability.

'Aunt Connie said you wanted to see me.'

'Eh? Ah! Oh! Yes.' Lord Emsworth pulled himself together. 'Yes, that's right. Yes, to be sure. Certainly I want to see you. What's all this, my boy, eh? Eh, what? What's all this?'

'What's all what, grandpapa?'

'Shooting people and all that sort of thing. Shooting Baxter and all that sort of thing. Mustn't do that, you know. Can't have that. It's very wrong and – er – very dangerous to shoot at people with a dashed great gun. Don't you know that, hey? Might put their eye out, dash it.'

'Oh, I couldn't have hit him in the eye, grandpapa. His back was turned and he was bending over, tying his shoelace.'

Lord Emsworth started.

'What! Did you get Baxter in the seat of the trousers?'

'Yes, grandpapa.'

'Ha, ha ... I mean, disgraceful ... I – er – I expect he jumped?'

'Oh, yes, grandpapa. He jumped like billy-o.'

'Did he, indeed? How this reminds me of Julia's governess.

Your Aunt Julia once shot her governess under precisely similar conditions. She was tying her shoelace.'

'Coo! Did *she* jump?'

'She certainly did, my boy.'

'Ha, ha!'

'Ha, ha!'

'Ha, ha!'

'Ha, h – . . . Ah . . . Er – well, just so,' said Lord Emsworth, a belated doubt assailing him as to whether this was quite the tone. "Well, George, I shall of course impound this – er – instrument.'

'Right ho, grandpapa,' said George, with the easy amiability of a boy conscious of having two catapults in his drawer upstairs.

'Can't have you going about the place shooting people.'

'Okay, Chief.'

Lord Emsworth fondled the gun. That nostalgic feeling was growing.

'Do you know, young man, I used to have one of these things when I was a boy.'

'Coo! Were guns invented then?'

'Yes, I had one when I was your age.'

'Ever hit anything, grandpapa?'

Lord Emsworth drew himself up a little haughtily.

'Certainly I did. I hit all sorts of things. Rats and things. I had a very accurate aim. But now I wouldn't even know how to load the dashed affair.'

'This is how you load it, grandpapa. You open it like this and shove the slug in here and snap it together again like that and there you are.'

'Indeed? Really? I see. Yes. Yes, of course, I remember now.'

'You can't kill anything much with it,' said George, with a wistfulness which betrayed an aspiration to higher things. 'Still, it's awfully useful for tickling up cows.'

'And Baxter.'

'Yes.'

'Ha, ha!'

'Ha, ha!'

26

Once more, Lord Emsworth forced himself to concentrate on the right tone.

'We mustn't laugh about it, my boy. It's no joking matter. It's very wrong to shoot Mr Baxter.'

'But he's a blister.'

'He is a blister,' agreed Lord Emsworth, always fair-minded. 'Nevertheless. . . . Remember, he is your tutor.'

'Well, I don't see why I've got to have a tutor right in the middle of the summer holidays. I sweat like the dickens all through the term at school,' said George, his voice vibrant with self-pity, 'and then plumb spank in the middle of the holidays they slosh a tutor on me. I call it a bit thick.'

Lord Emsworth might have told the little fellow that thicker things than that were going on in Blandings Castle, but he refrained. He dismissed him with a kindly, sympathetic smile and resumed his fondling of the airgun.

Like so many men advancing into the sere and yellow of life, Lord Emsworth had an eccentric memory. It was not to be trusted an inch as far as the events of yesterday or the day before were concerned. Even in the small matter of assisting him to find a hat which he had laid down somewhere five minutes ago it was nearly always useless. But by way of compensation for this it was a perfect encyclopedia on the remote past. It rendered his boyhood an open book to him.

Lord Emsworth mused on his boyhood. Happy days, happy days. He could recall the exact uncle who had given him the weapon, so similar to this one, with which Julia had shot her governess. He could recall brave, windswept mornings when he had gone prowling through the stable yard in the hope of getting a rat – and many a fine head had he secured. Odd that the passage of time should remove the desire to go and pop at things with an airgun. . . .

Or did it?

With a curious thrill that set his pince-nez rocking gently on his nose, Lord Emsworth suddenly became aware that it did not. All that the passage of time did was to remove the desire to pop temporarily – say for forty years or so. Dormant for a short while – we'll call it fifty years – that desire, he perceived, still lurked unquenched. Little by little it began to stir within him now. Slowly but surely, as he sat there fondling the gun, he was once more becoming a potential popper.

At this point, the gun suddenly went off and broke the bust of Aristotle.

It was enough. The old killer instinct had awakened. Reloading with the swift efficiency of some hunter of the woods, Lord Emsworth went to the window. He was a little uncertain as to what he intended to do when he got there, except that he had a clear determination to loose off at something. There flitted into his mind what his grandson George had said about tickling up cows, and this served to some extent to crystallize his aims. True, cows were not plentiful on the terrace of Blandings Castle. Still, one might have wandered there. You never knew with cows.

There were no cows. Only Rupert Baxter. The ex-secretary was in the act of throwing away a cigarette.

Most men are careless in the matter of throwing away cigarettes. The world is their ashtray. But Rupert Baxter had a tidy soul. He allowed the thing to fall to the ground like any ordinary young man, it is true, but immediately he had done so his better self awakened. He stooped to pick up the object that disfigured the smooth flagged stones, and the invitation of that beckoning trousers' seat would have been too powerful for a stronger man than Lord Emsworth to resist.

He pulled the trigger, and Rupert Baxter sprang into the air with a sharp cry. Lord Emsworth reseated himself and took up Whiffle on *The Care Of The Pig*.

Everyone is interested nowadays in the psychology of the criminal. The chronicler, therefore, feels that he runs no risk of losing his grip on the reader if he pauses at this point to examine and analyse the workings of Lord Emsworth's mind after the perpetration of the black act which has just been recorded.

At first, then, all that he felt as he sat turning the pages of his Whiffle was a sort of soft warm glow, a kind of tremulous joy such as he might have experienced if he had just been receiving the thanks of the nation for some great public service.

It was not merely the fact that he had caused his late employee to skip like the high hills that induced this glow. What pleased him so particularly was that it had been such a magnificent shot. He was a sensitive man, and though in his conversation with his grandson George he had tried to wear the mask, he had not been able completely to hide his annoyance at the boy's careless assumption that in his airgun days he had been an indifferent marksman.

'Did you ever hit anything, grandpapa?' Boys say these things with no wish to wound, but nevertheless they pierce the armour. 'Did you ever hit anything, grandpapa?' forsooth! He would have liked to see George stop putting finger to trigger for forty-seven years and then, first crack out of the box, pick off a medium-sized secretary at a distance like that! In rather a bad light, too.

But after he had sat for a while, silently glowing, his mood underwent a change. A gunman's complacency after getting his man can never remain for long an unmixed complacency. Sooner or later there creeps in the thought of Retribution. It did with Lord Emsworth. Quite suddenly, whispering in his ear, he heard the voice of Conscience say:

'What if your sister Constance learns of this?'

A moment before this voice spoke, Lord Emsworth had been smirking. He now congealed, and the smile passed from his lips like breath off a razor blade, to be succeeded by a tense look of anxiety and alarm.

Nor was this alarm unjustified. When he reflected how scathing and terrible his sister Constance could be when he committed even so venial a misdemeanour as coming down to dinner with a brass paper-fastener in his shirt front instead of the more conventional stud, his imagination boggled at the thought of what she would do in a case like this. He was appalled. Whiffle on *The Care Of The Pig* fell from his nerveless hand, and he sat looking like a dying duck. And Lady Constance, who now entered, noted the expression and was curious as to its cause.

'What is the matter, Clarence?'

'Matter?'

'Why are you looking like a dying duck?'

'I am not looking like a dying duck,' retorted Lord Emsworth with what spirit he could muster.

'Well,' said Lady Constance, waiving the point, 'have you spoken to George?'

'Certainly. Yes, of course I've spoken to George. He was in here just now and I – er – spoke to him.'

'What did you say?'

'I said' – Lord Emsworth wanted to make this very clear – 'I said that I wouldn't even know how to load one of those things.'

'Didn't you give him a good talking-to?'

'Of course I did. A very good talking-to. I said "Er – George, you know how to load those things and I don't, but that's no reason why you should go about shooting Baxter." '

'Was that all you said?'

'No. That was just how I began. I –'

Lord Emsworth paused. He could not have finished the sentence if large rewards had been offered to him to do so. For, as he spoke, Rupert Baxter appeared in the doorway, and he shrank back in his chair like some Big Shot cornered by G-men.

The secretary came forward limping slightly. His eyes behind their spectacles were wild and his manner emotional. Lady Constance gazed at him wonderingly.

'Is something the matter, Mr Baxter?'

'Matter?' Rupert Baxter's voice was taut and he quivered in every limb. He had lost his customary suavity and was plainly in no frame of mind to mince his words. 'Matter? Do you know what has happened? That infernal boy has shot me *again*!'

'What!'

'Only a few minutes ago. Out on the terrace.'

Lord Emsworth shook off his palsy.

'I expect you imagined it,' he said.

'Imagined it!' Rupert Baxter shook from spectacles to shoes. 'I tell you I was on the terrace, stooping to pick up my cigarette, when something hit me on the ... something hit me.'

'Probably a wasp,' said Lord Emsworth. 'They are very plentiful this year. I wonder,' he said chattily, 'if either of you are aware that wasps serve a very useful purpose. They keep down the leather-jackets, which, as you know, inflict serious injury upon –'

Lady Constance's concern became mixed with perplexity.

'But it could not have been George, Mr Baxter. The moment you told me of what he had done, I confiscated his airgun. Look, there it is on the table now.'

'Right there on the table,' said Lord Emsworth, pointing helpfully. 'If you come over here, you can see it clearly. Must have been a wasp.'

'You have not left the room, Clarence?'

'No. Been here all the time.'

'Then it would have been impossible for George to have shot you, Mr Baxter.'

'Quite,' said Lord Emsworth. 'A wasp, undoubtedly. Unless, as I say, you imagined the whole thing.'

The secretary stiffened.

'I am not subject to hallucinations, Lord Emsworth.'

'But you are, my dear fellow. I expect it comes from exerting your brain too much. You're always getting them.'

'Clarence!'

'Well, he is. You know that as well as I do. Look at that time he went grubbing about in a lot of flower-pots because he thought you had put your necklace there.'

'I did not –'

'You did, my dear fellow. I dare say you've forgotten it, but you did. And then, for some reason best known to yourself, you threw the flower-pots at me through my bedroom window.'

Baxter turned to Lady Constance, flushing darkly. The episode to which his former employer had alluded was one of which he never cared to be reminded.

'Lord Emsworth is referring to the occasion when your diamond necklace was stolen, Lady Constance. I was led to believe that the thief had hidden it in a flower-pot.'

'Of course, Mr Baxter.'

'Well, have it your own way,' said Lord Emsworth agreeably. 'But bless my soul, I shall never forget waking up and finding all those flower-pots pouring in through the window and then looking out and seeing Baxter on the lawn in lemon-coloured pyjamas with a wild glare in his –'

'Clarence!'

'Oh, all right. I merely mentioned it. Hallucinations – he gets them all the time,' he said stoutly, though in an undertone.

Lady Constance was cooing to the secretary like a mother to her child.

'It really is impossible that George should have done this, Mr Baxter. The gun has never left this –'

She broke off. Her handsome face seemed to turn suddenly to stone. When she spoke again the coo had gone out of her voice and it had become metallic.

'Clarence!'

'My dear?'

Lady Constance drew in her breath sharply.

'Mr Baxter, I wonder if you would mind leaving us for a moment. I wish to speak to Lord Emsworth.'

The closing of the door was followed by a silence, followed in its turn by an odd, whining noise like gas escaping from a pipe. It was Lord Emsworth trying to hum carelessly.

'Clarence!'

'Yes? Yes, my dear?'

The stoniness of Lady Constance's expression had become more marked with each succeeding moment. What had caused it in the first place was the recollection, coming to her like a flash, that when she had entered this room she had found her brother looking like a dying duck. Honest men, she felt, do not look like dying ducks. The only man whom an impartial observer could possibly mistake for one of these birds *in extremis* is the man with crime upon his soul.

'Clarence, was it you who shot Mr Baxter?'

Fortunately there had been that in her manner which led Lord Emsworth to expect the question. He was ready for it.

'Me? Who, me? Shoot Baxter? What the dooce would I want to shoot Baxter for?'

'We can go into your motives later. What I am asking you now is – Did you?'

'Of course I didn't.'

'The gun has not left the room.'

'Shoot Baxter, indeed! Never heard anything so dashed absurd in my life.'

32

'And you have been here all the time.'

'Well, what of it? Suppose I have? Suppose I had wanted to shoot Baxter? Suppose every fibre in my being had egged me on, dash it, to shoot the feller? How could I have done it, not even knowing how to load the contrivance?'

'You used to know how to load an airgun.'

'I used to know a lot of things.'

'It's quite easy to load an airgum. I could do it myself.'

'Well, I didn't.'

'Then how do you account for the fact that Mr Baxter was shot by an airgun which had never left the room you were in?'

Lord Emsworth raised pleading hands to heaven.

'How do you know he was shot with this airgun? God bless my soul, the way women jump to conclusions is enough to . . . How do you know there wasn't another airgun? How do you know the place isn't bristling with airguns? How do you know Beach hasn't an airgun? Or anybody?'

'I scarcely imagine that Beach would shoot Mr Baxter.'

'How do you know he wouldn't? He used to have an airgun when he was a small lad. He said so. I'd watch the man closely.'

'Please don't be ridiculous, Clarence.'

'I'm not being half as ridiculous as you are. Saying I shoot people with airguns. Why should I shoot people with airguns? And how do you suppose I could have potted Baxter at that distance?'

'What distance?'

'He was standing on the terrace, wasn't he? He specifically stated that he was standing on the terrace. And I was up here. It would take a most expert marksman to pot the fellow at a distance like that. Who do you think I am? One of those chaps who shoot apples off their son's heads?'

The reasoning was undeniably specious. It shook Lady Constance. She frowned undecidedly.

'Well, it's very strange that Mr Baxter should be so convinced that he was shot.'

'Nothing strange about it at all. There wouldn't be anything strange if Baxter was convinced that he was a turnip and had been bitten by a white rabbit with pink eyes. You know

33

perfectly well, though you won't admit it, that the fellow's a raving lunatic.'

'Clarence!'

'It's no good saying "Clarence". The fellow's potty to the core, and always has been. Haven't I seen him on the lawn at five o'clock in the morning in lemon-coloured pyjamas, throwing flower-pots in at my window? Pooh! Obviously, the whole thing is the outcome of the man's diseased imagination. Shot, indeed! Never heard such nonsense. And now,' said Lord Emsworth, rising firmly, 'I'm going out to have a look at my roses. I came to this room to enjoy a little quiet reading and meditation, and ever since I got here there's been a constant stream of people in and out, telling me they're going to marry men named Abercrombie and saying they've been shot and saying I shot them and so on and so forth. . . . Bless my soul, one might as well try to read and meditate in the middle of Piccadilly Circus. Tchah!' said Lord Emsworth, who had now got near enough to the door to feel safe in uttering this unpleasant exclamation. 'Tchah!' he said, and adding 'Pah!' for good measure made a quick exit.

But even now his troubled spirit was not to know peace. To reach the great outdoors at Blandings Castle, if you start from the library and come down the main staircase, you have to pass through the hall. To the left of this hall there is a small writing-room. And outside this writing-room Lord Emsworth's niece Jane was standing.

'Yoo-hoo,' she cried. 'Uncle Clarence.'

Lord Emsworth was in no mood for yoo-hooing nieces. George Abercrombie might enjoy chatting with this girl. So might Herbert, Lord Roegate. But he wanted solitude. In the course of the afternoon he had had so much female society thrust upon him that if Helen of Troy had appeared in the doorway of the writing-room and yoo-hooed at him, he would merely have accelerated his pace.

He accelerated it now.

'Can't stop, my dear, can't stop.'

'Oh, yes you can, old Sure-shot,' said Jane, and Lord Emsworth found that he could. He stopped so abruptly that he nearly dislocated his spine. His jaw had fallen and his pince-nez were dancing on their string like leaves in the wind.

'Two-Gun Thomas, the Marksman of the Prairie – He never misses. Kindly step this way, Uncle Clarence,' said Jane, 'I would like a word with you.'

Lord Emsworth stepped that way. He followed the girl into the writing-room and closed the door carefully behind him.

'You – you didn't see me?' he quavered.

'I certainly did see you,' said Jane. 'I was an interested eye-witness of the whole thing from start to finish.'

Lord Emsworth tottered to a chair and sank into it, staring glassily at his niece. Any Chicago business man of the modern school would have understood what he was feeling and would have sympathized with him.

The thing that poisons life for gunmen and sometimes makes them wonder moodily if it is worthwhile going on is this tendency of the outside public to butt in at inconvenient moments. Whenever you settle some business dispute with a commercial competitor by means of your sub-machine gun, it always turns out that there was some officious witness passing at the time, and there you are, with a new problem confronting you.

And Lord Emsworth was in worse case than his spiritual brother of Chicago would have been, for the latter could always have solved his perplexities by rubbing out the witness. To him this melancholy pleasure was denied. A prominent Shropshire landowner, with a position to keep up in the county, cannot rub out his nieces. All he can do, when they reveal that they have seen him wallowing in crime, is to stare glassily at them.

'I had a front seat for the entire performance,' proceeded Jane. 'When I left you, I went into the shrubbery to cry my eyes out because of your frightful cruelty and inhumanity. And while I was crying my eyes out, I suddenly saw you creep to the window of the library with a hideous look of low cunning on your face and young George's airgun in your hand. And I was just wondering if I couldn't find a stone and bung it at you, because it seemed to me that something along those lines was what you had been asking for from the start, when you raised the gun and I saw that you were taking aim. The next moment there was a shot, a cry, and Baxter weltering in his blood on the terrace. And as I stood there, a thought floated into my mind. It was – What will Aunt Constance have to say about this when I tell her?'

Lord Emsworth emitted a low, gargling sound, like the death rattle of that dying duck to which his sister had compared him.

'You – you aren't going to tell her?'

'Why not?'

An ague-like convulsion shook Lord Emsworth.

'I implore you not to tell her, my dear. You know what she's like. I should never hear the end of it.'

'She would give you the devil, you think?'

'I do.'

'So do I. And you thoroughly deserve it.'

'My dear!'

'Well, don't you? Look at the way you've been behaving. Working like a beaver to ruin my life's happiness.'

'I don't want to ruin your life's happiness.'

'You don't? Then sit down at this desk and dash off a short letter to George, giving him that job.'

'But –'

'What did you say?'

'I only said, "But –"'

'Don't say it again. What I want from you, Uncle Clarence, is prompt and cheerful service. Are you ready? "Dear Mr Abercrombie . . ."'

'I don't know how to spell it,' said Lord Emsworth, with the air of a man who has found a way out satisfactory to all parties.

'I'll attend to the spelling. A-b, ab; e-r, er; c-r-o-m, crom; b-i-e, bie. The whole constituting the word "Abercrombie", which is the name of the man I love. Got it?'

'Yes,' said Lord Emsworth sepulchrally. 'I've got it.'

'Then carry on. "Dear Mr Abercrombie. Pursuant" – one p, two u's – spread 'em about a bit, an r and s, and an ant – "Pursuant on our recent conversation –"'

'But I've never spoken to the man in my life.'

'It doesn't matter. It's just a form. "Pursuant on our recent conversation, I have much pleasure in offering you the post of land-agent at Blandings Castle, and shall be glad if you will take up your duties immediately. Yours faithfully, Emsworth." E-m-s-w-o-r-t-h.'

Jane took the letter, pressed it lovingly on the blotting-pad and placed it in the recesses of her costume. 'Fine,' she said. 'That's that. Thanks awfully, Uncle Clarence. This has squared you nicely for your recent foul behaviour in trying to ruin my life's happiness. You made a rocky start, but you've come through magnificently at the finish.'

Kissing him affectionately, she passed from the room, and Lord Emsworth, slumped in his chair, tried not to look at the vision of his sister Constance which was rising before his eyes. What Connie was going to say when she learned that in defiance of her direct commands he had given this young man . . .

He mused on Lady Constance, and wondered if there were any other men in the world so sister-pecked as he. It was weak of him, he knew, to curl up into an apologetic ball when assailed by a mere sister. Most men reserved such craven conduct for their wives. But it had always been so, right back to those boyhood days which he remembered so well. And too late to alter it now, he supposed.

The only consolation he was able to enjoy in this dark hour was the reflection that, though things were bad, they were unquestionably less bad than they might have been. At the least, his fearful secret was safe. That rash moment of recovered boyhood would never now be brought up against him. Connie would never know whose hand it was that had pulled the fatal trigger. She might suspect, but she could never know. Nor could Baxter ever know. Baxter would grow into an old, white-haired, spectacled pantaloon, and always this thing would remain an insoluble mystery to him.

Dashed lucky, felt Lord Emsworth, that the fellow had not been listening at the door during the recent conversation. . . .

It was at this moment that a sound behind him caused him to turn and, having turned, to spring from his chair with a convulsive leap that nearly injured him internally. Over the sill of the open window, like those of a corpse emerging from the tomb to confront its murderer, the head and shoulders of Rupert Baxter were slowly rising. The evening sun fell upon his spectacles, and they seemed to Lord Emsworth to gleam like the eyes of a dragon.

Rupert Baxter had not been listening at the door. There had been no necessity for him to do so. Immediately outside the writing-room window at Blandings Castle there stands a rustic garden seat, and on this he had been sitting from beginning to end of the interview which has just been recorded. If he had been actually in the room, he might have heard a little better, but not much.

When two men stand face to face, one of whom has recently shot the other with an airgun and the second of whom has just discovered who it was that did it, it is rarely that conversation flows briskly from the start. One senses a certain awkwardness – what the French call *gêne*. In the first half-minute of this encounter the only thing that happened in a vocal way was that Lord Emsworth cleared his throat, immediately afterwards becoming silent again. And it is possible that his silence might have prolonged itself for some considerable time, had not Baxter made a movement as if about to withdraw. All this while he had been staring at his former employer, his face an open book in which it was easy for the least discerning eye to read a number of disconcerting emotions. He now took a step backwards, and Lord Emsworth's asphasia left him.

'Baxter!'

There was urgent appeal in the ninth Earl's voice. It was not often that he wanted Rupert Baxter to stop and talk to him, but he was most earnestly desirous of detaining him now. He wished to soothe, to apologize, to explain. He was even prepared, should it be necessary, to offer the man his old post of private secretary as the price of his silence.

'Baxter! My dear fellow!'

A high tenor voice, raised almost to A in Alt by agony of soul, has a compelling quality which it is difficult even for a man in Rupert Baxter's mental condition to resist. Rupert Baxter had not intended to halt his backward movement, but he did so, and Lord Emsworth, reaching the window and thrusting his head out, was relieved to see that he was still within range of the honeyed word.

'Er – Baxter,' he said, 'could you spare me a moment?'

The secretary's spectacles flashed coldly.

'You wish to speak to me, Lord Emsworth?'

'That's exactly it,' assented his lordship, as if he thought it a very happy way of putting the thing. 'Yes, I wish to speak to you.' He paused, and cleared his throat again. 'Tell me, Baxter – tell me, my dear fellow – were you – er – were you sitting on that seat just now?'

'I was.'

'Did you, by any chance, overhear my niece and myself talking?'

'I did.'

'Then I expect – I fancy – perhaps – possibly – no doubt you were surprised at what you heard?'

'I was astounded,' said Rupert Baxter, who was not going to be fobbed off with any weak verbs at a moment like this.

Lord Emsworth cleared his throat for the third time.

'I want to tell you all about that,' he said.

'Oh?' said Rupert Baxter.

'Yes. I – ah – welcome this opportunity of telling you all about it,' said Lord Emsworth, though with less pleasure in his voice than might have been expected from a man welcoming an opportunity of telling somebody all about something. 'I fancy that my niece's remarks may – er – possibly have misled you.'

'Not at all.'

'They may have put you on the wrong track.'

'On the contrary.'

'But, if I remember correctly, she gave the impression – by what she said – my niece gave the impression by what she said – anybody overhearing what my niece said would have received the impression that I took deliberate aim at you with the gun.'

'Precisely.'

'She was quite mistaken,' said Lord Emsworth warmly. 'She has got hold of the wrong end of the stick completely. Girls say such dashed silly things . . . cause a lot of trouble . . . upset people. They ought to be more careful. What actually happened, my dear fellow, was that I was glancing out of the library window . . . with the gun in my hand . . . and without knowing it I must have placed my finger on the trigger . . . for suddenly . . . without the slightest warning . . . you could have knocked me down with a feather . . . the dashed thing went off. By accident.'

'Indeed?'

'Purely by accident. I should not like you to think that I was aiming at you.'

'Indeed?'

'And I should not like you to tell – er – anybody about the unfortunate occurrence in a way that would give her . . . I mean them . . . the impression that I aimed at you.'

'Indeed?'

Lord Emsworth could not persuade himself that his companion's manner was encouraging. He had a feeling that he was not making headway.

'That's how it was,' he said, after a pause.

'I see.'

'Pure accident. Nobody more surprised than myself.'

'I see.'

So did Lord Emsworth. He saw that the time had come to play his last card. It was no moment for shrinking back and counting the cost. He must proceed to that last fearful extremity which he had contemplated.

'Tell me, Baxter,' he said, 'are you doing anything just now, Baxter?'

'Yes,' replied the other, with no trace of hesitation. 'I am going to look for Lady Constance.'

A convulsive gulp prevented Lord Emsworth from speaking for an instant.

'I mean,' he quavered, when the spasm had spent itself, 'I gathered from my sister that you were at liberty at the moment – that you had left that fellow what's-his-name – the American fellow – and I was hoping, my dear Baxter,' said Lord Emsworth, speaking thickly, as if the words choked him, 'that I might be able to persuade you to take up – to resume – in fact, I was going to ask you if you would care to become my secretary again.'

He paused and, reaching for his handkerchief, feebly

mopped his brow. The dreadful speech was out, and its emergence had left him feeling spent and weak.

'You were?' cried Rupert Baxter.

'I was,' said Lord Emsworth hollowly.

A great change for the better had come over Rupert Baxter. It was as if those words had been a magic formula, filling with sweetness and light one who until that moment had been more like a spectacled thunder-cloud than anything human. He ceased to lower darkly. His air of being on the point of shooting out forked lightning left him. He even went so far as to smile. And if the smile was a smile that made Lord Emsworth feel as if his vital organs were being churned up with an egg-whisk, that was not his fault. He was trying to smile sunnily.

'Thank you,' he said. 'I shall be delighted.'

Lord Emsworth did not speak.

'I was always happy at the Castle.'

Lord Emsworth did not speak.

'Thank you very much,' said Rupert Baxter. 'What a beautiful evening.'

He passed from view, and Lord Emsworth examined the evening. As Baxter had said, it was beautiful, but it did not bring the balm which beautiful evenings usually brought to him. A blight seemed to hang over it. The setting sun shone bravely on the formal garden over which he looked, but it was the lengthening shadows rather than the sunshine that impressed themselves upon Lord Emsworth.

His heart was bowed down with weight of woe. Oh, says the poet, what a tangled web we weave when first we practise to deceive, and it was precisely the same, Lord Emsworth realized, when first we practise to shoot airguns. Just one careless, off-hand pop at a bending Baxter, and what a harvest, what a retribution! As a result of that single idle shot he had been compelled to augment his personal staff with a land-agent, which would infuriate his sister Constance, and a private secretary, which would make his life once again the inferno it had been in the old, bad Baxter days. He could scarcely have got himself into more trouble if he had gone blazing away with a machine gun.

It was with a slow and distrait shuffle that he eventually took himself from the writing-room and proceeded with his interrupted plan of going and sniffing at his roses. And so preoccupied was his mood that Beach, his faithful butler, who came to him after he had been smiling at them for perhaps half an hour, was obliged to speak twice before he could induce him to remove his nose from a Gloire de Dijon.

'Eh?'

'A note for you, m'lord.'

'A note? Who from?'

'Mr Baxter, m'lord.'

If Lord Emsworth had been less careworn, he might have noticed that the butler's voice had not its customary fruity ring. It had a dullness, a lack of tone. It was the voice of a butler who has lost the bluebird. But, being in the depths and so in no frame of mind to analyse the voice-production of butlers, he merely took the envelope from its salver and opened it listlessly, wondering what Baxter was sending him notes about.

The communication was so brief that he was enabled to discover this at a glance.

'LORD EMSWORTH,

'After what has occurred, I must reconsider my decision to accept the post of secretary which you offered me.

'I am leaving the Castle immediately.

'R. BAXTER.'

Simply that, and nothing more.

Lord Emsworth stared at the thing. It is not enough to say that he was bewildered. He was nonplussed. If the Gloire de Dijon at which he had recently been sniffing had snapped at his nose and bitten the tip off, he could scarcely have been more taken aback. He could make nothing of this.

As in a dream, he became aware that Beach was speaking.

'Eh?'

'My month's notice, m'lord.'

'Your what?'

'My month's notice, m'lord.'

'What about it?'

'I was saying that I wish to give my month's notice, m'lord.'

A weak irritation at all this chattering came upon Lord Emsworth. Here he was, trying to grapple with this frightful thing which had come upon him, and Beach would insist on weakening his concentration by babbling.

'Yes, yes, yes,' he said. 'I see. All right. Yes, yes.'

'Very good, m'lord.'

Left alone, Lord Emsworth faced the facts. He understood now what had happened. The note was no longer mystic. What it meant was that for some reason that trump card of his had proved useless. He had thought to stop Baxter's mouth with bribes, and he had failed. The man had seemed to accept the olive branch, but later there must have come some sharp revulsion of feeling, causing him to change his mind. No doubt a sudden twinge of pain in the wounded area had brought the memory of his wrongs flooding back upon him, so that he found himself preferring vengeance to material prosperity. And now he was going to blow the gaff. Even now the whole facts in the case might have been placed before Lady Constance. And even now, Lord Emsworth felt with a shiver, Connie might be looking for him.

The sight of a female form coming through the rose bushes brought him the sharpest shudder of the day, and for an instant he stood panting like a dog. But it was not his sister Constance. It was his niece Jane.

Jane was in excellent spirits.

'Hullo, Uncle Clarence,' she said. 'Having a look at the roses? I've sent that letter off to George, Uncle Clarence. I got the boy who cleans the knives and boots to take it. Nice chap. His name is Cyril.'

'Jane,' said Lord Emsworth, 'a terrible, a ghastly thing has happened. Baxter was outside the window of the writing-room when we were talking, and he heard everything.'

'Golly! He didn't?'

'He did. Every word. And he means to tell your aunt.'

'How do you know?'

'Read this.'

Jane took the note.

'H'm,' she said, having scanned it. 'Well, it looks to me, Uncle Clarence, as if there was only one thing for you to do. You must assert yourself.'

'Assert myself?'

'You know what I mean. Get tough. When Aunt Constance comes trying to bully you, stick your elbows out and put your head on one side and talk back at her out of the corner of your mouth.'

'But what shall I say?'

'Good heavens, there are a hundred things you can say. "Oh, yeah?" "Is zat so?" "Hey, just a minute," "Listen baby," "Scram" . . .'

'Scram?'

'It means "Get the hell outa here." '

'But I can't tell Connie to get the hell outa here.'

'Why not? Aren't you master in your own house?'

'No,' said Lord Emsworth.

Jane reflected.

'Then I'll tell you what to do. Deny the whole thing.'

'Could I, do you think?'

'Of course you could. And then Aunt Constance will ask me, and I'll deny the whole thing. Categorically. We'll both deny it categorically. She'll have to believe us. We'll be two to one. Don't you worry, Uncle Clarence. Everything'll be all right.'

She spoke with the easy optimism of Youth, and when she passed on a few moments later seemed to be feeling that she was leaving an uncle with his mind at rest. Lord Emsworth could hear her singing a gay song.

He felt no disposition to join in the chorus. He could not bring himself to share her sunny outlook. He looked into the future and still found it dark.

There was only one way of taking his mind off this dark future, only one means of achieving a momentary forgetfulness of what lay in store. Five minutes later, Lord Emsworth was in the library, reading Whiffle on *The Care Of The Pig*.

But there is a point beyond which the magic of the noblest writer ceases to function. Whiffle was good – no question about that – but he was not good enough to purge from the mind such a load of care as was weighing upon Lord Emsworth's. To expect him to do so was trying him too high. It was like asking Whiffle to divert and entertain a man stretched upon the rack.

Lord Emsworth was already beginning to find a difficulty in concentrating on that perfect prose, when any chance he might have had of doing so was removed. Lady Constance appeared in the doorway.

'Oh, here you are, Clarence,' said Lady Constance.

'Yes,' said Lord Emsworth in a low, strained voice.

A close observer would have noted about Lady Constance's manner, as she came into the room, something a little nervous and apprehensive, something almost diffident, but to Lord Emsworth, who was not a close observer, she seemed pretty much as usual, and he remained gazing at her like a man confronted with a ticking bomb. A dazed sensation had come upon him. It was in an almost detached way that he found himself speculating as to which of his crimes was about to be brought up for discussion. Had she met Jane and learned of the fatal letter? Or had she come straight from an interview with Rupert Baxter in which that injured man had told all?

He was so certain that it must be one of these two topics that she had come to broach that her manner as she opened the conversation filled him with amazement. Not only did it lack ferocity, it was absolutely chummy. It was as if a lion had come into the library and started bleating like a lamb.

'All alone, Clarence?'

Lord Emsworth hitched up his lower jaw, and said Yes, he was all alone.

'What are you doing? Reading?'

Lord Emsworth said Yes, he was reading.

'I'm not disturbing you, am I?'

Lord Emsworth, though astonishment nearly robbed him of speech, contrived to say that she was not disturbing him. Lady Constance walked to the window and looked out.

'What a lovely evening.'

'Yes.'

'I wonder you aren't out of doors.'

'I was out of doors. I came in.'

'Yes. I saw you in the rose garden.' Lady Constance traced a pattern on the window-sill with her finger. 'You were speaking to Beach.'

'Yes.'

'Yes, I saw Beach come up and speak to you.'

There was a pause. Lord Emsworth was about to break in by asking his visitor if she felt quite well, when Lady Constance spoke again. That apprehension in her manner, that nervousness, was now well marked. She traced another pattern on the window-sill.

'Was it important?'

'Was what important?'

'I mean, did he want anything?'

'Who?'

'Beach.'

'Beach?'

'Yes. I was wondering what he wanted to see you about.'

Quite suddenly there flashed upon Lord Emsworth the recollection that Beach had done more than merely hand him Baxter's note. With it – dash it, yes, it all came back to him – with it he had given his month's notice. And it just showed, Lord Emsworth felt, what a morass of trouble he was engulfed in that the fact of this superb butler handing in his resignation had made almost no impression on him. If such a thing had happened only as recently as yesterday, it would have constituted a major crisis. He would have felt that the foundations of his world were rocking. And he had scarcely listened. 'Yes, yes,' he had said, if he remembered correctly. 'Yes, yes, yes. All right.' Or words to that effect.

Bending his mind now on the disaster, Lord Emsworth sat stunned. He was appalled. Almost since the beginning of time, this super-butler had been at the Castle, and now he was about to melt away like snow in the sunshine – or as much like snow in the sunshine as was within the scope of a man who weighed sixteen stone in the buff. It was frightful. The thing was a nightmare. He couldn't get on without Beach. Life without Beach would be insupportable.

He gave tongue, his voice sharp and anguished.

'Connie! Do you know what's happened? Beach has given notice!'

'What!'

'Yes! His month's notice. He's given it. Beach has. And not a word of explanation. No reason. No —'

Lord Emsworth broke off. His face suddenly hardened. What seemed the only possible solution of the mystery had struck him. Connie was at the bottom of this. Connie must have been coming the *grande dame* on the butler, wounding his sensibilities.

Yes, that must be it. It was just the sort of thing she would do. If he had caught her being the Old English Aristocrat once, he had caught her a hundred times. That way of hers of pursing the lips and raising the eyebrows and generally doing the daughter-of-a-hundred-earls stuff. Naturally no butler would stand it.

'Connie,' he cried, adjusting his pince-nez and staring keenly and accusingly, 'what have you been doing to Beach?'

Something that was almost a sob burst from Lady Constance's lips. Her lovely complexion had paled, and in some odd way she seemed to have shrunk.

'I shot him,' she whispered.

Lord Emsworth was a little hard of hearing.

'You did what?'

'I shot him.'

'Shot him?'

'Yes.'

'You mean, *shot* him?'

'Yes, yes, yes! I shot him with George's airgun.'

A whistling sigh escaped Lord Emsworth. He leaned back in his chair, and the library seemed to be dancing old country dances before his eyes. To say that he felt weak with relief would be to understate the effect of this extraordinary communication. His relief was so intense that he felt absolutely boneless. Not once but many times during the past quarter of an hour he had said to himself that only a miracle could save him from the consequences of his sins, and now the miracle had happened. No one was more alive than he to the fact that women are abundantly possessed of crust, but after this surely even Connie could not have the crust to reproach him for what he had done.

'Shot him?' he said, recovering speech.

A fleeting touch of the old imperiousness returned to Lady Constance.

'Do stop saying "Shot him?" Clarence! Isn't it bad enough to have done a perfectly mad thing, without having to listen to you talking like a parrot? Oh, dear! Oh, dear!'

'But what did you do it for?'

'I don't know. I tell you I don't know. Something seemed suddenly to come over me. It was as if I had been bewitched. After you went out, I thought I would take the gun to Beach –'

'Why?'

'I . . . I . . . Well, I thought it would be safer with him than lying about in the library. So I took it down to his pantry. And all the way there I kept remembering what a wonderful shot I had been as a child –'

'What?' Lord Emsworth could not let this pass. 'What do you mean, you were a wonderful shot as a child? You've never shot in your life.'

'I have. Clarence, you were talking about Julia shooting Miss Mapleton. It wasn't Julia – it was I. She had made me stay in and do my rivers of Europe over again, so I shot her. I was a splendid shot in those days.'

'I bet you weren't as good as me,' said Lord Emsworth, piqued. 'I used to shoot rats.'

'So used I to shoot rats.'

'How many rats did you ever shoot?'

'Oh, Clarence, Clarence! Never mind about the rats.'

'No,' said Lord Emsworth, called to order. 'No, dash it. Never mind the rats. Tell me about this Beach business.'

'Well, when I got to the pantry, it was empty, and I saw Beach outside by the laurel bush, reading in a deck-chair –'

'How far away?'

'I don't know. What does it matter? About six feet, I suppose.'

'Six feet? Ha!'

'And I shot him. I couldn't resist it. It was like some horrible obsession. There was a sort of hideous picture in my mind of how he would jump. So I shot him.'

'How do you know you did? I expect you missed him.'

'No. Because he sprang up. And then he saw me at the window and came in, and I said, "Oh, Beach, I want you to take this airgun and keep it," and he said, "Very good, m'lady." '

'He didn't say anything about you shooting him?'

'No. And I have been hoping and hoping that he had not realized what had happened. I have been in an agony of suspense. But now you tell me that he has given his notice, so he must have done. Clarence,' cried Lady Constance, clasping her hands like a persecuted heroine, 'you see the awful position, don't you? If he leaves us he will spread the story all over the county and people will think I'm mad. I shall never be able to live it down. You must persuade him to withdraw his notice. Offer him double wages. Offer him anything. He must not be allowed to leave. If he does, I shall never . . . S'h!'

'What do you mean, S'. . . . Oh, ah,' said Lord Emsworth, at last observing that the door was opening.

It was his niece Jane who entered.

'Oh, hullo, Aunt Constance,' she said. 'I was wondering if you were in here. Mr Baxter's looking for you.'

Lady Constance was distraite.

'Mr Baxter?'

'Yes. I heard him asking Beach where you were. I think he wants to see you about something,' said Jane.

She directed at Lord Emsworth a swift glance, accompanied by a fleeting wink. 'Remember!' said the glance. 'Categorically!' said the wink.

Footsteps sounded outside. Rupert Baxter strode into the room.

At an earlier point in this chronicle, we have compared the aspect of Rupert Baxter, when burning with resentment, to a thunder-cloud, and it is possible that the reader may have formed a mental picture of just an ordinary thunder-cloud, the kind that rumbles a bit but does not really amount to anything very much. It was not this kind of cloud that the secretary resembled now, but one of those which burst over cities in the Tropics, inundating countrysides while thousands flee. He moved darkly towards Lady Constance, his hands outstretched. Lord Emsworth he ignored.

'I have come to say good-bye, Lady Constance,' he said.

There were not many statements that could have roused Lady Constance from her preoccupation, but this one did. She ceased to be the sportswoman brooding on memories of shikari, and stared aghast.

'Good-bye?'

'Good-bye.'

'But, Mr Baxter, you are not leaving us?'

'Precisely.'

For the first time, Rupert Baxter deigned to recognize that the ninth Earl was present.

'I am not prepared,' he said bitterly, 'to remain in a house where my chief duty appears to be to act as a target for Lord Emsworth and his airgun.'

'What!'

'Exactly.'

In the silence which followed these words, Jane once more gave her uncle that glance of encouragement and stimulation – that glance which said 'Be firm!' To her astonishment, she perceived that it was not needed. Lord Emsworth was firm already. His face was calm, his eye steady, and his pince-nez were not even quivering.

'The fellow's potty,' said Lord Emsworth in a clear resonant voice. 'Absolutely potty. Always told you he was. Target for my airgun? Pooh! Pah! What's he talking about?'

Rupert Baxter quivered. His spectacles flashed fire.

'Do you deny that you shot me, Lord Emsworth?'

'Certainly I do.'

'Perhaps you will deny admitting to this lady here in the writing-room that you shot me?'

'Certainly I do.'

'Did you tell me that you had shot Mr Baxter, Uncle Clarence?' said Jane. 'I didn't hear you.'

'Of course I didn't.'

'I thought you hadn't. I should have remembered it.'

Rupert Baxter's hands shot ceilingwards, as if he were calling upon heaven to see justice done.

'You admitted it to me personally. You begged me not to tell anyone. You tried to put matters right by engaging me as your secretary, and I accepted the position. At this time I was

50

perfectly willing to forget the entire affair. But when, not half an hour later . . .'

Lord Emsworth raised his eyebrows. Jane raised hers.

'How very extraordinary,' said Jane.

'Most,' said Lord Emsworth.

He removed his pince-nez and began to polish them, speaking soothingly the while. But his manner, though soothing, was very resolute.

'Baxter, my dear fellow,' he said, 'there's only one explanation of all this. It's just what I was telling you. You've been having these hallucinations of yours again. I never said a word to you about shooting you. I never said a word to my niece about shooting you. Why should I, when I hadn't? And as for what you say about engaging you as my secretary, the absurdity of the thing is manifest on the very face of it. There is nothing on earth that would induce me to have you as my secretary. I don't want to hurt your feelings, but I'd rather be dead in a ditch. Now, listen, my dear Baxter, I'll tell you what to do. You just jump on that motor-bicycle of yours and go on touring England where you left off. And soon you will find that the fresh air will do wonders for that pottiness of yours. In a day or two you won't know . . .'

Rupert Baxter turned and stalked from the room.

'Mr Baxter!' cried Lady Constance.

Her intention of going after the fellow and pleading with him to continue inflicting his beastly presence on the quiet home life of Blandings Castle was so plain that Lord Emsworth did not hesitate.

'Connie!'

'But, Clarence!'

'Constance, you will remain where you are. You will not stir a step.'

'But, Clarence!'

'Not a dashed step. You hear me? Let him scram!'

Lady Constance halted, irresolute. Then suddenly she met the full force of the pince-nez and it was as if she – like Rupert Baxter – had been struck by a bullet. She collapsed into a chair and sat there twisting her rings forlornly.

'Oh, and, by the way, Connie,' said Lord Emsworth, 'I've

been meaning to tell you. I've given that fellow Abercrombie that job he was asking for. I thought it all over carefully, and decided to drop him a line saying that pursuant on our recent conversation I was offering him Simmons's place. I've been making inquiries, and I find he's a capital fellow.'

'He's a baa-lamb,' said Jane.

'You hear? Jane says he's a baa-lamb. Just the sort of chap we want about the place.'

'So now we're going to get married.'

'So now they're going to get married. An excellent match, don't you think, Connie?'

Lady Constance did not speak. Lord Emsworth raised his voice a little.

'DON'T YOU, CONNIE?'

Lady Constance leaped in her seat as if she had heard the Last Trump.

'Very,' she said. 'Oh, very.'

'Right,' said Lord Emsworth. 'And now I'll go and talk to Beach.'

In the pantry, gazing sadly out on the stable yard, Beach the butler sat sipping a glass of port. In moments of mental stress, port was to Beach what Whiffle was to his employer, or, as we must now ruefully put it, his late employer. He flew to it when Life had got him down, and never before had Life got him down as it had now.

Sitting there in his pantry, that pantry which so soon would know him no more, Beach was in the depths. He mourned like some fallen monarch about to say good-bye to all his greatness and pass into exile. The die was cast. The end had come. Eighteen years, eighteen happy years, he had been in service at Blandings Castle, and now he must go forth, never to return. Little wonder that he sipped port. A weaker man would have swigged brandy.

Something tempestuous burst open the door, and he perceived that his privacy had been invaded by Lord Emsworth. He rose, and stood staring. In all the eighteen years during which he had held office, his employer had never before paid a visit to the pantry.

But it was not simply the other's presence that caused his gooseberry eyes to dilate to their full width, remarkable though that was. The mystery went deeper than that. For this was a strange, unfamiliar Lord Emsworth, a Lord Emsworth who glared where once he had blinked, who spurned the floor like a mettlesome charger, who banged tables and spilled port.

'Beach,' thundered this changeling, 'what the dooce is all this dashed nonsense?'

'M'lord?'

'You know what I mean. About leaving me. Have you gone off your head?'

A sigh shook the butler's massive frame.

'I fear that in the circumstances it is inevitable, m'lord.'

'Why? What are you talking about? Don't be an ass, Beach. Inevitable, indeed! Never heard such nonsense in my life. Why is it inevitable? Look me in the face and answer me that.'

'I feel it is better to tender my resignation than to be dismissed, m'lord.'

It was Lord Emsworth's turn to stare.

'Dismissed?'

'Yes, m'lord.'

'Beach, you're tight.'

'No, m'lord. Has not Mr Baxter spoken to you, m'lord?'

'Of course he's spoken to me. He's been gassing away half the afternoon. What's that got to do with it?'

Another sigh, seeming to start at the soles of his flat feet, set the butler's waistcoat rippling like corn in the wind.

'I see that Mr Baxter has not yet informed you, m'lord. I assumed that he would have done so before this. But it is a mere matter of time, I fear, before he makes his report.'

'Informed me of what?'

'I regret to say, m'lord, that in a moment of uncontrollable impulse I shot Mr Baxter.'

Lord Emsworth's pince-nez flew from his nose. Without them he could see only indistinctly, but he continued to stare at the butler, and in his eyes there appeared an expression which was a blend of several emotions. Amazement would have been chief of these, had it not been exceeded by affection. He did not speak, but his eyes said 'My brother!'

'With Master George's airgun, m'lord, which her ladyship left in my custody. I regret to say, m'lord, that upon receipt of the weapon I went out into the grounds and came upon Mr Baxter walking near the shrubbery. I tried to resist the temptation, m'lord, but it was too keen. I was seized with an urge which I have not experienced since I was a small lad, and, in short, I –'

'Plugged him?'

'Yes, m'lord.'

Lord Emsworth could put two and two together.

'So that's what he was talking about in the library. That's what made him change his mind and send me that note. . . . How far was he away when you shot him?'

'A matter of a few feet, m'lord. I endeavoured to conceal myself behind a tree, but he turned very sharply, and I was so convinced that he had detected me that I felt I had no alternative but to resign my situation before he could make his report to you, m'lord.'

'And I thought you were leaving because my sister Connie shot you!'

'Her ladyship did not shoot me, m'lord. It is true that the weapon exploded accidentally in her ladyship's hand, but the bullet passed me harmlessly.'

Lord Emsworth snorted.

'And she said she was a good shot! Can't even hit a sitting butler at six feet. Listen to me, Beach. I want no more of this nonsense of you resigning. Bless my soul, how do you suppose I could get on without you? How long have you been here?'

'Eighteen years, m'lord.'

'Eighteen years! And you talk of resigning! Of all the dashed absurd ideas!'

'But I fear, m'lord, when her ladyship learns –'

'Her ladyship won't learn. Baxter won't tell her. Baxter's gone.'

'Gone, m'lord?'

'Gone for ever.'

'But I understood, m'lord –'

'Never mind what you understood. He's gone. A few feet away, did you say?'

'M'lord?'

'Did you say Baxter was only a few feet away when you got him?'

'Yes, m'lord.'

'Ah!' said Lord Emsworth.

He took the gun absently from the table and absently slipped a slug into the breech. He was feeling pleased and proud, as champions do whose pre-eminence is undisputed. Connie had missed a mark like Beach – practically a haystack – at six feet. Beach had plugged Baxter – true – and so had young George – but only with the muzzle of the gun almost touching the fellow. It had been left for him, Clarence, ninth Earl of Emsworth, to do the real shooting. . . .

A damping thought came to diminish his complacency. It was as if a voice had whispered in his ear the word 'Fluke!' His jaw dropped a little, and he stood for a while, brooding. He felt flattened and discouraged.

Had it been merely a fluke, that superb shot from the library window? Had he been mistaken in supposing that the ancient skill still lingered? Would he – which was what the voice was hinting – under similar conditions miss nine times out of ten?

A stuttering, sputtering noise broke in upon his reverie. He raised his eyes to the window. Out in the stable yard, Rupert Baxter was starting up his motor-bicycle.

'Mr Baxter, m'lord.'

'I see him.'

An overwhelming desire came upon Lord Emsworth to put this thing to the test, to silence for ever that taunting voice.

'How far away would you say he was, Beach?'

'Fully twenty yards, m'lord.'

'Watch!' said Lord Emsworth.

Into the sputtering of the bicycle there cut a soft pop. It was followed by a sharp howl. Rupert Baxter, who had been leaning on the handle-bars, rose six inches with his hand to his thigh.

'There!' said Lord Emsworth.

Baxter had ceased to rub his thigh. He was a man of intelligence, and he realized that anyone on the premises of Blandings Castle who wasted time hanging about and rubbing thighs was simply asking for it. To one trapped in this inferno of Blandings Castle instant flight was the only way of winning to safety. The sputtering rose to a crescendo, diminished, died away altogether. Rupert Baxter had gone on, touring England.

Lord Emsworth was still gazing out of the window, raptly, as if looking at the X which marked the spot. For a long moment Beach stood staring reverently at his turned back. Then, as if performing some symbolic rite in keeping with the dignity of the scene, he reached for his glass of port and raised it in a silent toast.

Peace reigned in the butler's pantry. The sweet air of the summer evening poured in through the open window. It was as if Nature had blown the All Clear.

Blandings Castle was itself again.

Chapter Two
Buried Treasure

The situation in Germany had come up for discussion in the bar parlour of the Angler's Rest, and it was generally agreed that Hitler was standing at the crossroads and would soon be compelled to do something definite. His present policy, said a Whisky and Splash, was mere shilly-shallying.

'He'll have to let it grow or shave it off,' said the Whisky and Splash. 'He can't go on sitting on the fence like this. Either a man has a moustache or he has not. There can be no middle course.'

The thoughtful pause which followed these words was broken by a Small Bass.

'Talking of moustaches,' he said, 'you don't seem to see any nowadays, not what I call moustaches. What's become of them?'

'I've often asked myself the same question,' said a Gin and Italian Vermouth. 'Where, I've often asked myself, are the great sweeping moustaches of our boyhood? I've got a photograph of my grandfather as a young man in the album at home, and he's just a pair of eyes staring over a sort of quickset hedge.'

'Special cups they used to have,' said the Small Bass, 'to keep the vegetation out of their coffee. Ah, well, those days are gone for ever.'

Mr Mulliner shook his head.

'Not entirely,' he said, stirring his hot Scotch and lemon. 'I admit that they are rarer than they used to be, but in the remoter rural districts you will still find these curious growths flourishing. What causes them to survive is partly boredom and partly the good, clean spirit of amateur sport which has made us Englishmen what we are.'

The Small Bass said he did not quite get that.

'What I mean,' said Mr Mulliner, 'is that life has not much to offer in the way of excitement to men who are buried in the country all the year round, so for want of anything better to do they grow moustaches at one another.'

'Sort of competitively, as it were?'

'Exactly. One landowner will start to try to surpass his neighbour in luxuriance of moustache, and the neighbour, inflamed, fights back at him. There is often a great deal of very intense feeling about these contests, with not a little wagering on the side. So, at least, my nephew Brancepeth, the artist, tells me. And he should know, for his present affluence and happiness are directly due to one of them.'

'Did he grow a moustache?'

'No. He was merely caught up in the whirlwind of the struggle for supremacy between Lord Bromborough, of Rumpling Hall, Lower Rumpling, Norfolk, and Sir Preston Potter, Bart., of Wapleigh Towers in the same county. Most of the vintage moustaches nowadays are to be found in Norfolk and Suffolk. I suppose the keen, moist sea air brings them on. Certainly it, or some equally stimulating agency, had brought on those of Lord Bromborough and Sir Preston Potter, for in the whole of England at that time there were probably no two finer specimens than the former's Joyeuse and the latter's Love in Idleness.

It was Lord Bromborough's daughter Muriel (said Mr Mulliner) who had entitled these two moustaches in this manner. A poetic, imaginative girl, much addicted to reading old sagas and romances, she had adapted to modern conditions the practice of the ancient heroes of bestowing names on their favourite swords. King Arthur, you will remember, had his Excalibur, Charlemagne his Flamberge, Doolin of Mayence the famous Merveilleuse: and Muriel saw no reason why this custom should be allowed to die out. A pretty idea, she thought, and I thought it a pretty idea when my nephew Brancepeth told me of it, and he thought it a pretty idea when told of it by Muriel.

For Muriel and Brancepeth had made one another's acquaintance some time before this story opens. The girl, unlike her father, who never left the ancestral acres, came often to London, and on one of these visits my nephew was introduced to her.

With Brancepeth it seems to have been a case of love at first sight, and it was not long before Muriel admitted to returning his passion. She had been favourably attracted to him from the moment when she found that their dance steps fitted, and when some little while later he offered to paint her portrait for nothing there was a look in her eyes which it was impossible to mistake. As early as the middle of the first sitting he folded her in his arms, and she nestled against his waistcoat with a low, cooing gurgle. Both knew that in the other they had found a soul-mate.

Such, then, was the relationship of the young couple, when one summer morning Brancepeth's telephone rang and, removing the receiver, he heard the voice of the girl he loved.

'Hey, cocky,' she was saying .

'What ho, reptile,' responded Brancepeth. 'Where are you speaking from?'

'Rumpling. Listen, I've got a job for you.'

'What sort of job?'

'A commission. Father wants his portrait painted.'

'Oh yes?'

'Yes. His sinister design is to present it to the local Men's Club. I don't know what he's got against them. A nasty jar it'll be for the poor fellows when they learn of it.'

'Why, is the old dad a bit of a gargoyle?'

'You never spoke a truer word. All moustache and eyebrows. The former has to be seen to be believed.'

'Pretty septic?'

'My dear! Suppurating. Well, are you on? I've told Father you're the coming man.'

'So I am,' said Brancepeth. 'I'm coming this afternoon.'

He was as good as his word. He caught the 3.15 train from Liverpool Street and at 7.20 alighted at the little station of Lower Rumpling, arriving at the Hall just in time to dress for dinner.

Always a rapid dresser, tonight Brancepeth excelled himself, for he yearned to see Muriel once more after their extended separation. Racing down to the drawing-room, however, tying his tie as he went, he found that his impetuosity had brought him there too early. The only occupant of the room at the moment of his entrance was a portly man whom, from the evidence submitted, he took to be his host. Except for a few outlying ears and the tip of a nose, the fellow was entirely moustache, and until he set eyes upon it, Brancepeth tells me, he had never really appreciated the full significance of those opening words of Longfellow's Evangeline, 'This is the forest primeval.'

He introduced himself courteously.

'How do you do, Lord Bromborough? My name is Mulliner.'

The other regarded him – over the zareba – with displeasure, it seemed to Brancepeth.

'What do you mean – Lord Bromborough?' he snapped curtly.

Brancepeth said he had meant Lord Bromborough.

'I'm not Lord Bromborough,' said the man.

Brancepeth was taken aback.

'Oh, aren't you?' he said. 'I'm sorry.'

'I'm glad,' said the man. 'Whatever gave you the silly idea that I was old Bromborough?'

'I was told that he had a very fine moustache.'

'Who told you that?'

'His daughter.'

The other snorted.

'You can't go by what a man's daughter says. She's biased. Prejudiced. Blinded by filial love, and all that sort of thing. If I wanted an opinion on a moustache, I wouldn't go to a man's daughter. I'd go to somebody who knew about moustaches. "Mr Walkinshaw," I'd say, or whatever the name might be . . . Bromborough's moustache a very fine moustache, indeed! Pshaw! Bromborough *has* a moustache – of a sort. He is not clean-shaven – I concede that . . . but fine? Pooh. Absurd. Ridiculous. Preposterous. Never heard such nonsense in my life.'

He turned pettishly away, and so hurt and offended was his manner that Brancepeth had no heart to continue the conversation. Muttering something about having forgotten his handkerchief, he sidled from the room and hung about on the landing outside. And presently Muriel came tripping down the stairs, looking more beautiful than ever.

She seemed delighted to see him.

'Hullo, Brancepeth, you old bounder,' she said cordially. 'So you got here? What are you doing parked on the stairs? Why aren't you in the drawing-room?'

Brancepeth shot a glance at the closed door and lowered his voice.

'There's a hairy bird in there who wasn't any too matey. I thought it must be your father and accosted him as such, and he got extraordinarily peevish. He seemed to resent my saying that I had heard your father had a fine moustache.'

The girl laughed.

'Golly! You put your foot in it properly. Old Potter's madly jealous of Father's moustache. That was Sir Preston Potter, of Wapleigh Towers, one of our better-known local Barts. He and his son are staying here.' She broke off to address the butler, a kindly, silver-haired old man who at this moment mounted the stairs. 'Hullo, Phipps, are you ambling up to announce the tea and shrimps? You're a bit early. I don't think Father and Mr Potter are down yet. Ah, here's Father,' she said, as a brilliantly moustached man of middle age appeared. 'Father, this is Mr Mulliner.'

Brancepeth eyed his host keenly as he shook hands, and his heart sank a little. He saw that the task of committing this man to canvas was going to be a difficult one. The recent slurs of Sir Preston Potter had been entirely without justification. Lord Bromborough's moustache was an extraordinarily fine one, fully as lush as that which barred the public from getting a square view of the Baronet. It seemed to Brancepeth, indeed, that the job before him was more one for a landscape artist than a portrait painter.

Sir Preston Potter, however, who now emerged from the drawing-room, clung stoutly to his opinion. He looked sneeringly at his rival.

'You been clipping your moustache, Bromborough?'

'Of course I have not been clipping my moustache,' replied

Lord Bromborough shortly. It was only too plain that there was bad blood between the two men. 'What the dooce would I clip my moustache for? What makes you think I've been clipping my moustache?'

'I thought it had shrunk,' said Sir Preston Potter. 'It looks very small to me, very small. Perhaps the moth's been at it.'

Lord Bromborough quivered beneath the coarse insult, but his patrician breeding checked the hot reply which rose to his lips. He was a host. Controlling himself with a strong effort, he turned the conversation to the subject of early mangold-wurzels; and it was while he was speaking of these with eloquence and even fire that a young man with butter-coloured hair came hurrying down the stairs.

'Buck up, Edwin,' said Muriel impatiently. 'What's the idea of keeping us all waiting like this?'

'Oh, sorry,' said the young man.

'So you ought to be. Well, now you're here, I'd like to introduce you to Mr Mulliner. He's come to paint Father's portrait. Mr Mulliner . . . Mr Edwin Potter, my *fiancé*.'

'Dinner is served,' said Phipps the butler.

It was in a sort of trance that my nephew Brancepeth sat through the meal which followed. He toyed listlessly with his food and contributed so little to the conversation that a casual observer entering the room would have supposed him to be a deaf-mute who was on a diet. Nor can we fairly blame him for this, for he had had a severe shock. Few things are more calculated to jar an ardent lover and upset his poise than the sudden announcement by the girl he loves that she is engaged to somebody else, and Muriel's words had been like a kick in the stomach from an army mule. And in addition to suffering the keenest mental anguish, Brancepeth was completely bewildered.

It was not as if this Edwin Potter had been Clark Gable or somebody. Studying him closely, Brancepeth was unable to discern in him any of those qualities which win girls' hearts. He had an ordinary, meaningless face, disfigured by an eyeglass, and was plainly a boob of the first water. Brancepeth could make nothing of it. He resolved at the earliest possible moment to get hold of Muriel and institute a probe.

It was not until next day before luncheon that he found an opportunity of doing so. His morning had been spent in making preliminary sketches of her father. This task concluded, he came out into the garden and saw her reclining in a hammock slung between two trees at the edge of the large lawn.

He made his way towards her with quick, nervous strides. He was feeling jaded and irritated. His first impressions of Lord Bromborough had not misled him. Painting his portrait, he saw, was going to prove, as he had feared it would prove, a severe test of his courage and strength. There seemed so little about Lord Bromborough's face for an artist to get hold of. It was as if he had been commissioned to depict a client who, for reasons of his own, insisted on lying hid behind a haystack.

His emotions lent acerbity to his voice. It was with a sharp intonation that he uttered the preliminary 'Hoy!'

The girl sat up.

'Oh, hullo,' she said.

'Oh, hullo, yourself, with knobs on,' retorted Brancepeth. 'Never mind the "Oh, hullo." I want an explanation.'

'What's puzzling you?'

'This engagement of yours.'

'Oh, that?'

'Yes, that. A nice surprise that was to spring on a chap, was it not? A jolly way of saying "Welcome to Rumpling Hall," I don't think.' Brancepeth choked. 'I came here thinking that you loved me . . .'

'So I do.'

'What!'

'Madly. Devotedly.'

'Then why the dickens do I find you betrothed to this blighted Potter?'

Muriel sighed.

'It's the old, old story.'

'What's the old, old story?'

'This is. It's all so simple, if you'd only understand. I don't suppose any girl ever worshipped a man as I worship you,

Brancepeth, but Father hasn't a bean . . . you know what it's like owning land nowadays. Between ourselves, while we're on the subject, I'd stipulate for a bit down in advance on that portrait, if I were you. . . .'

Brancepeth understood.

'Is this Potter rotter rich?'

'Rolling. Sir Preston was Potter's Potted Table Delicacies.'

There was a silence.

'H'm,' said Brancepeth.

'Exactly. You see now. Oh, Brancepeth,' said the girl, her voice trembling, 'why haven't you money? If you only had the merest pittance – enough for a flat in Mayfair and a little week-end place in the country somewhere and a couple of good cars and a villa in the South of France and a bit of trout fishing on some decent river, I would risk all for love. But as it is . . .'

Another silence fell.

'What you ought to do,' said Muriel, 'is invent some good animal for the movies. That's where the money is. Look at Walt Disney.'

Brancepeth started. It was as if she had read his thoughts. Like all young artists nowadays, he had always held before him as the goal of his ambition the invention of some new comic animal for the motion pictures. What he burned to do, as Velazquez would have burned to do if he had lived today, was to think of another Mickey Mouse and then give up work and just sit back and watch the money roll in.

'It isn't so easy,' he said sadly.

'Have you tried?'

'Of course I've tried. For years I have followed the gleam. I thought I had something with Hilda the Hen and Bertie the Bandicoot, but nobody would look at them. I see now that they were lifeless, uninspired. I am a man who needs the direct inspiration.'

'Doesn't Father suggest anything to you?'

Brancepeth shook his head.

'No. I have studied your father, alert for the slightest hint . . .'

'Walter the Walrus?'

'No. Lord Bromborough looks like a walrus, yes, but unfortunately not a funny walrus. That moustache of his is majestic rather than diverting. It arouses in the beholder a feeling of awe, such as one gets on first seeing the pyramids. One senses the terrific effort behind it. I suppose it must have taken a lifetime of incessant toil to produce a cascade like that?'

'Oh, no. Father hadn't a moustache at all a few years ago. It was only when Sir Preston began to grow one and rather flaunt it at him at District Council meetings that he buckled down to it. But why,' demanded the girl passionately, 'are we wasting time talking about moustaches? Kiss me, Brancepeth. We have just time before lunch.'

Brancepeth did as directed, and the incident closed.

I do not propose (resumed Mr Mulliner, who had broken off his narrative at this point to request Miss Postlethwaite, our able barmaid, to give him another hot Scotch and lemon) to dwell in detail on the agony of spirit endured by my nephew Brancepeth in the days that followed this poignant conversation. The spectacle of a sensitive artist soul on the rack is never a pleasant one. Suffice it to say that as each day came and went it left behind it an increased despair.

What with the brooding on his shattered romance and trying to paint Lord Bromborough's portrait and having his nerves afflicted by the incessant bickering that went on between Lord Bromborough and Sir Preston Potter and watching Edwin Potter bleating round Muriel and not being able to think of a funny animal for the movies, it is little wonder that his normally healthy complexion began to shade off to a sallow pallor and that his eyes took on a haunted look. Before the end of the first week he had become an object to excite the pity of the tender-hearted.

Phipps the butler was tender-hearted, and had been since a boy. Brancepeth excited his pity, and he yearned to do something to ameliorate the young man's lot. The method that suggested itself to him was to take a bottle of champagne to his room. It might prove a palliative rather than a cure, but he was convinced that it would, if only temporarily, bring the roses back to Brancepeth's cheeks. So he took a bottle of champagne to his room on the fifth night of my nephew's visit, and found him lying on his bed in striped pyjamas and a watered silk dressing-gown, staring at the ceiling.

The day that was now drawing to a close had been a particularly bad one for Brancepeth. The weather was unusually warm, and this had increased his despondency, so that he had found himself chafing beneath Lord Bromborough's moustache in a spirit of sullen rebellion. Before the afternoon sitting was over, he had become conscious of a vivid feeling of hatred for the thing. He longed for the courage to get at it with a hatchet after the manner of a pioneer in some wild country hewing a clearing in the surrounding jungle. When Phipps found him, his fists were clenched and he was biting his lower lip.

'I have brought you a little champagne, sir,' said Phipps, in his kindly, silver-haired way. 'It occurred to me that you might be in need of a restorative.'

Brancepeth was touched. He sat up, the hard glare in his eyes softening.

'That's awfully good of you,' he said. 'You are quite right. I could do with a drop or two from the old bin. I am feeling rather fagged. The weather, I suppose.'

A gentle smile played over the butler's face as he watched the young man put away a couple, quick.

'No, sir. I do not think it is the weather. You may be quite frank with me, sir. I understand. It must be a very wearing task, painting his lordship. Several artists have had to give it up. There was a young fellow here in the spring of last year who had to be removed to the cottage hospital. His manner had been strange and moody for some days, and one night we found him on a ladder, in the nude, tearing away at the ivy on the west wall. His lordship's moustache had been too much for him.'

Brancepeth groaned and refilled his glass. He knew just how his brother brush must have felt.

'The ironical thing,' continued the butler, 'is that conditions would be just as bad, were the moustache non-existent. I have been in service at the Hall for a number of years, and I can assure you that his lordship was fully as hard on the eye when he was clean-shaven. Well, sir, when I tell you that I was actually relieved when he began to grow a moustache, you will understand.'

66

'Why, what was the matter with him?'

'He had a face like a fish, sir.'

'A fish?'

'Yes, sir.'

Something resembling an electric shock shot through Brancepeth, causing him to quiver in every limb.

'A funny fish?' he asked in a choking voice.

'Yes, sir. Extremely droll.'

Brancepeth was trembling like a saucepan of boiling milk at the height of its fever. A strange, wild thought had come into his mind. A funny fish . . .

There had never been a funny fish on the screen. Funny mice, funny cats, funny dogs . . . but not a funny fish. He stared before him with glowing eyes.

'Yes, sir, when his lordship began to grow a moustache, I was relieved. It seemed to me that it must be a change for the better. And so it was at first. But now . . . you know how it is, sir. . . . I often find myself wishing those old, happy days were back again. We never know when we are well off, sir, do we?'

'You would be glad to see the last of Lord Bromborough's moustache?'

'Yes, sir. Very glad.'

'Right,' said Brancepeth. 'Then I'll shave it off.'

In private life butlers relax that impassive gravity which the rules of their union compel them to maintain in public. Spring something sensational on a butler when he is chatting with you in your bedroom, and he will leap and goggle like any ordinary man. Phipps did so now.

'Shave it off, sir?' he gasped, quaveringly.

'Shave it off,' said Brancepeth, pouring out the last of the champagne.

'Shave off his lordship's moustache?'

'This very night. Leaving not a wrack behind.'

'But, sir . . .'

'Well?'

'The thought that crossed my mind, sir, was – how?'

Brancepeth clicked his tongue impatiently.

'Quite easily. I suppose he likes a little something last thing at night? Whisky or what not?'

'I always bring his lordship a glass of warm milk to the smoking-room.'

'Have you taken it to him yet?'

'Not yet, sir. I was about to do so when I left you.'

'And is there anything in the nature of a sleeping draught in the house?'

'Yes, sir. His lordship is a poor sleeper in the hot weather and generally takes a tablet of Slumberola in his milk.'

'Then, Phipps, if you are the pal I think you are, you will slip into his milk tonight not one tablet but four tablets.'

'But, sir . . .'

'I know, I know. What you are trying to say, I presume, is – What is there in it for you? I will tell you, Phipps. There is a packet in it for you. If Lord Bromborough's face in its stark fundamentals is as you describe it, I can guarantee that in less than no time I shall be bounding about the place trying to evade super-tax. In which event, rest assured that you will get your cut. You are sure of your facts? If I make a clearing in the tangled wildwood, I shall come down eventually to a face like a fish?'

'Yes, sir.'

'A fish with good comedy values?'

'Oh, yes, sir. Till it began to get me down, many is the laugh I had at the sight of it.'

'That is all I wish to know. Right. Well, Phipps, can I count on your co-operation? I may add, before you speak, that this means my life's happiness. Sit in, and I shall be able to marry the girl I adore. Refuse to do your bit, and I drift through the remainder of my life a soured, blighted bachelor.'

The butler was plainly moved. Always kindly and silver-haired, he looked kindlier and more silver-haired than ever before.

'It's like that, is it, sir?'

'It is.'

'Well, sir, I wouldn't wish to come between a young gentleman and his life's happiness. I know what it means to love.'

'You do?'

'I do indeed, sir. It is not for me to boast, but there was a time when the girls used to call me Saucy George.'

'And so –?'

'I will do as you request, sir.'

'I knew it, Phipps,' said Brancepeth with emotion. 'I knew that I could rely on you. All that remains, then, is for you to show me which is Lord Bromborough's room.' He paused. A disturbing thought had struck him. 'I say! Suppose he locks his door?'

'It is quite all right, sir,' the butler reassured him. 'In the later summer months, when the nights are sultry, his lordship does not sleep in his room. He reposes in a hammock slung between two trees on the large lawn.'

'I know the hammock,' said Brancepeth tenderly. 'Well that's fine, then. The thing's in the bag. Phipps,' said Brancepeth, grasping his hand, 'I don't know how to express my gratitude. If everything develops as I expect it to ; if Lord Bromborough's face gives me the inspiration which I anticipate and I clean up big, you, I repeat, shall share my riches. In due season there will call at your pantry elephants laden with gold, and camels bearing precious stones and rare spices. Also apes, ivory and peacocks. And . . . you say your name is George?'

'Yes, sir.'

'Then my eldest child shall be christened George. Or, if female, Georgina.'

'Thank you very much, sir.'

'Not at all,' said Brancepeth. 'A pleasure.'

*

Brancepeth's first impression on waking next morning was that he had had a strange and beautiful dream. It was a vivid, lovely thing, all about stealing out of the house in striped pyjamas and a watered silk dressing-gown, armed with a pair of scissors, and stooping over the hammock where Lord Bromborough lay and razing his great moustache Joyeuse to its foundations. And he was just heaving a wistful sigh and wishing it were true, when he found that it was. It all came back to him – the furtive sneak downstairs, the wary passage of the lawn, the snip-snip-snip of the scissors blending with a strong man's snores in the silent night. It was no dream. The thing had actually occurred. His host's upper lip had became a devastated area.

It was not Brancepeth's custom, as a rule, to spring from his bed at the beginning of a new day, but he did so now. He was consumed with a burning eagerness to gaze upon his handiwork, for the first time to see Lord Bromborough steadily and see him whole. Scarcely ten minutes had elapsed before he was in his clothes and on his way to the breakfast-room. The other, he knew, was an early riser, and even so great a bereavement as he had suffered would not deter him from getting at the coffee and kippers directly he caught a whiff of them.

Only Phipps, however, was in the breakfast-room. He was lighting wicks under the hot dishes on the sideboard. Brancepeth greeted him jovially.

'Good morning, Phipps. What ho, what ho, with a hey nonny nonny and a hot cha-cha.'

The butler was looking nervous, like Macbeth interviewing Lady Macbeth after one of her visits to the spare room.

'Good morning, sir. Er – might I ask, sir . . .'

'Oh, yes,' said Brancepeth. 'The operation was a complete success. Everything went according to plan.'

'I am very glad to hear it, sir.'

'Not a hitch from start to finish. Tell me, Phipps,' said Brancepeth, helping himself buoyantly to a fried egg and a bit of bacon and seating himself at the table, 'what sort of a fish did Lord Bromborough look like before he had a moustache?'

The butler reflected.

'Well, sir, I don't know if you have seen Sidney the Sturgeon?'

'Eh?'

'On the pictures, sir. I recently attended a cinematograph performance at Norwich – it was on my afternoon off last week – and,' said Phipps, chuckling gently at the recollection, 'they were showing a most entertaining new feature, "The Adventures of Sidney the Sturgeon." It came on before the big picture, and it was all I could do to keep a straight face. This sturgeon looked extremely like his lordship in the old days.'

He drifted from the room and Brancepeth stared after him, stunned. His castles had fallen about him in ruins. Fame, fortune and married bliss were as far away from him as ever. All his labour had been in vain. If there was already a funny fish functioning on the silver screen, it was obvious that it would be mere waste of time to do another. He clasped his head in his hands and groaned over his fried egg. And, as he did so, the door opened.

'Ha,' said Lord Bromborough's voice. 'Good morning, good morning.'

Brancepeth spun round with a sharp jerk which sent a piece of bacon flying off his fork as if it had been shot from a catapult. Although his host's appearance could not affect his professional future now, he was consumed with curiosity to see what he looked like. And, having spun round, he sat transfixed. There before him stood Lord Bromborough, but not a hair of his moustache was missing. It flew before him like a banner in all its pristine luxuriance.

'Eh, what?' said Lord Bromborough, sniffing. 'Kedgeree? Capital, capital.'

He headed purposefully for the sideboard. The door opened again, and Edwin Potter came in, looking more of a boob than ever.

In addition to looking like a boob, Edwin Potter seemed worried.

'I say,' he said, 'my father's missing.'

'On how many cylinders?' asked Lord Bromborough. He was a man who liked his joke of a morning.

'I mean to say,' continued Edwin Potter. 'I can't find him. I went to speak to him about something just now, and his room was empty and his bed had not been slept in.'

Lord Bromborough was dishing out kedgeree on to a plate.

'That's all right,' he said. 'He wanted to try my hammock last night, so I let him. If he slept as soundly as I did, he slept well. I came over all drowsy as I was finishing my glass of hot milk and I woke this morning in an arm-chair in the smoking-room. Ah, my dear,' he went on, as Muriel entered, 'come along and try this kedgeree. It smells excellent. I was just telling our young friend here that his father slept in my hammock last night.'

Muriel's face was wearing a look of perplexity.

'Out in the garden, do you mean?'

'Of course I mean out in the garden. You know where my hammock is. I've seen you lying in it.'

'Then there must be a goat in the garden.'

'Goat?' said Lord Bromborough, who had now taken his place at the table and was shovelling kedgeree into himself like a stevedore loading a grain ship. 'What do you mean, goat? There's no goat in the garden. Why should there be a goat in the garden?'

'Because something has eaten off Sir Preston's moustache.'

'What!'

'Yes. I met him outside, and the shrubbery had completely disappeared. Here he is. Look.'

What seemed at first to Brancepeth a total stranger was standing in the doorway. It was only when the newcomer folded his arms and began to speak in a familiar rasping voice that he recognized Sir Preston Potter, Bart., of Wapleigh Towers.

'So!' said Sir Preston, directing at Lord Bromborough a fiery glance full of deleterious animal magnetism.

Lord Bromborough finished his kedgeree and looked up.

'Ah, Potter,' he said. 'Shaved your moustache, have you? Very sensible. It would never have amounted to anything, and you will be happier without it.'

Flame shot from Sir Preston Potter's eyes. The man was plainly stirred to his foundations.

'Bromborough,' he snarled, 'I have only five things to say to you. The first is that you are the lowest, foulest fiend that ever disgraced the pure pages of Debrett; the second that your dastardly act in clipping off my moustache shows you a craven, who knew that defeat stared him in the eye and that only thus he could hope to triumph; the third that I intend to approach my lawyer immediately with a view to taking legal action; the fourth is good-bye for ever; and the fifth —'

'Have an egg,' said Lord Bromborough.

'I will not have an egg. This is not a matter which can be lightly passed off with eggs. The fifth thing I wish to say –.'

'But, my dear fellow, you seem to be suggesting that I had something to do with this. I approve of what has happened, yes. I approve of it heartily. Norfolk will be a sweeter and better place to live in now that this has occurred. But it was none of my doing. I was asleep in the smoking-room all night.'

'The fifth thing I wish to say –'

'In an arm-chair. If you doubt me, I can show you the arm-chair.'

'The fifth thing I wish to say is that the engagement between my son and your daughter is at an end.'

'Like your moustache. Ha, ha!' said Lord Bromborough, who had many good qualities but was not tactful.

'Oh, but, Father!' cried Edwin Potter. 'I mean, dash it!'

'And *I* mean,' thundered Sir Preston, 'that your engagement is at an end. You have my five points quite clear, Bromborough?'

'I think so,' said Lord Bromborough, ticking them off on his fingers. 'I am a foul fiend, I'm a craven, you are going to institute legal proceedings, you bid me good-bye for ever, and my daughter shall never marry your son. Yes, five in all.'

'Add a sixth. I shall see that you are expelled from all your clubs.'

'I haven't got any.'

'Oh?' said Sir Preston, a little taken aback. 'Well, if ever you make a speech in the House of Lords, beware. I shall be up in the gallery, booing.'

He turned and strode from the room, followed by Edwin, protesting bleatingly. Lord Bromborough took a cigarette from his case.

'Silly old ass,' he said. 'I expect that moustache of his was clipped off by a body of public-spirited citizens. Like the Vigilantes they have in America. It is absurd to suppose that a man could grow a beastly, weedy caricature of a moustache like Potter's without inflaming popular feelings. No doubt they have been lying in wait for him for months. Lurking. Watching their opportunity. Well, my dear, so your wedding's off. A nuisance in a way of course, for I'd just bought a new pair of trousers to give you away in. Still it can't be helped.'

'No, it can't be helped,' said Muriel. 'Besides there will be another one along in a minute.'

She shot a tender smile at Brancepeth, but on his lips there was no answering simper. He sat in silence, crouched over his fried egg.

What did it profit him, he was asking himself bitterly, that the wedding was off? He himself could never marry Muriel. He was a penniless artist without prospects. He would never invent a comic animal for the movies now. There had been an instant when he had hoped that Sir Preston's uncovered face might suggest one, but the hope had died at birth. Sir Preston Potter, without his moustache, had merely looked like a man without a moustache.

He became aware that his host was addressing him.

'I beg your pardon?'

'I said, "Got a light?" '

'Oh, sorry,' said Brancepeth.

He took out his lighter and gave it a twiddle. Then, absently, he put the flame to the cigarette between his host's lips.

Or, rather, for preoccupation had temporarily destroyed his judgement of distance, to the moustache that billowed above and around it. And the next moment there was a sheet of flame and a cloud of acrid smoke. When this had cleared away, only a little smouldering stubble was left of what had once been one of Norfolk's two most outstanding eyesores.

A barely human cry rent the air, but Brancepeth hardly heard it. He was staring like one in a trance at the face that confronted him through the shrouding mists, fascinated by the short, broad nose, the bulging eyes, the mouth that gaped and twitched. It was only when his host made a swift dive across the table with bared teeth and clutching hands that Prudence returned to its throne. He slid under the table and came out on the other side.

'Catch him!' cried the infuriated peer. 'Trip him up! Sit on his head!'

'Certainly not,' said Muriel. 'He is the man I love.'

'Is he!' said Lord Bromborough, breathing heavily as he

crouched for another spring. 'Well, he's the man I am going to disembowel with my bare hands – when I catch him.'

'I think I should nip through the window, darling,' said Muriel gently.

Brancepeth weighed the advice hastily and found it good. The window, giving on to the gravel drive, was, he perceived, open at the bottom. The sweet summer air floated in, and an instant later he was floating out. As he rose from the gravel, something solid struck him on the back of the head. It was a coffee-pot.

But coffee-pots, however shrewdly aimed, mattered little to Brancepeth now. This one had raised a painful contusion and he had in addition skinned both hands and one of his knees. His trousers, moreover, a favourite pair, had a large hole in them. Nevertheless, his heart was singing within him.

For Phipps had been wrong. Phipps was an ass. Phipps did not know a fish when he saw one. Lord Bromborough's face did not resemble that of a fish at all. It suggested something much finer, much fuller of screen possibilities, much more box-office than a fish. In that one blinding instant of illumination before he had dived under the table, Brancepeth had seen Lord Bromborough for what he was – Ferdinand the Frog.

He turned, to perceive his host in the act of hurling a cottage loaf.

'Muriel!' he cried.

'Hullo?' said the girl, who had joined her father at the window and was watching the scene with great interest.

'I love you, Muriel.'

'Same here.'

'But for the moment I must leave you.'

'I would,' said Muriel. She glanced over her shoulder. 'He's gone to get the kedgeree.' And Brancepeth saw that Lord Bromborough had left his butt. 'He is now,' she added, 'coming back.'

'Will you wait for me, Muriel?'

'To all eternity.'

'It will not be necessary,' said Brancepeth. 'Call in six months or a year. By that time I shall have won fame and fortune.'

He would have spoken further, but at this moment Lord

75

Bromborough reappeared, poising the kedgeree. With a loving smile and a wave of the hand, Brancepeth leaped smartly to one side. Then, turning, he made his way down the drive, gazing raptly into a future of Rolls-Royces, caviare and silk underclothing made to measure.

Chapter Three
The Letter of the Law

'Fo-o-o-re!'

The cry, in certain of its essentials not unlike the wail of a soul in torment, rolled out over the valley, and the young man on the seventh tee, from whose lips it had proceeded, observing that the little troupe of spavined octogenarians doddering along the fairway, paid no attention whatever, gave his driver a twitch as if he was about to substitute action for words. Then he lowered the club and joined his companion on the bench.

'Better not, I suppose,' he said, moodily.

The Oldest Member, who often infested the seventh tee on a fine afternoon, nodded.

'I think you are wise,' he agreed. 'Driving into people is a thing one always regrets. I have driven into people in my golfing days, and I was always sorry later. There is something about the reproachful eye of the victim as you meet it subsequently in the bar of the clubhouse which cannot fail to jar the man of sensibility. Like a wounded oyster. Wait till they are out of distance, says the good book. The only man I ever knew who derived solid profit from driving into somebody who was not out of distance was young Wilmot Byng. . . .'

The two young men started.

'Are you going to tell us a story?'

'I am.'

'But –'

'I knew you would be pleased,' said the Oldest Member.

Wilmot Byng at the time of which I speak (the sage proceeded) was an engaging young fellow with a clear-cut face and a drive almost as long as the Pro's. Strangers, watching him at his best, would express surprise that he had never taken a couple of days off and won the Open Championship, and you could have knocked them down with a putter when you informed them that his handicap was six. For Wilmot's game had a fatal defect. He was impatient. If held up during a round, he tended to press. Except for that, however, he had a sterling nature and frank blue eyes which won all hearts.

It was the fact that for some days past I had observed in these eyes a sort of cloud that led me to think that the lad had something on his mind. And when we were lunching together in the clubhouse one afternoon and he listlessly refused a most admirable steak and kidney pudding I shot at him a glance so significant that, blushing profusely, he told me all.

He loved, it seemed, and the partner he had selected for life's medal round was a charming girl named Gwendoline Poskitt.

I knew the girl well. Her father was one of my best friends. We had been at the University together. As an undergraduate, he had made a name as a hammer thrower. More recently, he had taken up golf and, being somewhat short-sighted and completely muscle-bound, had speedily won for himself in our little community the affectionate sobriquet of the First Grave Digger.

'Indeed?' I said. 'So you love Gwendoline Poskitt, do you? Very sensible. Were I a younger man, I would do it myself. But she scorns your suit?'

'She doesn't scorn any such dashed thing,' rejoined Wilmot with some heat. 'She is all for my suit.'

'You mean she returns your love?'

'She does.'

'Then why refuse steak and kidney pudding?'

'Because her father will never consent to her becoming my wife. And it's no good saying Why not elope? because I suggested that and she would have none of it. She loves me dearly, she says – as a matter of fact, she admitted in so many words that I was the tree on which the fruit of her life hung – but she can't bring herself to forgo the big church wedding, with full choral effects and the Bishop doing his stuff and photographs in the illustrated weekly papers. As she quite rightly pointed out, were we to sneak off and get married at the registrar's, bim would go the Bishop and phut the photographs. I can't shake her.'

'You ought not to want to shake her.'

'Move her, I mean. Alter her resolution. So I've got to get her father's consent. And how can I, when he has it in for me the way he has?'

He gave a groan and began to crumble my bread. I took another piece and put it on the opposite side of my plate.

'Has it in for you?'

'Yes. It's like this. You know the Wrecking Crew.'

He was alluding to the quartet of golfing cripples of which Joseph Poskitt was a regular member. The others were Old Father Time, The Man With The Hoe, and Consul, The Almost Human.

'You know the way they dodder along and won't let anyone through. There have been ugly mutterings about it in the Club for months, and it came even harder on me than on most of the crowd, for, as you know, I like to play quick. Well, the other day I cracked under the strain. I could endure it no longer. I –'

'Drove into them?'

'Drove into them. Using my brassie for the shot. I took a nice easy stance, came back slow, keeping my head well down, and let fly – firing into the brown, as it were, and just trusting to luck which of them I hit. The man who drew the short straw was old Poskitt. I got him on the right leg. Did you tell me he got his blue at Oxford for throwing the hammer?'

'Throwing the hammer, yes.'

'Not the high jump?'

'No.'

'Odd. I should have said –'

I was deeply concerned. To drive into the father of the girl you love, no matter what the provocation, seemed to me an act of the most criminal folly and so I told him.

He quivered and broke a tumbler.

'Now there,' he said, 'you have touched on another cause for complaint. At the time, I had no notion that he was the father of the girl I loved. As a matter of fact, he wasn't, because I had not met Gwendoline then. She blew in later, having been on one of those round-the-world cruises. I must say I think that old buffers who hold people up and won't let them through ought to wear some sort of label indicating that they

79

have pretty daughters who will be arriving shortly. Then one would know where one was and act accordingly. Still, there it is. I gave old Poskitt this juicy one, as described, and from what he said to me later in the changing room I am convinced that any suggestion on my part that I become his son-in-law will not be cordially received.'

I ate cheese gravely. I could see that the situation was a difficult one.

'Well, the only thing I can advise,' I said, 'is that you culti- vate him assiduously. Waylay him and give him cigars. Ask after his slice. Tell him it's a fine day. He has a dog named Edward. Seek Edward out and pat him. Many a young man has won over the father of the girl he loves by such tactics, so why not you?'

He agreed to do so, and in the days which followed Poskitt could not show his face in the clubhouse without having Wil- mot spring out at him with perfectos. The dog Edward began to lose hair off his ribs through incessant patting. And gradually, as I had hoped, the breach healed. Came a morning when Wil- mot, inquiring after my old friend's slice, was answered not with the usual malevolent grunt but with a reasonably cordial statement that it now showed signs of becoming a hook.

'Ah?' said Wilmot. 'A cigar?'

'Thanks,' said Poskitt.

'Nice doggie,' said Wilmot pursuing his advantage by ad- ministering a hearty buffet to Edward's aching torso before the shrinking animal could side-step.

'Ah,' said Poskitt.

That afternoon, for the first time for weeks, Wilmot Byng took twice of steak and kidney pudding at lunch and followed it up with treacle tart and a spot of Stilton.

And so matters stood when the day arrived for the annual contest for the President's Cup.

The President's Cup, for all its high-sounding name, was one of the lowliest and most humble trophies offered for compe- tition to the members of our club, ranking in the eyes of good judges somewhere between the Grandmothers' Umbrella and the Children's All-Day Sucker (open to boys and girls not yet having celebrated their seventh birthday). It had been instituted by a kindly committee for the benefit of the *canaille* of our little golfing world, those retired military, naval and business men who withdraw to the country and take up golf in their fifties. The contest was decided by medal play, if you could call it that, and no exponent with a handicap of under twenty-four was allowed to compete.

Nevertheless, there was no event on the fixture list which aroused among those involved a tenser enthusiasm. Centenarians sprang from their bathchairs to try their skill, and I have seen men with waistlines of sixty doing bending and stretching exercises for weeks in advance in order to limber themselves up for the big day. Form was eagerly discussed in the smoking-room, and this year public opinion wavered between two men: Joseph Poskitt, the First Grave Digger, and Wadsworth Hemmingway, better known in sporting circles as Palsied Percy.

The betting, as I say, hovered uncertainly between these two, but there was no question as to which was the people's choice. Everybody was fond of Poskitt. You might wince as you saw his iron plough through the turf, but you could not help liking him, whereas Hemmingway was definitely unpopular. He was a retired solicitor, one of those dark, subtle, sinister men who carry the book of rules in their bag, and make it their best club. He was a confirmed hole-claimer, and such are never greatly esteemed by the more easy-going. He had, moreover, a way of suddenly clearing his throat on the greens which alone would have been sufficient to ensure dislike.

The President's Cup was an event which I always made a point of watching, if I could, considering it a spectacle that purged the soul with pity and terror: but on this occasion business in London unfortunately claimed me and I was compelled to deprive myself of my annual treat. I had a few words with Wilmot before leaving to catch my train. I was pleased with the lad.

'You've done splendidly, my boy,' I said. 'I notice distinct signs of softening on our friend's part.'

'Me too,' agreed Wilmot jubilantly. 'He thanks me now when I give him a cigar.'

'So I observed. Well, continue to spare no effort. Did you wish him success for this afternoon?'

'Yes. He seemed pleased.'

'It might be a good idea if you were to offer to caddy for him. He would appreciate your skilled advice.'

'I thought of that, but I'm playing myself.'

'Today?'

I was surprised, for President's Cup day is usually looked on as a sort of Walpurgis Night, when fearful things are abroad and the prudent golfer stays at home.

'I promised a fellow a game, and I can't get out of it.'

'You will be held up a good deal, I'm afraid.'

'I suppose so.'

'Well, don't go forgetting yourself and driving into Poskitt.'

'I should say not, ha, ha! Not likely, ho, ho! One doesn't do that sort of thing twice, does one? But excuse me now, if you don't mind. I have an appointment to wander in the woods with Gwendoline.'

It was late in the evening when I returned home. I was about to ring up Poskitt to ask how the contest had come out, when the telephone rang and I was surprised to hear Hemmingway's voice.

'Hullo,' said Hemmingway. 'Are you doing anything tomorrow morning?'

'Nothing,' I replied. 'How did things come out this afternoon?'

'That is what I rang up about. Poskitt and I tied for a low score at a hundred and fifteen. I put the matter up to the Committee and they decided that there must be a play off – match play.'

'You mean stroke play?'

'No, match play. It was my suggestion. I pointed out to Poskitt that by this method he would only have to play the first ten holes, thus saving wear and tear on his niblick.'

'I see. But why was it necessary to refer the thing to the Committee?'

'Oh, there was some sort of foolish dispute. It turned on a question of rubs of the green. Well, if you aren't doing anything tomorrow, will you referee the play-off?'

'Delighted.'

'Thanks. I want somebody who knows the rules. Poskitt does not seem to realize that there are any.'

'Why do you say that?'

'Well, he appears to think that when you're playing in a medal competition you can pick and choose which strokes you are going to count and which you aren't. Somebody drove into him when he was addressing his ball at the eleventh and he claims that that is what made him send it at right angles into a bush. As I told him, and the Committee supported me . . .'

A nameless fear caused the receiver to shake in my hand.

'Who drove into him?'

'I forget his name. Tall, good-looking young fellow with red hair –'

I had heard enough. Five minutes later, I was at Wilmot's door, beating upon it. As he opened it, I noticed that his face was flushed, his eye wild.

'Wilmot!' I cried.

'Yes, I know,' he said impatiently, leading the way to the sitting-room. 'I suppose you've been talking to Poskitt.'

'To Hemmingway. He told me –'

'I know, I know. You were surprised?'

'I was shocked. Shocked to the core. I thought there was better stuff in you, young Byng. Why, when the desire to drive into people grips you, do you not fight against it and conquer it like a man? Have you no will power? Cannot you shake off this frightful craving?'

'It wasn't that at all.'

'What wasn't what at all?'

'All that stuff about having no will power. I was in full possession of my faculties when I tickled up old Poskitt this afternoon. I acted by the light of pure reason. Seeing that I had nothing to lose –'

'Nothing to lose?'

'Not a thing. Gwendoline broke off the engagement this morning.'

'What?'

'Yes. As you are aware, we went to wander in the woods. Well, you know how you feel when you are wandering in the woods with a girl you adore. The sunlight streamed through the overhanging branches, forming a golden pattern on the green below: the air was heavy with fragrant scents and murmurous with the drone of fleeting insects, and what with one thing and another I was led to remark that I loved her as no one had ever loved before. Upon which, she said that I did not love her as much as she loved me. I said yes, I did, because my love stood alone. She said no, it didn't, because hers did. I said it couldn't, because mine did.

'Hot words ensued, and a few moments later she was saying that she never wanted to see or speak to me again, because I was an obstinate, fat-headed son of an Army mule. She then handed back my letters, which she was carrying in a bundle tied round with lilac ribbon somewhere in the interior of her costume, and left me. Naturally, then, when Poskitt and his accomplice held us up for five minutes on the eleventh, I saw no reason to hesitate. My life's happiness was wrecked, and I found a sort of melancholy consolation in letting him have it on the seat of the pants with a wristy spoon shot.'

In the face of the profounder human tragedies there is little that one can say. I was pondering in gloomy silence on this ruin of two young lives, when the doorbell rang. Wilmot went to answer it and came back carrying a letter in his hand. There was a look upon his face which I had not seen since the occasion when he missed the short putt on the eighteenth which would have given him the Spring medal.

'Listen,' said Wilmot. 'Cyanide. Do you happen to have any cyanide on you?'

'Cyanide?'

'Or arsenic would do. Read this. On second thought, I'll give you the gist. There is some rather fruity stuff in Para. One which I feel was intended for my eye alone. The nub is that Gwendoline says she's sorry and it's all on again.'

The drama of the situation hit me like a stuffed eelskin.

'She loves you as of yore?'

'Rather more than of yore, if anything, I gather.'

'And you –'

'And I –'

'Have driven –'

'Have driven –'

'Into –'

'Into old Poskitt, catching him bending –'

'Causing him to lose a stroke and thereby tie for the President's Cup instead of winning it.'

I had not thought that the young fellow's jaw could drop any farther, but at these words it fell another inch.

'You don't mean that?'

'Hemmingway rang me up just now to tell me that he and Poskitt turned in the same score and are playing it off tomorrow.'

'Gosh!'

'Quite.'

'What shall I do?'

I laid my hand upon his shoulder.

'Pray, my boy, that Poskitt will win tomorrow.'

'But even then –'

'No. You have not studied the psychology of the long-handicap golfer as I have. It would not be possible for a twenty-four handicap man who had just won his first cup to continue to harbour resentment against his bitterest foe. In the hour of triumph Poskitt must inevitably melt. So pray, my boy.'

A quick-gleam lit up Wilmot Byng's blue eyes.

'You bet I'll pray,' he said. 'The way I'll pray will be nobody's business. Push off, and I'll start now.'

At eleven o'clock the following morning I joined Poskitt and Hemmingway on the first tee, and a few minutes later the play-off for the President's Cup had begun. From the very outset it was evident that this was to be a battle of styles. Two men of more sharply contrasted methods can seldom have come together on a golf course.

Poskitt, the d'Artagnan of the links, was a man who brought to the tee the tactics which in his youth had won him such fame as a hammer thrower. His plan was to clench his teeth, shut his eyes, whirl the club round his head and bring it down with sickening violence in the general direction of the sphere. Usually, the only result would be a ball topped along the ground or – as had been known to happen when he used his niblick – cut in half. But there would come times when by some mysterious dispensation of Providence he managed to connect, in which event the gallery would be stunned by the spectacle of a three-hundred-yarder down the middle. The whole thing, as he himself recognized, was a clean, sporting venture. He just let go and hoped for the best.

In direct antithesis to these methods were those of Wadsworth Hemmingway. It was his practice before playing a shot to stand over the ball for an appreciable time, shaking gently in every limb and eyeing it closely as if it were some difficult point of law. When eventually he began his back swing, it was with a slowness which reminded those who had travelled in Switzerland of moving glaciers. A cautious pause at the top, and the clubhead would descend to strike the ball squarely and dispatch it fifty yards down the course in a perfectly straight line.

The contest, in short, between a man who – on, say, the long fifteenth – oscillated between a three and a forty-two and one who on the same hole always got his twelve – never more, never less. The Salt of Golf, as you might say.

And yet, as I took my stand beside the first tee, I had no feeling of pleasurable anticipation. To ensure the enjoyment of the spectator of a golf match, one thing is essential. He must feel that the mimic warfare is being conducted in the gallant spirit of a medieval tourney, not in the mood of a Corsican vendetta. And today it was only too plain from the start that bitterness and hostility were rampant.

The dullest mind would have been convinced of this by the manner in which, when Hemmingway had spun a half-crown and won the honour, Poskitt picked up the coin and examined it on both sides with a hard stare. Reluctantly convinced by his inspection that there was no funny business afoot, he drew back and allowed his opponent to drive. And presently Hemmingway had completed his customary fifty-yarder, and it was Poskitt's turn to play.

A curious thing I have noticed about golf is that a festering grievance sometimes does wonders for a man's drive. It is as if pent-up emotion added zip to his swing. It was so on the present occasion. Assailing his ball with hideous violence,

Poskitt sent it to within ten yards of the green, and a few moments later, despite the fact that Hemmingway cleared his throat both before and during the first, second and third putts, he was one up.

But this pent-up emotion is a thing that cuts both ways. It had helped Poskitt on the first. On the second, the short lake hole, it undid him. With all this generous wrath surging about inside him, he never looked like accomplishing the restrained mashie shot which would have left him by the pin. Outdriving the green by some hundred and seventy yards, he reached the woods that lay behind it, and before he could extricate himself Hemmingway was on the green and he was obliged to concede. They went to the third all square.

Here Poskitt did one of his celebrated right-angle drives and took seven to get out of the rough. Hemmingway, reaching the green with a steady eight, had six for it and won without difficulty.

The fourth is a dog-leg. Hemmingway drove short of the bunker. Poskitt followed with a stroke which I have never seen executed on the links before or since, a combination hook and slice. The ball, starting off as if impelled by dynamite, sailed well out to the left, then, after travelling one hundred and fifty yards, seemed to catch sight of the hole round the bend, paused in mid-air and, turning sharply to the right, soared on to the green.

All square once more, a ding-dong struggle brought them to the seventh, which Poskitt won. Hemmingway, recovering, secured the eighth.

The ninth brings you back to the water again, though to a narrower part of it, and when Poskitt. with another of his colossal drives, finished within fifty yards of the pin, it seemed as if the hole must be his. Allowing him four approach shots and three putts, he would be down in eight, a feat far beyond the scope of his opponent. He watched Hemmingway's drive just clear the water, and with a grunt of satisfaction started to leave the tee.

'One moment,' said Hemmingway.

'Eh?'

'Are you not going to drive?'

'Don't you call that a drive?'

'I do not. A nice practice shot, but not a drive. You took the honour when it was not yours. I, if you recollect, won the last hole. I am afraid I must ask you to play again.'

'What?'

'The rules are quite definite on this point,' said Hemmingway, producing a well-thumbed volume.

There was an embarrassing silence.

'And what do the rules say about clearing your throat on the green when your opponent is putting?'

'There is no rule against that.'

'Oh no?'

'It is recognized that a tendency to bronchial catarrh is a misfortune for which the sufferer should be sympathized with rather than penalized.'

'Oh yes?'

'Quite.' Hemmingway glanced at his watch. 'I notice that three minutes have elapsed since I made my drive. I must point out to you that if you delay more than five minutes, you automatically lose the hole.'

Poskitt returned to the tee and put down another ball. There was a splash.

'Playing three,' said Hemmingway.

Poskitt drove again.

'Playing five,' said Hemmingway.

'Must you recite?' said Poskitt.

'There is no rule against calling the score.'

'I concede the hole,' said Poskitt.

Wadsworth Hemmingway was one up at the turn.

There is nothing (said the Oldest Member) which, as a rule, I enjoy more than recounting stroke by stroke the course of a golf match. Indeed I have been told that I am sometimes almost too meticulous in my attention to detail. But there is one match which I have never been able to bring myself to report in this manner, and that is the play-off for the President's Cup between Wadsworth Hemmingway and Joseph Poskitt.

The memory is too painful. As I said earlier, really bad golf is a thing which purges the soul, and a man becomes a better and broader man from watching it. But this contest, from the tenth hole – where Poskitt became all square – onwards, was so poisoned by the mental attitude of the principals that to recall it even today makes me shudder. It resolved itself into a struggle between a great-souled slosher, playing far above his form, and a subtle Machiavellian schemer who, outdriven on every hole, held his own by constant reference to the book of rules.

I need merely say that Poskitt, after a two-hundred-and-sixty yard drive at the eleventh, lost the hole through dropping his club in a bunker, that, having accomplished an equally stupendous stroke at the twelfth, he became two down owing to a careless inquiry as to whether I did not think he could get on from there with a mashie ('seeking advice of one who was not his caddy') and that, when he had won the thirteenth, he became two down once more at the short fourteenth when a piece of well-timed throat-clearing on the part of his opponent caused him to miss the putt which should have given him a half.

But there was good stuff in Joseph Poskitt. He stuck to it manfully. The long fifteenth I had expected him to win, and he did, but I had not been prepared for his clever seven on the sixteenth. And when he obtained a half on the seventeenth by holing out from a bunker a hundred and fifty yards short of the green, I felt that all might yet be well. I could see that Hemmingway, confident that he would be dormy one, was a good deal shaken at coming to the eighteenth all square.

The eighteenth was one of those objectionable freak holes, which, in my opinion, deface a golf course. Ten yards from the tee the hill rose almost sheer to the table-land where the green had been constructed. I suppose that from tee to pin was a distance of not more than fifty yards. A certain three if you were on, anything if you were not.

It was essentially a hole unsuited to Poskitt's particular style. What Poskitt required, if he was to give of his best, was a great wide level prairie stretching out before him into the purple distance. Conditions like those of the eighteenth hole put him very much in the position of a house-painter who is suddenly called upon to execute a miniature. I could see that he was ill at ease as he teed his ball up, and I was saddened, but not surprised, when he topped it into the long grass at the foot of the hill.

But the unnerving experience of seeing his opponent hole out from bunkers had taken its toll of Hemmingway. He, too, was plainly not himself. He swung with his usual care, but must have swerved from the policy of a lifetime and lifted his head. He finished his stroke with a nice, workmanlike follow-through but this did him no good, for he had omitted to hit the ball. When he had disentangled himself, there it was, still standing up on its little mountain of sand.

'You missed it,' said Poskitt.

'I am aware of the fact,' said Hemmingway.

'What made you do that? Silly. You can't expect to get anywhere if you don't hit the ball.'

'If you will kindly refrain from talking, I will play my second.'

'Well, don't miss this one.'

'Please.'

'You'll never win at golf if you do things in this slipshod way. The very first thing is to hit the ball. If you don't you cannot make real progress. I should have thought you would have realized that.'

Hemmingway appealed to me.

'Umpire, I should be glad if you would instruct my opponent to be quiet. Otherwise, I shall claim the hole and the match.'

'There is nothing in the rules,' I said, 'against the opponent offering genial sympathy and advice.'

'Exactly,' said Poskitt. 'You don't want to miss it again, do you? Very well. All I'm doing is telling you not to.'

I pursed my lips. I was apprehensive. I knew Hemmingway. Another man in his position might have been distracted by these cracks, but I could see that they had but solidified his determination to put his second up to the pin. I had seen wrath and resentment work a magic improvement in Poskitt's game, and I felt sure that they were about to do so in Wadsworth Hemmingway.

Nor was I mistaken. Concentration was written in every line of the man's face as he swung back. The next moment, the ball was soaring through the air, to fall three feet from the hole. And there was Poskitt faced with the task of playing two from the interior of a sort of jungle. Long grass twined itself about his ball, wild flowers draped it, a beetle was sitting on it. His caddie handed him a niblick, but I could not but feel that what was really required was a steam-shovel. It was not a golf shot at all. The whole contract should have been handed to some capable excavation company.

But I had not realized to what lengths an ex-hammer-thrower can go, when armed with a niblick and really up against it. Just as film stars are happiest among their books, so was Joseph Poskitt happiest among the flowering shrubs with his niblick. His was a game into which the niblick had always entered very largely. It was the one club with which he really felt confident of expressing his personality. It removed all finicky science from the proceedings and put the issue squarely up to the bulging biceps and the will to win.

Even though the sight of his starting eyes and the knotted veins on his forehead had prepared me for an effort on the major scale, I gave an involuntary leap as the club came down. It was as if a shell had burst in my immediate neighbourhood. Nor were the effects so very dissimilar to those which a shell would have produced. A gaping chasm opened in the hillside. The air became full of a sort of macedoine of grass, dirt, flowers and beetles. And dimly, in the centre of this moving hash, one perceived the ball, travelling well. Accompanied by about a pound of mixed solids, it cleared the brow and vanished from our sight.

But when we had climbed the steep ascent and reached the green, my heart bled for Poskitt. He had made a gallant effort as ever man made and had reduced the lower slopes to what amounted to a devastated area, but he was lying a full ten feet from the hole and Hemmingway, an unerring putter over the short distance, was safe for three. Unless he could sink this ten-footer and secure a half, it seemed to me inevitable that my old friend must lose the match.

He did not sink it. He tried superbly, but when the ball stopped rolling three inches separated it from the hole.

One could see from Hemmingway's bearing as he poised his

club that he had no doubts or qualms. A sinister smile curved his thin lips.

'This for it,' he said, with sickening complacency.

He drew back the clubhead, paused for an instant, and brought it down.

And, as he did so, Poskitt coughed.

I have heard much coughing in my time. I am a regular theatre-goer, and I was once at a luncheon where an operatic basso got a crumb in his windpipe. But never have I heard a cough so stupendous as that which Joseph Poskitt emitted at this juncture. It was as if he had put a strong man's whole soul into the thing.

The effect on Wadsworth Hemmingway was disintegrating. Not even his cold self-control could stand up against it. A convulsive start passed through his whole frame. His club jerked forward, and the ball, leaping past the hole, skimmed across the green, took the edge in its stride and shot into the far bunker.

'Sorry,' said Poskitt. 'Swallowed a fly or something.'

There was a moment when all Nature seemed to pause, breathless.

'Umpire,' said Hemmingway.

'It's no good appealing to the umpire,' said Poskitt. 'I know the rules. They covered your bronchial catarrh, and they cover my fly or something. You had better concede the hole and match.'

'I will not concede the hole and match.'

'Well, then, hurry up and shoot,' said Poskitt, looking at his watch, 'because my wife's got a big luncheon party today, and I shall get hell if I'm late.'

'Ah!' said Hemmingway.

'Well, snap into it,' said Poskitt.

'I beg your pardon?'

'I said, "Snap into it." '

'Why?'

'Because I want to go home.'

Hemmingway pulled up the knees of his trousers and sat down.

'Your domestic arrangements have nothing to do with me,'

he said. 'The rules allow me five minutes between strokes. I propose to take them.'

I could see that Poskitt was shaken. He looked at his watch again.

'All right,' he said. 'I can manage another five minutes.'

'You will have to manage a little more than that,' said Hemmingway. 'With my next stroke I shall miss the ball. I shall then rest for another five minutes. I shall then miss the ball again. . . .'

'But we can't go on all day.'

'Why not?'

'I must be at that lunch.'

'Then what I would suggest is that you pick up and concede the hole and match.'

'Caddy,' said Poskitt.

'Sir?' said the caddy.

'Go to the club and get my house on the phone and tell my wife that I am unavoidably detained and shall not be able to attend that luncheon party.'

He turned to me.

'Is this five-minutes business really right?'

'Would you care to have a look at my book of the rules?' said Hemmingway. 'I have it here in my bag.'

'Five minutes,' mused Poskitt.

'And as four and a half have now elapsed,' said Hemmingway, 'I will now go and play my third.'

He disappeared.

'Missed it,' he said, returning and sitting down again. The caddy came back.

'Well?'

'The lady said, "Oh, yeah?"'

'She said what?'

' "Oh, yeah?" I tell her what you tell me to tell her and she said, "Oh, yeah?"'

I saw Poskitt's face pale. Nor was I surprised. Any husband would pale if his wife, in response to his telephone message that he proposed to absent himself from her important luncheon party, replied 'Oh, yeah?' And of all such husbands, Joseph Poskitt was the one who might be expected to pale most. Like so many of these big, muscle-bound men, he was a mere serf in the home. His wife ruled him with an unremitting firmness from the day they had stepped across the threshold of St Peter's, Eaton Square.

He chewed his lower lip thoughtfully.

'You're sure it wasn't "Oh, *yes*" – like that – without the mark of interrogation – as much as to say that she quite understood and that it would be perfectly all right?'

'She said, "Oh, yeah?" '

'H'm,' said Poskitt.

I walked away. I could not bear the spectacle of this old friend of mine in travail. What wives do to their husbands who at the eleventh hour edge out of important luncheon parties I am not able, as a bachelor, to say, but a mere glance was enough to tell me that in the Poskitt home, at least, it was something special. And yet to pick up and lose the first cup he had ever had a chance of winning. . . . No wonder Joseph Poskitt clutched his hair and rolled his eyes.

And so, as I say, I strolled off, and my wandering footsteps took me in the direction of the practice tee. Wilmot Byng was there, with an iron and a dozen balls.

He looked up, as I approached, with a pitiful eagerness.

'Is it over?'

'Not yet.'

'They haven't holed out?'

'Not yet.'

'But they must have done,' said Wilmot, amazed. 'I saw them both land on the green.'

'Poskitt has played three and is lying dead.'

'Well, where's Hemmingway?'

I peered round the bush which hides the eighteenth green from the practice tee.

'Just about to play five from the far bunker.'

'And Poskitt is dead in three?'

'Yes.'

'Well, then . . .'

I explained the circumstances. Wilmot was aghast.

'But what's going to happen?'

I shook my head sadly.

'I fear that Poskitt has no alternative but to pick up. His wife, informed over the telephone that he would not be back to lunch, said, "Oh, yeah?"'

For a space Wilmot Byng stood brooding.

'You'd better be getting along,' he advised. 'From what you tell me, this seems to be one of those matches where an umpire on the spot is rather required.'

I did so, for I could see that there was much in what he said. I found Poskitt pacing the green. Hemmingway climbed out of the bunker a moment later to announce that he had once more been unsuccessful in striking the ball.

He seemed disposed to conversation.

'A lot of wasps there are about this summer,' he said. 'One sang right past my ear just then.'

'I wish it had bitten you,' said Poskitt.

'Wasps,' replied Hemmingway, who dabbled in Natural History, 'do not bite. They sting. You are thinking of snakes.'

'Your society would make anyone think of snakes.'

'Gentlemen,' I said. 'Gentlemen!'

Saddened, I strolled away again. Golf to me is a sacred thing, and it pained me to see it played in this spirit. Moreover, I was beginning to want my lunch. It was partly the desire to converse with a rational human being and partly the reflection that he could pop into the clubhouse and bring me out a couple of ham sandwiches that led me to seek Wilmot Byng again. I made my way to the practice tee, and as I came in sight of it I stopped dead.

Wilmot Byng, facing the bunker, was addressing a ball with his iron. And standing in the bunker, his club languidly raised for his sixth, or it may have been his seventh, was Wadsworth Hemmingway.

The next moment Wilmot had swung, and almost simultaneously a piercing cry of agony rang out over the countryside. A magnificent low, raking shot, with every ounce of wrist and weight behind it, had taken Hemmingway on the left leg.

Wilmot turned to me, and in his eyes there was the light which comes into the eyes of those who have set themselves a task and accomplished it.

'You'll have to disqualify that bird,' he said. 'He has dropped his club in a bunker.'

Little (said the Oldest Member) remains to be told. When, accompanied by Wilmot, I returned to the green, I formally awarded the match and cup to Poskitt, at the same time condoling with his opponent on having had the bad luck to be in the line of flight of somebody's random practice drive. These things, I pointed out, were all in the game and must be accepted as rubs of the green. I added that Wilmot was prepared to apologize, and Wilmot said, Yes, fully prepared. Hemingway was, however, none too well pleased, I fear, and shortly afterwards he left us, his last words being that he proposed to bring an action against Wilmot in the civil courts.

The young fellow appeared not to have heard the threat. He was gazing at Poskitt, pale but resolute.

'Mr Poskitt,' he said. 'May I have a word with you?'

'A thousand,' replied Poskitt, beaming on his benefactor, for whom it was plain that he had now taken a fancy amounting to adoration. 'But later on, if you don't mind. I have to run like a . . .'

'Mr Poskitt, I love your daughter.'

'So do I,' said Poskitt. 'Very nice girl.'

'I want to marry her.'

'Well, why don't you?'

'You will give your consent?'

A kindly smile flickered over my old friend's face. He looked at his watch again, then patted Wilmot affectionately on the shoulder.

'I will do better than that, my boy,' he said. 'I will formally refuse my consent. I will forbid the match *in toto* and oppose it root and branch. That will fix everything nicely. When you have been married as long as I have, you will know that what these things require is tact and the proper handling.'

And so it proved. Two minutes after Poskitt announced that young Wilmot Byng wished to marry their daughter Gwendoline and that he, Poskitt, was resolved that this should be done only over his, Poskitt's, dead body, Mrs Poskitt was

sketching out the preliminary arrangements for the sacred cere-
mony. It took place a few weeks later at a fashionable church
with full choral effects, and all were agreed that the Bishop
had seldom been in finer voice. The bride, as one was able to
see from the photographs in the illustrated weekly papers,
looked charming.

Chapter Four
Farewell to Legs

Squeals of feminine merriment woke the Oldest Member from the doze into which he had fallen. The door of the cardroom, in which it was his custom to take refuge when there was Saturday-night revelry at the clubhouse, had opened to admit a gloomy young man.

'Not butting in, am I?' said the gloomy young man. 'I can't stand it out there any longer.'

The Sage motioned him to a chair. He sank into it and for a while sat glowering darkly.

'Tricks with string!' he muttered at length.

'I beg your pardon?'

'Josh Hook is doing tricks with bits of string, and the girls are fawning on him as if he were Clark Gable. Makes me sick.'

The Oldest Member began to understand.

'Is your *fiancée* among them?'

'Yes, she is. She keeps saying. "Oh, Mr *Hook*!" with a sort of rising inflection and giving him pats on the arm. Loving pats, or so it seemed to me.'

The Sage smiled sympathetically. In his hot youth he had been through this sort of thing himself. 'Cheer up,' he said. 'I know just how you feel, but rest assured that all will be well. Josh Hook's string tricks may be sweeping the girl off her feet for the moment, but his glamour will pass. She will wake tomorrow morning her true self again, thankful that she has the love of a good man who seldom shoots worse than eighty-three.'

His companion brightened. His face lost its drawn look.

'You think so?'

'I am convinced of it. I have seen so many of these party hounds. They dazzle for a while, but they never last. I have observed this Hook. His laughter is as the crackling of thorns under the pot and his handicap is twenty-four. Just another Legs Mortimer.'

'Who was Legs Mortimer?'

'That was precisely what Angus McTavish wanted to know when he saw him blowing kisses at Evangeline Brackett from the clubhouse verandah.'

Angus McTavish (said the Oldest Member), as one might infer from his name, was a man who all his life had taken golf with a proper seriousness, and in Evangeline Brackett he seemed to have found his female counterpart. She was not one of those girls who titter 'tee-hee' when they top a drive. It was, indeed, her habit of biting her lips and rolling her eyes on such occasions which had first drawn Angus to her. On her side, respect for a man who, though slight of build and weighing ten stone two, could paste the ball two hundred yards from the tee, had speedily ripened into passion, and at the time of which I speak they had just become engaged; and the only cloud on Angus's happiness, until the series of events began which I am about to describe, was the fact that his great love occasionally caused him to fluff a chip shot. He would be swinging and he would suddenly think of Evangeline and jerk his head towards the sky, as if asking Heaven to make him worthy of her, thus shanking. He told me he had lost several holes that way.

However, the iron self-control of the McTavishes was rendering these lapses less frequent, and, as I say, there was virtually no flaw in his happiness until the spring morning when, coming up from the eighteenth green with the girl of his dreams, to whom he had been giving a third, he was shocked to observe that there was a young man on the clubhouse verandah, leaning over the rail and blowing kisses at her.

Now, no recently betrothed lover likes this sort of thing, and it jars him all the more sharply when, as in the present case, the blower is a man of extraordinary physical attractions, with large brown eyes and a natural wave in his hair. There was a certain coldness in Angus's voice as he spoke.

'Who,' he asked, 'is that bird?'

'Eh?' said Evangeline. She was polishing her ball with a sponge and her head was bent.

'Fellow on the verandah. Seems to know you.'

Evangeline looked up. She stared for a moment, then uttered a delighted yowl.

'Why, it's Legs! Yoo-hoo!'

'Yoo-hoo!'

'Yoo-hoo!'

'Yoo-hoo!'

As, at the beginning of the episode, they had not been more than four Yoo-hoos' length from the verandah, they were now standing beside the handsome stranger.

'Why, Legs Mortimer!' said Evangeline. 'Whatever are you doing here?'

The young man explained – in a manner which may have been merely brotherly, but which seemed to Angus McTavish rather fresher than an April breeze – that he had come to settle in the neighbourhood and that while his bungalow was being made ready he was temporarily established at the clubhouse. In making this statement, he addressed Evangeline once as 'sweetness', twice as 'kid', and three times as 'darling'.

'Splendid!' said Evangeline. 'You'll wake the place up.'

'Trust me, beautiful. Trust old Legs, kid. There will be many a jocund party thrown in yonder clubhouse.'

'Well, mind you invite me. By the way, this is my *fiancé*, Angus McTavish.'

'Angus McTavish,' cried Legs Mortimer. 'Hoots, mon! Scots wha hae! Hoo's a' wi' ye the morn's morn?'

And Angus, hearing these words and watching their speaker break into what appeared to be a Highland fling, became aware with a sinking heart that here, as he had already begun to suspect, was a life-and-soul-of-the-party man, a perfect scream, and an absolutely priceless fellow who simply makes you die with the things he says.

He was thoughtful as he accompanied Evangeline to her home.

'This Mortimer,' he said dubiously.

'What about him?'

'Well, what about him? Who is he? Where did you meet him? What is his handicap?'

'I met him when I was over in Switzerland last winter. He

was staying at the hotel. I believe he has a lot of money of his own. He doesn't play golf.'

'Doesn't play golf?' said Angus incredulously.

'No. But he's wonderful at ski-ing.'

'Faugh!'

'What?'

'I said "Faugh!" Ski-ing, indeed! What on earth does the fellow want to ski for? Isn't there enough sadness in life without going out of your way to fasten long planks to your feet and jump off mountains? And don't forget this – from ski-ing to yodelling is but a short step. Do we want a world full of people going about the place singing, "Ti-ra-ra-ra-la-i-te," or something amounting to very much the same thing? I'll bet this Mortimer man of yours is a confirmed yodeller.'

'He did yodel a good deal,' admitted Evangeline. 'He yodelled to the waiters.'

'Why to the waiters?'

'They were Swiss, you see. So he yodelled to them. He made us all scream. And he was always playing jokes on people.'

'Jokes?'

'Like giving them trick cigars, you know. There was a Bishop staying at the hotel, and Legs gave him a cigar and the Bishop went off with a bang. We all expired with mirth.'

Angus drew his breath in sharply.

'So,' he said, 'the man is not only a dangerous incendiary, but utterly lacking in respect for the Cloth. Faugh!'

'I wish you wouldn't say "Faugh!"'

'Enough to make one say "Faugh!"' said Angus sombrely.

The joy had gone out of his world. A dark fog seemed to be spreading over the sunlit uplands of his bliss, and there was a marked shortage of bluebirds.

He viewed the future with concern. And he had good reason to do so. Little by little, as the days went by, the conviction was forced upon him that Evangeline Brackett was becoming infatuated with this yodelling, trick-cigar merchant. That very first morning he had thought them a great deal too matey. A week later, he was compelled to recognize that matiness was a feeble and inadequate word. It was Legs this and Legs that and Oh, Legs, and Yoo-hoo, Legs, till he began to feel like a super standing in the wings watching Romeo and Juliet play their balcony scene. A great bitterness of spirit began to descend on Angus McTavish, and he twice took sixes at holes at which in happier days he had often got threes.

There is no question (said the Oldest Member) that these party lizards like Legs Mortimer are a terrible menace when they sneak out into the rural districts. In a great city their noxious influence is less marked. The rushing life of a metropolis seems to fortify girls against their meretricious spell. But in a peaceful hamlet like that in which Angus McTavish and Evangeline Brackett resided there are so few counter-attractions that the poison may be said to work without anything in the nature of an antidote.

Except, of course, golf. The one consolation which Angus had during this dark period was the fact that Evangeline had not yet faltered in her devotion to golf. She was practising diligently for the Ladies' Spring Medal.

And yet, though, as I say, this consoled Angus, it did so only faintly. If Evangeline could still turn out with her bag of clubs and practise for the Spring Medal, it showed, of course, that her better self was not entirely dead. But of what avail was it to practise, he asked himself, if Legs Mortimer gave almost nightly parties and she persisted in attending them? Until the other's arrival, Evangeline had been accustomed to go to bed at eleven after spending the evening with some good book such as *Braid on Taking Turf*. Now, it seemed a perpetual race between her and the milkman as to which should reach her door first, with the milkman winning three times out of four.

He tried to reason with her one morning when a sudden yawn had caused her to top a mashie niblick shot which a month before she would have laid dead to the pin.

'What can you expect,' he said, 'if you stop up half the night at parties?'

She was plainly impressed.

'You don't really think it's hurting my game, do you?'

'It is ruining your game.'

'But everybody goes to parties.'

'Not when they have an important match in prospect.'

'And Legs's parties are such fun. He makes them go so.'

'Oh yes?' said Angus coldly.

'He's a perfect scream. You should have seen him last night. He told Jack Prescott he wanted him to help him with a trick, and he got him to lay his hands on the table, palms downward. Then he put a full glass of water on each hand ...'

'And then –?' said Angus, with deepening gloom, for his whole soul was revolted at the thought of Jack Prescott, a four handicap man, lending himself to such childishness.

'Why, then he just walked away and left him, and Jack couldn't get his hands free without drenching himself with water. We simply howled.'

'Well,' said Angus, when he had ceased shuddering, 'if you will take my advice, you will cut out these orgies from now on.'

'I must go to the one next week.'

'Why?'

'I promised I would. It's Legs's birthday.'

'Then,' said Angus, 'I shall come, too.'

'But you'll only go to sleep. You ought to see Legs's imitation of you going to sleep at a party. It's a scream.'

'Possibly,' said Angus stiffly. 'I may doze off for a while. But I shall wake up in time to take you home at a reasonable hour.'

'But I don't want to go home at a reasonable hour.'

'You would prefer to finish about sixteenth in the Spring Medal?'

The girl paled.

'Don't say that.'

'I do say that.'

'Sixteenth?'

'Or seventeenth.'

She drew in her breath sharply.

'All right, then. You shall take me home before midnight.'

'Good,' said Angus.

Being of Scottish descent, he never smiled, but he came within an ace of smiling as he heard those words. For the first time in weeks he was conscious of something that might roughly be called a gleam of light on the darkness of his horizon.

Nothing but love and his determination to save the girl he

worshipped from crawling into bed at four in the morning could have forced Angus McTavish, when the appointed night arrived, to fish out the old stiff shirt and put on dress clothes and present himself at the clubhouse. The day had been unusually warm for the time of year and he had played three rounds and was feeling that desire for repose and solitude which comes to men who have done their fifty-four holes under a hot sun. But tomorrow was the day of the Ladies' Spring Medal, and at whatever cost to himself it was imperative that Evangeline be withdrawn from the revels at an hour which would enable her to get a good night's sleep. So he fought down the desire to put on pyjamas, and presently was mingling with Legs Mortimer's guests, trying to stifle the yawns which nearly tore him asunder.

Equally hard to stifle was the austere disgust which swept over him as he surveyed his surroundings. Legs Mortimer was a man who prided himself on doing these things well, and the clubhouse had broken out into an eruption of roses, smilax, Chinese lanterns, gold-toothed saxophonists, giggling girls and light refreshments. An inhabitant of ancient Babylon would have beamed approvingly on the spectacle, but it made Angus McTavish sick. His idea of a clubhouse was a sort of cathedral filled with serious-minded men telling one another in quiet undertones how they got a four on the long fifteenth.

His rising nausea was in no way allayed by the sight of Evangeline treading the measure in the arms of his host. Angus had never learned to dance, fearing that it might spoil his game, and so knew nothing of the technicalities of the modern fox-trot. He was unable to say, accordingly, whether Legs Mortimer should or should not have been holding Evangeline like that. It might be all right. On the other hand, it might not be all right. All Angus knew was that he had seen melodramas on the stage in which heroines had told villains to unhand them on far less provocation.

Finally, he could endure the thing no longer. There was a sort of annexe, soothingly dark, at the end of the room, and into this he withdrew. He sank into a chair, and almost immediately fell into a restful slumber.

How long he slept, he could not have said. It seemed to him

104

but a moment, but no doubt it was in reality a good deal longer. He was aroused by someone shaking his shoulder and, blinking up, perceived Legs Mortimer at his side. Legs Mortimer's face was contorted with alarm, and he was shouting something which, after a brief interval of dazed misapprehension, Angus discovered was the word 'Fire!'

The last mists of sleep rolled away from Angus McTavish. He was his keen, alert self once more. He had grasped the situation and realized what must be done.

His first thought was of Evangeline. He must start by saving her. Then he must save the trophies in the glass case on the smoking-room mantelpiece, including the ball used by Henry Cotton when breaking the course record. After that he must attend to the female guests, and after that rescue the man who mixed the club's special cocktails, and finally, if there was still time, he must save himself.

It was a comprehensive programme, calling for prompt action and an early start, and he embarked upon it immediately. With a cry of 'Evangeline!' he sprang to his feet, and the next moment had shot into the ballroom with incredible velocity and was skidding along the polished floor on one ear.

Only then did he observe that during his slumbers some hidden hand had fastened roller-skates to his feet with stout straps. Simultaneously with this discovery came the sound of musical mirth on every side, and looking up he found himself the centre of a ring of merry, laughing faces. The merriest of these faces, and the one that laughed most, was that of Evangeline Brackett.

It was a grim, moody Angus McTavish who, some five minutes later, after taking three more tosses in a manner which he distinctly heard Evangeline compare to the delivery of coals in sacks, withdrew on all fours to the kitchen, where a kindly waiter cut the straps with a knife. It was a stern, soured Angus McTavish who, having tipped his preserver, strode off through the night to his cottage. He had a nasty bruise on his right thigh, but it was in his soul that he suffered most.

His love, he told himself, was dead. He felt that he had been deceived in Evangeline. A girl capable of laughing like a hyena at her betrothed in the circumstances in which Evangeline

Brackett had laughed like a hyena at him was not, he reasoned, worthy of a good man's devotion. If this was the sort of girl she was, let her link her lot with that of Legs Mortimer. If her spiritual mate was a fellow who could outrage all the sacred laws of hospitality by fastening roller-skates to his guests' feet and then shouting 'Fire!' in their ears, let her have him.

He rubbed himself with liniment and went to bed.

When he woke on the morrow, however, his mood, as so often happens, had become softer and gentler. He still chafed at the thought that Evangeline could have lowered herself to behave like a hyena, and a mentally arrested hyena at that, but now he was charitably inclined to put her conduct down to cerebral excitement induced by the insidious atmosphere of Chinese lanterns and smilax. Briefly, what he felt was that the girl had been temporarily led astray, and that it must be his task to win her back to the straight and narrow fairway. When, therefore, the telephone rang and he heard her voice, he greeted her amiably.

'How's the boy?' asked Evangeline. 'All right?'

'Splendid,' said Angus.

'No ill effects after last night?'

'None.'

'You're caddying for me in the Ladies' Medal today, aren't you?'

'Of course.'

'That's good. I was afraid you might want to be off somewhere, roller-skating. Ha, ha, ha,' said Evangeline, laughing a silvery laugh. 'He, he, he,' she added, laughing another.

Now, against silvery laughs *qua* silvery laughs there is, of course, nothing to be said. But there are moments in a man's life when he is ill-attuned to them, and it must be confessed that this particular couple, proceeding whence they did, stirred Angus McTavish up to no little extent. A good deal of the softness and gentleness was missing from his composition when he presented himself on the first tee. In fact, not to put too fine a point upon it, he was as sore as a gumboil. And as this showed plainly in his demeanour, and as Evangeline was noticeably off her game during the opening holes, they came to the ninth green with a certain constraint between them. Angus was still

106

thinking of those silvery laughs and feeling that they had been, all things considered, in the most dubious taste, while Evangeline, on her side, was asking herself petulantly how on earth a girl could be expected to shoot to form in the society of a caddy who looked like a V-shaped depression off the coast of Ireland.

And at this crucial point in the affairs of the young couple, when it needed but a spark to precipitate an explosion, whom should they see leaning over the clubhouse verandah but Legs Mortimer.

'Greetings, fair gentles,' said Legs Mortimer. 'And how is our bright and beautiful Evangeline this bright and beautiful morning?'

'Oh, Legs, you're a scream,' said Evangeline. 'Did you,' she inquired of her betrothed, 'speak?'

'I did not,' said Angus, who had snorted.

'And the McTavish of McTavish,' proceeded Legs Mortimer. 'How is the McTavish of McTavish? Listen,' he said, 'I think it's all right. I've been in communication with the management of an important circus this morning, and they tell me if that roller-skating act of yours is as good as I say it is they will book you solid.'

'Oh, yes?' said Angus.

He was well aware that it was not much of a retort, but then no mere verbal thrust would have satisfied him. What he would have liked to do was to take Legs Mortimer's neck in his two hands, twist it, and continue twisting till it came unstuck. But he was slender of physique, and the other, like so many ski-ers and yodellers, was massive and well-proportioned, so he was compelled to confine himself to saying 'Oh yes?' and adding, 'Is that so?' His deportment, while making these observations, was that of an offended cobra.

'Well, boys and girls,' said Legs Mortimer, 'I will now withdraw to the bar and take a short, quick one. I have a slight headache, and meseems a hair of the dog that bit me is indicated.'

Beaming in the insufferable manner that is so frequent with these party lizards, he walked away, and Evangeline, turning imperiously on Angus, said: 'Oh, for goodness' sake.' And when Angus said What did she mean by saying 'Oh for good-

ness' sake,' she said that he knew very well what she meant by
saying 'Oh, for goodness' sake.'

'Behaving like that to poor Legs!'

'Like what?'

'Like a sulky schoolboy.'

'Faugh!'

'I was ashamed of you.'

'Faugh!'

'Don't say "Faugh!"'

'Pshaw!'

'And don't say "Pshaw," either.'

'Can't I speak?'

'Not if you're only going to say "Faugh!" and "Pshaw!"'

Angus was half inclined to remark that he had also been
going to say 'Tchah!' and 'Pah!' but he restrained himself and
kicked moodily at the woodwork.

'I simply can't understand you.'

'You can't, can't you?'

'Any man with a grain of humour would have laughed himself sick at what happened last night.'

'He would, would he?'

'Yes, he would. When Legs played that trick on the Prince
of Schlossing-Lossing, the prince was fearfully amused.'

'He was, was he?'

'Yes, he was. He laughed heartily, looking bronzed and fit.'

'He did, did he?'

'Yes, he did.'

'Well, I'm not a prince.'

'I'll say you're not.'

'What do you mean by that?'

'You're a – well, I don't know what you are.'

'Is that so?'

'Yes, that is so.'

'Indeed?'

'Yes, indeed.'

The hot blood of the McTavishes boiled over.

'Well, I'll tell you,' said Angus, 'what you are.'

'What?'

'You want to know?'

'I do.'

'All right, then. You're the girl who's going to finish twenty-seventh in the Ladies' Medal.'

'Don't talk nonsense.'

'I'm not talking nonsense.'

'Then it's the first time.'

'I'm talking cold sense. You know as well as I do that all this party stuff has turned you from a fine, resolute, upstanding beater of the ball to a wretched, wobbling foozler who ought never to have entered her name for so important a contest as the Ladies' Medal. You have your little mirror with you, I presume? Gaze into it, Evangeline Brackett, and read its message. Your eye is dull and fishy, woman. Your hand trembles. You waggle your putter as if it were a cocktail shaker. And as for the way you have been playing – if I may employ the word "playing" – with your wooden clubs . . .'

Evangeline's face was very cold and hard.

'Yes?' she said. 'Proceed.'

'No,' replied Angus. 'The subject is too painful. But I will say this: If I were you, I'd keep my wood in the bag from now on.'

It was the unforgivable insult. A sock on the jaw Evangeline Brackett might have condoned, a kick in the eye she might have overlooked, but this was too much. Now that Angus McTavish had forfeited her affection by his uncouth and sullen behaviour there were two things only that she loved – her mother and her steel-shafted driver.

'Good morning, Mr McTavish,' she said. 'If you will kindly hand me that bag of clubs, I will not trouble you to come round with me any longer.'

A swift revulsion of feeling swept over Angus McTavish. He perceived that he had gone too far. He loved this girl, and he had hurt her.

'Evangeline!' he cried.

'My name,' said the girl, 'is Brackett. A "Miss" goes with it.'

'But listen,' pleaded Angus. 'This is absurd. You know I worship the very tee you walk on. Are we to part like this just because that Mortimer excrescence has come into our lives? Shall our dream Paradise be shattered by a snake in the bosom

109

– or is it grass – who is not worth a thought from either of us? If you will but reflect, you will see how right I am in regarding him as a worm and a pustule. Consider. The man yodels. He does not play golf. He . . .'

'My bag of clubs, if you please,' said Evangeline haughtily, 'and look slippy with it, if you will be so good. I do not wish to remain here all day. Ah, here comes Legs. Dear old Legs! Legs, darling, will you carry for me?'

'Carry what, sweetest of your sex?'

'My clubs.'

'Oh, the jolly old hockey-knockers? Certainly, certainly, certainly.'

'Hockey-knockers!' hissed Angus in her ear. 'You heard what he said! One of the finest steel-shafted, rubber-grip, self-compensating sets of clubs ever made by the Pro, and he called them hockey-knockers. I warn you, girl, have a care. Do not trust that man. Somehow, somewhere, in some manner, at some time and place, he will let you down, and with a bump. Beware!'

'Come on, Legs darling,' said Evangeline, laughing a silvery laugh. 'My partner's waiting.'

Standing there on the verandah with folded arms, Angus McTavish watched them depart. Evangeline, her face like stone, did not vouchsafe him so much as a glance over her shoulder. Cold and aloof, she made her way to the tenth tee, and Legs Mortimer, having tilted his hat to one side, put on a false moustache which he produced from an inner pocket, and danced a few steps, said 'Hot dog,' shouldered the bag and followed her.

Now, it may well be (said the Oldest Member) that, listening to what I have been telling you and particularly taking into consideration the remarks of Angus McTavish during the scene which I have just described, you will have formed the impression that after her performance going out it was scarcely worth Evangeline Brackett's while to bother to play the second nine. Having made a start like that, you probably feel, she might just as well, for all the chance she had of winning the Ladies' Medal, have torn up her card and gone home.

But you must make allowances for the exaggeration – shall I say the imagery? – of a jealous lover still smarting from the fact of having had roller-skates put on him by his rival in the presence of the adored object, and then having been laughed at by her, first in a hyena-like and then in a silvery manner. These things distort the judgement and lend acid to the tongue. When Angus had referred so bitingly to Evangeline's ineffici-ency with the wood, he had had in mind merely the circum-stance of her having topped a couple of spoon shots. His remark about the putter and the cocktail shaker was based on a slight disposition on her part to fail to lay approach shots dead. The truth was that Evangeline, though perhaps five strokes in excess of what a pure-minded girl with her handicap might have expected to take on nine holes, was still well in the running. And the resentment with which she was seething as the result of her ex-*fiancé*'s uncouth behaviour resulted now, as resentment so often does on the golf course, in her striking a patch of positive brilliance.

The thought of Angus McTavish and those low cracks of his lent her an almost superhuman vigour. Every time she drove off the tee she did it with a sort of controlled fury, as if she were imagining that she had seen Angus McTavish standing in the middle of the fairway and that a well-directed shot would catch him on the spot where it would do him most good. When she chipped, it was as if she were chipping Angus. And whenever she made a recovery from a bunker with her niblick, she hit the ball as though it were Angus McTavish's shin.

By these means, she was enabled to get fours on the tenth, eleventh and twelfth, a five on the thirteenth, and on the short fourteenth one of those lucky twos which, as James Braid once said to J. H. Taylor, seem like a dome of many-coloured glass to stain the white radiance of Eternity. In short, to condense the thing into cold figures, by the time she had holed out at the seventeenth, she had played a net seventy-three. And when she learned from a bystander that her only two possible rivals had each turned in net seventy-nine, she not unnaturally considered that the contest was as good as over. The eighteenth had always been a favourite hole of hers, and she was supremely confident of securing a four on it. Not even in the stress of a medal round had she the slightest apprehension of failing to be on near the pin with, at the worst, her third.

In these circumstances, it is not to be wondered at that she gazed at Legs Mortimer with an affection bordering on something even warmer. As was his practice when wearing a false moustache, he was waggling the ends of it, and she thought she had never seen anything so droll. How vast an improvement, she felt, not only in the capacity of a caddy but in that of a mate for life, was this sunny, light-hearted merrymaker on such a human pain in the tonsils as Angus McTavish. Going round with Angus McTavish carrying your bag, she mused, was equivalent to about four bisques to the opposition. Angus McTavish was the sort of man who, just by going about looking like a frozen asset, takes all the edge and zip out of a girl's game. She felt that she had had a merciful escape from Angus McTavish.

'What I love about you, Legs,' she said, as they walked to the eighteenth tee, 'is your wonderful sense of humour. Don't you hate people with no sense of humour? Scotchmen, I mean, and people like that. I mean people who get stuffy if somebody plays a harmless good-natured practical joke on them. Like – well, Scotchmen, I mean.'

'Quite,' said Legs Mortimer, putting on a false nose.

'I'm sure I should be the first to laugh if anything of that sort ever happened to me. But then, thank goodness, I have always had a sense of humour.'

'Great gift,' said Legs.

'Well, it's just the way one happens to be born, I suppose,' said Evangeline modestly. 'You either have it or you haven't. I think I'll have a new ball here, Legs, darling. I don't want to make any mistake over this hole.'

The confidence which Evangeline Brackett had felt on holing out at the seventeenth had lost none of its force at this supreme moment. It seemed to inflate her as with some invisible gas as she surveyed the glistening white globe perched up on its wooden tee. Every golfer knows that sensation of power and mastery which comes when he has just played a series of holes in perfect style and is conscious that his stance is right and his wrists are right and all things working together for good. Evangeline had it now. Here was she and there was the ball, and in another moment she was going to slap it squarely in the tummy and send it a mile and a quarter. Her only fear was lest she might overdrive the green, which was a mere three hundred and eighty yards distant.

She waggled for an instant. Then, raising her club with an effortless swing, she brought it down.

And what of Angus, meanwhile? For some little time after Evangeline had left him, he stood rooted to the spot. For some little time after that, he had paced the terrace with knitted brow, reminding not a few of the members who watched him through the windows of Napoleon at St Helena. Eventually, finding conditions rather cramped and feeling that he needed more space in which to express himself, he had gone for a walk round the links, and by one of those odd coincidences was approaching the eighteenth tee from the rear at the exact moment when Evangeline made her drive. And as he drew near his reverie was suddenly shattered by a hideous, cackling shout of laughter from the other side of the bushes which hid the tee from his view.

He stopped, frowning. Laughter on the links was a thing which always offended his sense of the reverent, and the current burst of merriment he had recognized immediately as emanating from Legs Mortimer. Nobody else's mirth had just that quacking sound.

'Faugh!' said Angus, and was about to repeat the word, when it died on his lips, and he stood gaping. There was a sort of thudding sound as of feet spurning the turf, and then round the corner of the bushes came Legs Mortimer, cutting out an excellent pace, and after him, her face flushed, her eyes staring, Evangeline Brackett, brandishing in her hand a steel-shafted driver. She seemed to be endeavouring to brain the other, if it is possible to brain a man like Legs Mortimer.

There was very little vulgar curiosity in the composition of Angus McTavish, but what there was was sufficient to make him follow the pair at his best speed. He came up with the hunt just as Legs, apparently despairing of shaking off the girl's challenge, dodged behind a leafy tree and, with an adroitness born, no doubt, of his Swiss mountaineering, shinned up it like a squirrel and remained there.

It was at this moment that Evangeline saw Angus.

'Oh, Angus!' she cried, and the next moment she was in his arms.

Scotch blood, it has always been my experience, makes for solid worth rather than nimbleness of wit, for a certain rugged stability of character rather than quick intuition, but even a man as Scotch as Angus McTavish was able to perceive – and that without delay – that here was a good thing which should be pushed along. He would have been the first to admit that he did not quite follow the run of the scenario, but he divined that for some reason which would doubtless be made clear at a later date the past was forgotten and Evangeline's heart his once more. Reaching out, accordingly, he clasped her to his bosom, and for a space she remained there, hiccoughing.

'Oh, Angus!' she sobbed at length. 'How right you were!'

'When?' asked Angus McTavish.

'When you warned me against that man. "Do not trust him," you said. "Somehow, somewhere, in some manner, at some time or place, he will let you down, and with a bump." '

'And did he?'

'Did he not!' replied Evangeline Brackett. 'I needed a five on the eighteenth to win the medal, and I asked him to get me out a new ball and do you know what he did?'

'What?'

'I'll tell you what. He put down a s-s-s-s-s.'

Anguish robbed Evangeline of speech. There was something scarcely human in her expression, and in endeavouring to frame the last word she had sunk to the level of a soda-siphon.

Angus groped for her meaning.

'He put down what?'

'A s-s-s-s-s.'

'Sand?'

She shook her head violently.

'No, no! Not s-s-s-s-s. A s-s-s-s-s.'

'S-s-s-s-s?'

'S-s-s-s-s.'

'S-s-s-s?'

'A soap-ball,' said Evangeline, suddenly becoming articulate.

If he had not been holding on to the girl, Angus McTavish would have reeled – Scotch-reeled, as no doubt Legs Mortimer would have described it. If his reverent nature revolted at smilax in the clubhouse and laughter on the links it revolted with a far greater sensation of outraged nausea at the sight of those cakes of soap which manufacturers, dead to every decent instinct and making a mockery out of sacred things, turn out in the shape of regulation golf-balls. Many a time, going into a chemist's shop to purchase a tube of toothpaste, he had re-coiled with a hoarse cry on seeing them on the counter, to take his custom elsewhere. And until now he had always supposed that the ultimate depth possible for Humanity to reach had been reached by the perpetrators of these loathsome travesties.

And now a new low level had been hit. A man – or, rather, a creature bearing the outward semblance of a man – had teed up one of the dreadful things for a girl, a fragile, sensitive girl, to drive – not, which would have been bad enough, in some casual morning round, but at the very crisis of the Ladies' Spring Medal Competition.

'I came down on it like a thousand of bricks,' proceeded Evangeline, quivering at the memory, 'with every ounce of weight and muscle behind the shot. I thought for a moment I had broken in half. And talking,' she went on, a more cheerful note creeping into her voice, 'of breaking things in half, if you wouldn't mind, darling, just climbing that tree and handing me down its contents, I will see what can be done with this driver.'

But Angus McTavish, who had been scanning the tree closely, shook his head. It was as if he deprecated the violence at which she hinted. Gently he led her from the spot, and it was not until they were the distance of a good iron shot away that he released her and replied to the protestations which she had been uttering.

'It is quite all right, dear,' he said. 'Everything is in order.'

'Everything in order?' She faced him passionately. 'What do you mean?'

Angus patted her hand.

'You were a little too overwrought to observe it, no doubt,' he said, 'but there was a hornets' nest two inches above his head. I think we cannot be accused of being unduly sanguine if we assume that when he starts to ... Ah!' said Angus. 'Hark!'

Unmusical cries were ruining the peace of the spring evening.

'And look,' added Angus.

As he spoke, a form came sliding hastily down out of the tree. At a rapid pace it moved across the turf to the water beyond the eighteenth tee. It dived in and, having done so, seemed anxious to remain below the surface, for each time a head emerged from those smelling depths it went under again.

'Nature's remedy,' said Angus.

For a long minute Evangeline Brackett stood gazing silently with parted lips. Then she threw her head back and from those parted lips there proceeded a silvery laugh so piercing in its timbre that an old gentleman practising approach shots at the seventeenth jerked his mashie sharply and holed out from eighty yards.

Angus McTavish patted her hand fondly. He was broadminded, and felt that there were moments when laughter on the links was permissible.

Chapter Five
There's Always Golf

It was the day of the annual contest for the Mixed Foursomes Cup, and the Oldest Member, accompanied by the friend who was visiting him for the week-end, had strolled to the edge of the terrace to watch the first of the competitors drive off. As they came in sight of the tee the friend uttered an exclamation of astonishment, almost of awe.

'What an extraordinarily handsome woman,' he whispered.

He was alluding to the girl who had just teed up her ball and was now inspecting, with a sort of queenly dignity, the bag of clubs offered to her by her caddy – who, one felt, had he any sense of the fitness of things, not that caddies ever have, would have dropped on one knee like a medieval page in the presence of royalty.

The Oldest Member nodded.

'Yes,' he agreed. 'Mrs Plinlimmon is much admired in our little circle.'

'Her face seems oddly familiar. I have seen it before somewhere.'

'No doubt in the newspapers. As Clarice Fitch she was a good deal in the public eye.'

'Clarice Fitch? The girl who used to fly oceans and things and cross Africa on foot and what not?'

'Precisely. She is now Mrs Ernest Plinlimmon.'

The Oldest Member's friend eyed her thoughtfully as she took a driver from the bag.

'So that is Clarice Fitch. It must require a good deal of nerve to marry a girl like that. She reminds me of Cleopatra. What sort of fellow is her husband?'

'You see him now, going up to speak to her. The smallish man with spectacles.'

'What! The little chap who looks like the second vice-president of something?'

'Darling,' said the small man in the spectacles.

'Yes, darling?'

'Not the driver, darling.'

'Oh, darling!'

'No, darling. You know how shaky you are with the wood, darling. Take your iron, darling.'

'Must I, darling?'

'Yes, darling.'

'Very well. You know best, darling.'

On the face of the Oldest Member's friend, as the Sage led him back to their table, there was a look of profound amazement.

'Well,' he said, 'if I hadn't heard it with my own ears, I would never have believed it. If you had told me that a girl like that would merely coo meekly when informed that she was incapable of using her wooden clubs, I should have laughed derisively. If ever a wife had all the earmarks of being the dominant member of the firm—'

'Quite,' assented the Oldest Member. 'I admit that that is the impression she conveys. But I can assure you that ever since they were united it is Ernest Plinlimmon who, kindly but with quiet decision, has ruled the home.'

'What is he? A lion tamer?'

'No. He is, and has been for many years, an average-adjuster.'

'Good at his job, I'll bet.'

'Very. I am told by those in a position to know that he adjusts a beautiful average. He is also a devout and quite skilful golfer, playing nowadays to a handicap of four. The inside story of his wooing is a curious one, and affords a striking illustration of a truth in which I have always been a firm believer – that there is a Providence which watches over all pious golfers. In the events which led up to the union of Ernest Plinlimmon and Clarice Fitch one sees the hand of this Providence clearly in operation.'

When Clarice Fitch, some two years ago, came to spend the

summer with an aunt who resides in this neighbourhood, the effect of her advent upon the unattached males of the place was, as you can readily imagine (said the Oldest Member), stupendous. There was a sort of universal gasp, and men who had been playing for years in baggy flannel trousers with mud stains on them rushed off in a body to their tailors, bidding them work night and day on form-fitting suits of plus-fours. Moustaches were curled, ties straightened, and shoes cleaned that had not been cleaned for months.

And of all those stunned by the impact of her personality, none was more powerfully affected than Ernest Faraday Plinlimmon. Within half an hour of their first meeting, he had shaved twice, put on three clean collars, given all his hats to the odd-job man, and started reading Portuguese Love Sonnets. I met him later in the day at the chemist's. He was buying Stick-o, a preparation for smoothing the hair and imparting to it a brilliant gloss, and inquiring of the man behind the counter if he knew of anything that would be good for freckles.

But, like all the others, he made no progress in his wooing, and eventually, as nearly everybody does around these parts sooner or later, he came to consult me.

'It is killing me, this great love of mine,' he said. 'I cannot eat, cannot sleep. It has begun to affect my work. Sometimes in my office, as I start to adjust an average, her face rises between me and it, so that I adjust it all crooked and have to start over again. What can I do to melt that proud, cold heart? There must be some method, if one only knew.'

One of the compensations of age is that it enables a man to stand aside from the seething cauldron of sex, and note in a calm and dispassionate spirit what is going on inside the pot. In my capacity of oldest inhabitant of this hamlet I have often been privileged to see more than can the hot-blooded young principals involved. I had very clear ideas as to what Clarice Fitch found wrong with the attentions to which she had been subjected since her arrival, and these I imparted now to Ernest Plinlimmon.

'What none of you young fellows appear to realize,' I said, 'is that Clarice Fitch is essentially a romantic girl. The fact that she crosses Africa on foot, when it would be both quicker and cheaper to take a train, proves this. And, being romantic, she demands a romantic lover. You, like all the rest, cringe before her. Naturally, she compares you to your disadvantage with such a man as 'Mgoopi 'Mgwumpi.'

Ernest Plinlimmon's eyes widened and his mouth fell open, causing him to look exactly like a fish I once caught off Brighton pier.

'Such a man as – what was that name again?'

' 'Mgoopi 'Mgwumpi. He was the chief, if I remember rightly, of the Lesser 'Mgowpi. I gather that his personality made a deep impression upon Miss Fitch, and that, but for the fact that he was as black as the ace of spades and already had twenty-seven wives and a hundred spares, something might have come of it. At any rate, she as good as told me the other day that what she was looking for was someone who, while possessing the engaging spiritual qualities of this chief, was rather blonder and a bachelor.'

'H'm,' said Ernest Plinlimmon.

'I can give you another pointer,' I proceeded. 'She was speaking to me yesterday in terms of admiration of the hero of a novel by a female writer, whose custom it was to wear riding-boots and to kick the girl of his heart with them.'

Ernest paled.

'You don't really think she wants a man like that?'

'I do.'

'You don't feel that if a fellow had a nice singing voice and was gentle and devoted –'

'I do not.'

'But this kicking business . . . I mean, to start with, I haven't any riding-boots. . . .'

'Sir Jasper Medallion-Carteret would also on occasion drag the girl round the room by her hair.'

'He would?'

'He would.'

'And Miss Fitch appeared to approve?'

'She did.'

'I see,' said Ernest Plinlimmon. 'I see. Yes. Yes, I see. Well, good night.'

He withdrew with bent head, and I watched him go with a

pang of pity. It all seemed so hopeless, and I knew it would be futile to try to console him with any idle talk about time effecting a cure. Ernest Plinlimmon was not one of your butterflies who flit from flower to flower. He was an average-adjuster, and average-adjusters are like chartered accountants. When they love, they give their hearts for ever.

Nor did it seem likely that any words of mine to Clarice would bring about an improvement in the general conditions. Still, I supposed I had better try what I could do. My advanced years had enabled me to form an easy friendship with the girl, so it was not difficult for me to bring the conversation round to her intimate affairs. What in a younger man would be impertinence becomes, when the hair has whitened, mere kindly interest.

Taking advantage, accordingly, of a statement on her part to the effect that she was bored, that life seemed to stretch before her, arid and monotonous, like the Gobi Desert, I ventured to suggest that she ought to get married.

She raised her shapely eyebrows.

'To one of these local stiffs, do you mean?'

I sighed. I could not feel that this was promising.

'You are not attracted by the young bloods of our little community?'

A laugh like the screech of a parakeet in the jungles of Peru broke from her lips.

'Young what? Of all the human rabbits I ever encountered, of all the corpses that had plainly been some little time in the water . . .' She paused for an instant, and seemed to muse. 'Listen,' she went on, her voice soft with a kind of wistfulness, 'do you think that novelists draw their characters from real people?'

I sighed again.

'I was reading Chapter Twenty-six of that book last night. There's a meet, and Lady Pamela rides over hounds, and Sir Jasper catches her a juicy one with his hunting-crop just on the spot where it would make her think a bit. What a man!'

I sighed for the third time. It seemed so useless to try to give my unhappy young friend a build-up. When a woman is to all intents and purposes wailing for a demon lover, it requires super-salesmanship to induce her to accept on the this-is-just-as-good principle an Ernest Plinlimmon.

However, I made the attempt.

'I know a man living in this vicinity who loves you fondly.'

'I know fifty, the poor jellyfish. To which of the prawns in aspic do you refer?'

'Ernest Plinlimmon.'

She laughed again, jovially this time.

'Oh, golly! The "Trees" bird.'

'I beg your pardon?'

'He was round at our house last night, and my aunt dragged him to the piano, and he sang "Only God Can Make A Tree".'

My heart sank. I was stunned that Ernest Plinlimmon could have been guilty of such a piece of mad folly. I could have warned him, had I known that he was a man who had it in his system, that there is something about that particular song which seems to take all the virility out of the singer and leave him spiritually filleted. Genghis Khan or Attila the Hun, singing that passage about 'Troubled with birds' nests in the hair,' or whatever it is, would have seemed mild and spineless.

'You have mentioned,' said Clarice Fitch, sneering visibly, 'the one man on this earth whom I wouldn't marry to please a dying grandfather.'

'He has a handicap of seven,' I urged.

'What at?'

'I refer to the game of golf.'

'Well, I don't play golf, so that's wasted on me. All I know is that he's the worst yesser in a neighbourhood congested with yes-men and looks like a shrimp with dyspepsia. Weedy little brute. Wears spectacles. Sort of fellow who couldn't say Bo to a cassowary. What do you imagine this Plinlimmon pimple would do if he had to face a leaping lion?'

'I have no doubt that he would conduct himself like a perfect gentleman,' I said, a little coldly, for the girl's hard arrogance had annoyed me.

'Well, you can tell him from me,' said Clarice Fitch, 'that if he was the last man in the world, I wouldn't give him a second look. Nothing could be fairer that that.'

I broke the news to Ernest that evening. It seemed to me kinder to acquaint him with the true position of affairs than to allow him to go on eating his heart out in empty hope. I found him practising chip shots near the seventh green and put the thing to him squarely.

I could see that he was sorely shaken. He topped a shot into the bunker.

'Weedy little brute, did she say?'

'That's right. Weedy little brute.'

'And she wouldn't marry me to please a dying uncle?'

'Grandfather.'

'Well, I'll tell you,' said Ernest Plinlimmon. 'The way it looks to me is that I haven't much chance.'

'Not a great deal. Of course, if you could bring yourself to hit her over the head with your number three iron –'

He frowned petulantly.

'I won't,' he said sharply. 'Once and for all, I will not hit her over the head with my number three iron. No, I shall try to forget.'

'It seems the only thing to do.'

'I shall thrust her image from my mind. Immerse myself in my work. Stay longer at the office. Adjust more averages. And,' he said, forcing a brave smile, 'there is always golf.'

'Well spoken, Ernest Plinlimmon!' I cried. 'Yes, there is always golf. And from the way you're hitting them these days it seems to me that, receiving seven, you might quite easily win the summer medal.'

A gleam that I liked to see shone through the young fellow's spectacles.

'You think so?'

'Quite easily, if you practise hard.'

'You bet I'll practise hard. It has always been the dream of my life to win a medal competition. The only trouble is, I've always felt that half the fun would be telling one's grandchildren about it. And now, apparently, there aren't going to be any grandchildren.'

'There will be other people's grandchildren.'

'That's right, too. Very well, then. From now on, I stifle my love and buckle down to it.'

I must confess, however, that, though speaking in airy fashion about winning summer medals, I had done so rather with the idea of giving the unfortunate young man an interest in life than because I actually fancied his chances. It was true that, receiving seven strokes, he might come quite near the top of the list, but there were at least three men in the club who were capable of giving him ten and beating him. Alfred Jukes, for one. Wilberforce Bream, for another. And, for a third, George Peabody.

Still, when I watched him practising, I felt that I had been justified in falsifying the facts. There is something about practice at golf, about the steady self-discipline of playing shot after shot with the same club at the same objective, that gives strength to the soul, and it seemed to me that, as the days went by, Ernest Plinlimmon was becoming a stronger, finer man. And an incident that occurred the day before the competition gave proof of this. I was enjoying a quiet smoke on the terrace, when Clarice Fitch came out of the clubhouse. It was plain that something had upset her, for there was a frown on her lovely forehead and she was breathing through the nose with a low, whistling sound, like an escape of steam.

'Little worm!' she said.

'I beg your pardon?'

'Miserable undersized microbe!'

'You allude to –?'

'That bacillus in the goggles. The germ with the headlights. The tree crooner. Ernest Plinlimmon, in short. The nerve of the little glass-eyed insect!'

'What has Ernest Plinlimmon been doing to incur your displeasure?'

'Why, I told him to take my aunt to a matinée tomorrow, and he had the crust to say he couldn't.'

'But, my dear child, tomorrow is the day of the summer medal competition.'

'What in the name of the eight bearded gods of the Isisi is a summer medal competition?'

I explained.

'What!' cried Clarice Fitch. 'You mean that he refused to do what I asked him simply because he wanted to stay here and fool about with golf balls? Well, I'm –! Of all the –! Can you beat it! I never heard of such a thing.'

She strode off, fuming like an Oriental queen who has been having trouble with the domestic staff, and I resumed my cigar with an uplifted heart. I was proud of Ernest Plinlimmon. This incident showed that he had at last remembered that he was a golfer and a man. I felt that all he needed now was to do well in this medal competition, and the thrall in which Clarice Fitch held him would be broken for ever. I have seen it happen so many times. Golfers go off their drive or their approaches or, it may be, their putting, and while in the enfeebled state induced by this loss of form fall in love. Then one day they try a new stance and get back on their game and do not give the girl another thought. My knowledge of human nature told me that, should Ernest Plinlimmon by some miracle win the summer medal competition, he would have no time for mooning about and pining for Clarice Fitch. His whole being would be absorbed by the effort to bring himself down to scratch.

I was delighted, therefore, when I woke next morning, to see that the weather was fine and the breeze mild, for this meant that play would take place under conditions most favourable to Ernest's game. He was one of those golfers whom rain or a high wind upset. It looked as if this might be the young fellow's day.

And so it proved. Confidence gleamed from his spectacles as he strode on to his first tee, and his opening drive sent the ball sweetly down the middle of the course. He holed out in a nice four.

It was an auspicious start, and had I been younger and more lissom I would have liked to follow him round. Nowadays, however, I find that I enjoy these contests more from a chair on the terrace, relying for my information on those who drop in from time to time from the Front. It was thus that I learned that Ernest's most dangerous rivals were decidedly off their game. Their tee shots at the third had been weak, and at the lake hole Wilberforce Bream had put two into the water. And an hour or so later there came another bulletin. Wilberforce Bream had torn up his card, George Peabody had got into a casual sardine tin in the rough on the eleventh and had taken ten, and Alfred Jukes would be lucky if he did a ninety.

'Right off it, all three of them,' said Alexander Bassett, who was my informant.

'Strange.'

'Not so very. I happen to know,' said Alexander Bassett, who knows everything, 'that that Fitch girl turned them down, one after the other, at intervals during yesterday evening. This has naturally affected them – off the tee mostly. You know how it is. If you have a broken heart, it's bound to give you a twinge every now and then, and if this happens when you are starting your down swing you neglect to let the club-head lead.'

Well, I was sorry, of course, in a way, for one does not like to think of tragedy entering the lives of scratch men, but my commiseration waned as I reflected what this would mean to Ernest Plinlimmon. There is always, in these medal competitions, the danger of a long-handicap man striking his big day and turning in a net sixty-eight, but apart from such a contingency it seemed to me that, if he had kept his early form, he ought now to win. And Alexander's next words encouraged this hope.

'Plinlimmon's playing a nice game,' he said. 'Nice and steady. Now that the tigers are off the map, I'm backing him. Though there is one of the submerged tenth, they tell me – twenty-four-handicap man named Perkins – who seems in the money.'

Alexander Bassett left me, to resume his inspection of the contest, and I think that shortly afterwards I must have fallen into a doze, for when I opened my eyes, which I had closed for a moment in order to meditate, I found that the sun was perceptibly lower. The cool of the evening was in the air, and I realized that by this time the competition must be drawing to a close. I was about to rise and cross the green to see if there was anything of interest happening on the eighteenth fairway, when Clarice Fitch came over the brow of the hill.

I gave you a description of her aspect on the occasion when

she had been telling me how Ernest Plinlimmon, with splendid firmness, had refused to take her aunt to the matinée. She was looking very much like that now. There was the same frown, the same outraged glitter in her imperious eyes, the same escape-of-steam effects through the delicately chiselled nostrils. In addition, she appeared to be walking with some difficulty.

'Has something happened?' I asked, concerned. 'You are limping.'

She uttered a sharp, staccato howl, not unlike the battle-cry of the West African wild cat.

'So would you be limping, if a human boll-weevil had just hit you with a hard ball.'

'What!'

'Yes. I was strolling along and I had stopped to tie my shoe-lace, when suddenly something came whizzing along like a bullet and struck me.'

'Good heavens! Where?'

'Never mind,' said Clarice Fitch austerely.

'I mean,' I hastened to explain, 'where did this happen?'

'Down in that field there.'

'You mean the eighteenth fairway?'

'I don't know what you call it.'

'Was the man driving off the tee?'

'He was standing on a sort of grass platform thing, if that is what you mean.'

'What did he say when he came up to you?'

'He hasn't come up to me yet. Wait till he does! Yes, by the sacred crocodile of the Zambesi, just give me two minutes to rub in arnica and another to powder my nose, and I'll be ready for him. Ready and waiting! I'll startle his weak intellect, the miserable little undersized microbe!'

I started at the familiar phrase.

'Was it Ernest Plinlimmon who did this?'

'It was. Well, wait till I meet him.'

She limped into the clubhouse, and I hurried down to the eighteenth fairway. I felt that Ernest Plinlimmon should be warned that there lurked against his coming an infuriated female explorer whose bite might well be fatal.

The course has been altered recently, but at the time of which I am speaking the eighteenth hole was the one which terminated below the terrace. It was a nice two-shotter – uphill, but with nothing to trouble the man who was steady off the tee. A good drive left you with a mashie-niblick chip for your second: after a drive that was merely moderate a full mashie or even an iron was required. As I came over the hill, I saw Ernest Plinlimmon and his partner, in whom I recognized a prominent local dub, emerging from the rough on the right. Apparently, the latter had sliced from the tee, and Ernest had been helping him find his ball. Ernest's own blue dot was lying well up the slope, some eighty yards short of the green. I eyed it with respect. Clarice Fitch's evidence had shown that it had been travelling with considerable speed when it encountered her person. But for that unfortunate incident, therefore, it would, presumably, have been good for at least another fifty yards. A superb drive.

The dub played a weak and sinful spoon shot out to the right, and I met Ernest where his ball lay. He blinked at me inquiringly, as he came up, and I saw with surprise that his face was totally bare of glass.

'Oh, it's you,' he said. 'I didn't recognize you at first. I broke my spectacles at the fifteenth, and can't see a thing unless it's within a dozen yards or so.'

I clicked my tongue sympathetically.

'Then you are out of the running, I suppose?'

'Out of the running?' cried Ernest Plinlimmon jubilantly. 'I should say not. I've been playing like a book. Not being able to see seems to help me to concentrate. Knowing that I can't follow the ball, I don't loft my head. I've got this medal competition in the bag.

'You have?'

'Definitely in the good old sack. I've just been talking to Bassett, and he tells me that Perkins, leading the field by a matter of three strokes, has finished in a net seventy-five. There's nobody behind me, so that when I finish the returns will be all in. I have just played a net seventy-one. I shall be on with a net seventy-two. Then lay it dead with my approach putt and stuff it in with my second, and there I shall be – net seventy-four.

It's a walk-over. The thing that makes me a little sore, though, is that, if it hadn't been for the sheep, I might have chipped to the pin and needed only one putt. The animal must have lost me a full fifty yards.'

'Ernest,' I began.

'My drive – an absolute pippin – was stopped by a sheep. It was standing in the middle of the fairway when I teed up just now. I should have waited, I suppose, but I hate waiting on the tee. So I took a chance, and, apparently, plugged it. Infernal nuisance. It was one of those low, skimming shots and would have run a mile but for that. Still, it doesn't really matter. I can get down in three more on my head.'

I reconsidered my intention of warning the young man of what awaited him at journey's end. Obviously, if the state of the score was as he had said, nothing would deter him from holing out. It might be, I felt, that he would be able to make a quick getaway after sinking the winning putt. After all, Clarice Fitch, though she had talked lightly of taking two minutes for the rubbing of arnica on her wounds, would probably not emerge once more into public life for much nearer ten. I said nothing, accordingly, and watched him play a nice mashie shot.

'Where did it go?' he asked.

'On,' I replied, 'but a little wide of the pin.'

'How wide?'

'Possibly fifteen feet.'

'Easy,' said Ernest Plinlimmon. 'I've been laying fifteen-footers dead all the way round.'

I preserved a tactful silence, but I was disturbed in my mind. I had not liked the airy way in which he had spoken of being on with a net seventy-two, and I did not like the airy way in which he now spoke of laying fifteen-foot putts dead. Confidence, of course, is an admirable asset to a golfer, but it should be an unspoken confidence. It is perilous to put it into speech. The gods of golf lie in wait to chasten the presumptuous.

Ernest Plinlimmon did not lay his approach putt dead. The green was one of those tricky ones. It undulated. Sometimes at the close of a tight match I have fancied that I have seen it heave, like a stage sea. Ernest putted well, but not well enough. A hummock for which he had not allowed caught the ball and deflected it, leaving him a yard and a half from the hole, that fatal distance which has caused championships to change hands.

He shaped for the shot, however, with undiminished confidence.

'And now,' Ernest Plinlimmon, 'to stuff it in.'

His partner, who had picked up and joined us, caught my eye. He had pursed his lips gravely. He was thinking, I knew, as I was, that no good could come of this loose talk.

Ernest Plinlimmon addressed his ball. The line was quite straight and clear, and all that was needed was the right strength. But, alas, nothing is more difficult at the end of a tense round than to estimate strength. As the ball left the club-head, it looked to me destined for the happy ending. It trickled straight for the hole, and I was just expecting the joyful rattle which would signify that all was well, when it seemed to falter. Two feet . . . one foot . . . six inches . . . it was still moving. Three inches . . . two inches. . . . I held my breath.

Would it? Could it?

No! Barely an inch from the cup it wavered, hesitated and stopped. He tapped it in, but it was too late. Ernest Plinlimmon had merely tied for the summer medal, and would have to undergo all the spiritual agonies of a play-off.

It was a moment when unthinking men would have said 'Tough luck!' or some such banality. But Ernest's partner and I were seasoned golfers and knew that on these occasions silence is best. We exchanged a mute glance of pity and terror, and then our attention was diverted to the noticeable behaviour of the young man himself.

I had always known Ernest Plinlimmon as a mild, reserved man, and the sight of his contorted face gave me, I must confess, a rather painful shock. His eyes were wild, and the veins stood out on his forehead. I waited with something like apprehension for his first words, but when he spoke it was to utter a simple query.

'Where,' inquired Ernest Plinlimmon, 'is that sheep?'

'What sheep?' said his partner.

'*The* sheep. The sheep I drove into.' His eyes rolled. 'The best drive I ever made in my life, a drive that would have put me within easy chip shot of the pin, ruined by a blasted sheep. I now wish to be led into the presence of that sheep so that I may strangle it with my bare hands.'

'It didn't look like a sheep to me,' said his partner. 'More like Miss Fitch, if you follow what I mean.'

'Miss Fitch?'

I gave a violent start. The excitement of watching those final putts had driven everything from my mind. I now remembered that the lad stood in imminent peril, and must be warned to fly while there was yet time. At any moment Clarice Fitch would be coming out of the clubhouse, breathing fire.

'Ernest,' I said rapidly, 'our friend here is quite correct. Miss Fitch was on the fairway, tying her shoelace . . .'

'What!'

'Tying her shoelace.'

'What!'

Tying her . . .'

My voice died away. Clarice Fitch was standing on the edge of the green, her arms folded, her eyes shooting out little sparks.

'Let us get this straight,' said Ernest Plinlimmon, in a strange quiet voice. 'You say that this infernal girl stopped in the middle of the eighteenth fairway, in the middle of a medal competition, in the middle of a man's drive who only needed a four to win, in order to tie her shoelace . . . her blasted shoelace . . . her damned blanked . . .'

A dark flood swept over the young man's face. His teeth came together with a click. For an instant, his mouth opened and his nose twitched and he seemed to be struggling for utterance: then, as if realizing the futility of trying to find words that would do justice to his feelings, he raised his putter and hurled it violently from him. And Clarice Fitch, who had unfolded her arms and was advancing with a slow, sinister stride, like the snow leopard of the Himalayas, got it squarely on the shin-bone.

It was a moment which I shall not readily forget. I have always ranked it, indeed, among the high spots of my life.

Looking back, I find each smallest detail of the scene rising before my eyes as if it had happened yesterday. I see the setting sun crimsoning the western sky. I see the long shadows creeping over the terrace. I see Clarice Fitch hopping about on one leg, while Ernest Plinlimmon, his wrath turned off as if with a tap, stands gaping at the sight of what he has done. And over all, after that first sharp, shrill, piercing cry of agony, there broods a strange, eerie silence.

How long this silence lasted I am not able to say, for at these supreme moments one cannot measure time. But presently Clarice Fitch ceased to hop and, coming to a halt with a hand pressed to her shin, began to speak.

One of the advantages enjoyed by a girl who gets about a bit is that in the crisis of life she is not confined to the poor resources of her native tongue. I doubt if Clarice Fitch would have been able to say a tithe of the things she wished to say, had she been compelled to say them in English. The fact that as the result of her travels she had at her command a round dozen or so of African dialects enabled her now to express herself with a rich breadth which could not but awe even one who, like myself, did not understand a single word. There was no need to understand words. Given the situation, one got the general sense, and as the address gathered speed and volume I found myself edging away from Ernest Plinlimmon, fearful lest the lightning playing about his head might include me in its activities. So might the children of Israel have edged away from one of their number who had been so unfortunate as to fall out with the prophet Jeremiah.

And Ernest, as I say, stood gaping. One can dimly picture the young man's feelings. There before him was the shin he loved to touch, and he had sloshed it with a putter. In a similar situation, no doubt, Sir Jasper Medallion-Carteret would merely have sneered. Or he might even have followed up the putter with the number four iron. But Ernest was no Sir Jasper. He had the air of one who is out on his feet.

Over the quiet green the stream of words flowed on without a break. There seemed to be no reason why it should not go on for ever. And then, suddenly, in the very midst of what appeared to be a particularly powerful passage, Clarice Fitch broke down. Bursting into tears, she buried her face in her hands and began hopping again.

I cannot explain this. An instant before, one would have said she was incapable of such a feminine weakness. The only theory I can advance is that, having reached this point in her remarks, she had suddenly become aware once more of the agony which oratory had for the time enabled her to forget. At any rate, be that as it may, she now burst into tears and buried her face in her hands.

The effect on Ernest Plinlimmon was as if some magic spell had been removed, bringing life again to his congealed frame. He had been standing transfixed, incapable of movement. He now gave a convulsive start, like a somnambulist rudely awakened, and bounded forward – unless I am mistaken in my conjecture – with the idea of grovelling at her feet and beating his head upon the ground. His eyes were glaring. His lips were twisted. He waved his arms in frantic appeal. And just as he reached the girl she raised her head, and his fist, shooting out in a passionate gesture of remorse, caught her on the right eye.

The result was extraordinary. If he had been practising for weeks with a punching bag he could not have brought off a sweeter left jab. It travelled about eight inches with all his weight behind it, and it sent Clarice Fitch over the side of the green as if she had been shot from a gun. One moment, she was among those present; the next, she had disappeared and a fountain of sand showed that she had found the pot bunker which stands at the base of the slope to catch a hooked second.

Ernest Plinlimmon congealed once more, and again time stood still.

As before, one could, in a dim way, picture his feelings. Plainly, he was running over in his mind the recent series of events. He loved this girl and yearned for her to be his. And, in addition to singing 'Only God Can Make A Tree' in her presence, he had – in the course of some fifteen minutes – biffed her with a golf-ball, cracked her over the shin with a putter and pasted her in the right eye with his fist. Not so good, he was evidently thinking. I saw him put a hand up to straighten his spectacles, only to lower it again on finding no spectacles there. The action was that of a man in a trance.

And he was still standing there, when there was a scrambling sound and Clarice's head appeared over the edge of the green. And at the sight of it I uttered an involuntary cry of joy, for in her left eye – the other was closed and already assuming a blackish tint – I saw the light of love.

A moment ago, I said that I had been able to read Ernest Plinlimmon's mind. Now, even more clearly, I could read that of Clarice Fitch. It did not need words to tell me that she had been thinking things over in the bunker and had arrived at an arresting conclusion.

That drive that had struck her amidships she had attributed to carelessness. That hurled putter had seemed to her a putter hurled at random. But this punch in the eye had put an entirely different complexion on the matter. That, she knew, had been deliberate and calculated, the violent attempt at self-expression of a man who, though mild of aspect and intensely spectacled, possessed the soul of an infuriated rhinoceros and did not intend to allow girls to abuse him in Swahili without lodging a protest. And if that blow had been deliberate, so must the assault with the driver and putter have been deliberate. In other words, this man, crazed with love, had been wooing her just as she had hoped some day some man would come and woo her. Even the chief of the Lesser 'Mgowpi had not been so rough as this, and, as for Sir Jasper Medallion-Carteret, he became, in comparison with Ernest Plinlimmon, mere small-town stuff.

For an instant, she stood there, rubbing her shin and her eye alternately. Then with outstretched hands she advanced towards young Plinlimmon.

'My man!' she said.

Ernest Plinlimmon did not appear to get it.

'Eh?' he said, blinking. 'Your what?'

'My great, strong, wonderful man!'

Once more, he blinked.

'Who, me?'

She flung her arms about his neck in an ecstasy of devotion, so that even Ernest Plinlimmon was able, though still somewhat fogged, to get the general idea. He was bewildered, yes, but he retained sufficient intelligence to do his bit. I saw him

stand on tiptoe, for she was considerably the taller, and kiss
her. Then with a little sigh of happiness he adjusted himself to
her embrace as if he had been an average, and I turned to his
partner who, during the recent events, had been practising short
putts.

'Come,' I said. 'Let us leave them together.'

Chapter Six
The Masked Troubadour

A young man came out of the Drones Club and paused on the steps to light a cigarette. As he did so, there popped up – apparently through the pavement, for there had been no sign of him in the street a moment before – a seedy individual who touched his hat and smiled ingratiatingly. The young man seemed to undergo a brief struggle – then he felt in his pocket, pressed a coin into the outstretched palm, and passed on.

It was a pretty, heart-warming little scene, the sort of thing you see in full-page pictures in the Christmas numbers, but the only emotion it excited in the bosoms of the two Beans who had witnessed it from the window of the smoking-room was amazement.

'Well, stap my vitals,' said the first Bean. 'If I hadn't seen it with my own eyes I wouldn't have believed it.'

'Nor me,' said the second Bean.

'Believed what?' asked a Crumpet, who had come up behind them.

The two Beans turned to him as one Bean and spoke in alternate lines, like a Greek chorus.

'Freddie Widgeon –'

'– was outside there a moment ago –'

'– and a chap came up and touched his hat –'

'– and then he touched Freddie.'

'And Freddie, though he was on the steps at the time –'

'– and so had only to leap backwards in order to win to safety –'

'– stood there and let the deal go through.'

The Crumpet clicked his tongue.

'What sort of a looking chap was he? Small and a bit greasy?'

'Quite fairly greasy.'

'I thought as much,' said the Crumpet. 'I know the bird. He's a fellow named Waterbury, a pianist by profession. He's a sort of pensioner of Freddie's. Freddie is always slipping him money – here a tanner, there a bob.'

The astonishment of the two Beans deepened.

'But Freddie's broke,' said the senior Bean.

'True,' said the Crumpet. 'He can ill spare these bobs and tanners, but that old *noblesse oblige* spirit of his has cropped up again. He feels that he must allow himself to be touched, because this greasy bird has a claim on him. He saved his life!'

'The greasy bird saved Freddie's life?'

'No. Freddie saved the greasy bird's life.'

'Then Freddie ought to be touching the greasy bird.'

'Not according to the code of the Widgeons.' The Crumpet sighed. 'Poor old Freddie – it's a shame, this constant drain on his meagre resources, after all he's been through.'

'What's he been through?' asked the junior Bean.

'You would not be far out,' replied the Crumpet gravely, 'if you said that he had been through the furnace.'

At the time when this story opens (said the Crumpet) Freddie was feeling a bit low. His heart had just been broken, and that always pulls him down. He had loved Dahlia Prenderby with every fibre of his being, and she had handed him the horse's laugh. He was, therefore, as you may suppose, in no mood for social gaiety: and when he got a note from his uncle, old Blicester, asking him to lunch at the Ritz, his first impulse was to refuse.

But as Lord Blicester was the source from which proceeded his quarterly allowance, he couldn't do that, of course. The old boy's invitations were commands. So he turned up at the eating-house and was sitting in the lobby, thinking long, sad thoughts of Dahlia Prenderby, when his host walked in.

'Ah, Frederick,' he said, having eased his topper and umbrella off on to a member of the staff. 'Glad you were able to come. I want to have a serious talk with you. I've been thinking a lot about you lately.'

'Have you, uncle?' said Freddie, touched.

'Yes,' said old Blicester. 'Wondering why you were such a

blasted young blot on the escutcheon and trying to figure out some way of stopping you being the world's worst ass and pest. And I think I've found the solution. It would ease the situation very much, in my opinion, if you got married. Don't puff like that. What the devil are you puffing for?'

'I was sighing, uncle.'

'Well, don't. Good God! I thought you'd got asthma. Yes,' said Lord Blicester, 'I believe that if you were married and settled down, things might brighten considerably all round. I've known bigger ... well, no, scarcely that, perhaps.... I've known very nearly as big fools as you improve out of all recognition by marriage. And here is what I wanted to talk to you about. You will, no doubt, have been wondering why I am buying you a lunch in an infernally expensive place like this. I will tell you. My old friend, Lady Pinfold, is joining us in a few minutes with her daughter Dora. I have decided that she is the girl you shall marry. Excellent family, plenty of money of her own, and sense enough for two – which is just the right amount. So mind you make yourself attractive, if that is humanly possible, to Dora Pinfold.'

A weary, mirthless smile twisted Freddie's lips.

'All this –' he began.

'And let me give you a warning. She is not one of your fast modern girls, so bear in mind when conversing with her that you are not in the smoking-room of the Drones Club. Only carefully selected stories, and no limericks whatsoever.'

'All this –' began Freddie again.

'Don't drink anything at lunch. She is strict in her views about that. And, talking of lunch, when the waiter comes round with the menu, don't lose your head. Keep an eye on the prices in the right-hand column.'

'All this,' said Freddie at last, getting a word in, 'is very kind of you, uncle, and I appreciate it. Your intentions are good. But I cannot marry this girl.'

Old Blicester nodded intelligently.

'I see what you mean. You feel it would be a shabby trick to play on any nice girl. True. There is much in what you say. But somebody has got to suffer in this world. You can't make an omelette without breaking eggs. So never mind the ethics of the thing. You go ahead and fascinate her, or I'll ... S'h. Here they come.'

He got up and started to stump forward to greet a stout, elderly woman who was navigating through the doorway, and Freddie, following, suddenly halted in his tracks and nearly took a toss. He was looking at the girl floating along in the wake of the stout woman. In a blinding flash of revelation he saw Dahlia Prenderby and all the other girls who had turned him down. Just boyish infatuations, he could see now. This was his soulmate. There was none like her, none. Freddie, as you know, always falls in love at first sight, and he had done so on this occasion, with a wallop.

His knees were wobbling under him as he went in to lunch and he was glad to be able to sit down and take the weight off them.

The girl seemed to like him. Girls always do like Freddie at first. It is when the gruelling test of having him in their hair for several weeks comes that they throw in the towel. Over the fish and chips he and this Dora Pinfold fraternized like billy-o. True, it was mostly a case of her telling him about her dreams and ideals and him saying 'Oh, ah' and 'Oh, absolutely,' but that did not alter the fact that the going was good.

So much so that with the cheese Freddie, while not actually pressing her hand, was leaning over towards her at an angle of forty-five and saying why shouldn't they lap up their coffee quick at the conclusion of the meal and go and see a picture or something. And she said she would have loved it, only she had to be in Notting Hill at a quarter to three.

'I'm interested in a sort of Mission there,' she said.

'Great Scott!' said Freddie. 'Cocoa and good works, do you mean?'

'Yes. We are giving an entertainment this afternoon, to the mothers.'

Freddie nearly choked over his Camembert. A terrific idea had come to him.

If, he reflected, he was going to meet this girl again only at dinners and dances – the usual social round, I mean to say – all she would ever get to know about him was that he had a good appetite and india-rubber legs. Whereas, if he started frequenting Notting Hill in her company, he would be able to flash his deeper self on her. He could be suave, courteous, the *preux chevalier,* and shower her with those little attentions which make a girl sit up and say to herself: 'What ho!'

'I say,' he said, 'couldn't I come along?'

'Oh, it would bore you.'

'Not a bit. I could hover round and shove the old dears into their seats and so on. I'm good at that. I've been an usher at dozens of weddings.'

The girl reflected.

'I'll tell you what you can do, if you really want to help,' she said. 'We are a little short of talent. Can you sing?'

'Rather!'

'Then will you sing?'

'Absolutely.'

'That would be awfully kind of you. Any old song will do.'

'I shall sing,' said Freddie, directing at her a glance which he rather thinks – though he is not sure – made her blush in modest confusion, 'a number entitled, "When the Silver of the Moonlight Meets the Lovelight in Your Eyes".'

So directly lunch was over, off they popped, old Blicester beaming on Freddie and very nearly slapping him on the back – and no wonder, for his work had unquestionably been good – and as the clocks were striking three-thirty Freddie was up on the platform with the Vicar and a Union Jack behind him, the girl Dora at the piano at his side, and about two hundred Notting Hill mothers in front of him, letting it go like a Crosby.

He was a riot. Those mothers, he tells me, just sat back and ate it up. He did two songs, and they wanted a third. He did a third, and they wanted an encore. He did an encore, and they started whistling through their fingers till he came on and bowed. And when he came on and bowed, they insisted on a speech. And it was at this point, as he himself realizes now, that Freddie lost his cool judgement. He allowed himself to be carried away by the intoxication of the moment and went too far.

Briefly, what happened was that in a few cordial words he invited all those present to be his guests at a binge to be held in the Mission hall that day week.

'Mothers,' said Freddie, 'this is on me. I shall expect you to the last mother. And if any mothers here have mothers of their own, I hope they will bring them along. There will be no stint. Buns and cocoa will flow like water. I thank you one and all.'

And it was only when he got home, still blinking from the bright light which he had encountered in the girl Dora's eyes as they met his and still deafened by the rousing cheers which had greeted his remarks, that he remembered that all he had in the world was one pound, three shillings and fourpence.

Well, you can't entertain a multitude of mothers in slap-up style on one pound, three and fourpence, so it was obvious that he would be obliged to get into somebody's ribs for something substantial. And the only person he could think of who was good for the sum he required – twenty quid seemed to him about the figure – was old Blicester.

It would not be an easy touch. He realized that. The third Earl of Blicester was a man who, though well blessed with the world's goods, hated loosening up. Moths had nested in his pocket-book for years and raised large families. However, one of the fundamental facts of life is that you can't pick and choose when you want twenty quid – you have to go to the man who's got twenty quid. So he went round to tackle the old boy.

There was a bit of a lull when he got to the house. Some sort of by-election, it appeared, was pending down at Bottleton in the East End, and Lord Blicester had gone off there to take the chair at a meeting in the Conservative interest. So Freddie had to wait. But eventually he appeared, a bit hoarse from addressing the proletariat but in excellent feitle. He was very bucked at the way Freddie had shaped at the luncheon table.

'You surprised me, my boy,' he said. 'I am really beginning to think that if you continue as you have begun and are careful, when you propose, to do it in a dim light so that she can't get a good look at you, you may win that girl.'

'And you want me to win her, don't you, uncle?'

'I do, indeed.'

'Then will you give me twenty pounds?'

The sunlight died out of Lord Blicester's face.

'Twenty pounds? What do you want twenty pounds for?'

'It is vital that I acquire that sum,' said Freddie. And in a few words he explained that he had pledged himself to lush up the mothers of Notting Hill on buns and cocoa a week from that day, and that if he welshed and failed to come through the girl would never forgive him – and rightly.

Lord Blicester listened with growing gloom. He had set his heart on this union, but the overhead made him quiver. The thought of parting with twenty pounds was like a dagger in his bosom.

'It won't cost twenty pounds.'

'It will.'

'You can do it on much less than that.'

'I don't see how. There must have been fully two hundred mothers present. They will bring friends and relations. Add gate-crashers, and I can't budget for less than four hundred. At a bob a nob.'

Lord Blicester pshawed. 'Preposterous!' he cried. 'A bob a nob, forsooth! Cocoa's not expensive.'

'But the buns. You are forgetting the buns.'

'Buns aren't expensive, either.'

'Well, how about hard-boiled eggs? Have you reflected, uncle, that there may be hard-boiled eggs?'

'Hard-boiled eggs? Good God, boy, what is this thing you're planning. A Babylonian orgy? There will be no question of hard-boiled eggs.'

'Well, all right. Then let us return to the buns. Allowing twelve per person . . .'

'Don't be absurd. Twelve indeed! These are simple, God-fearing English mothers you are entertaining – not tape-worms. I'll give you ten pounds. Ten is ample.'

And nothing that Freddie could say would shake him. It was with a brace of fivers in his pocket that he left the other's presence, and every instinct in him told him that they would not be enough. Fifteen quid, in his opinion, was the irreducible minimum. He made his way to the club in pensive mood, his brain darting this way and that in the hope of scaring up some scheme for adding to his little capital. He was still brooding on a problem which seemed to grow each moment more hopeless of solution, when he entered the smoking-room and found a group of fellows there, gathered about a kid in knickerbockers. And not only were they gathered about this kid – they were practically fawning on him.

This surprised Freddie. He knew that a chap has to have something outstanding about him to be fawned upon at the Drones, and nothing in this child's appearance suggested that he was in any way exceptional. The only outstanding thing about him was his ears.

'What's all this?' he asked of Catsmeat Potter-Pirbright, who was hovering on the outskirts of the group.

'It's Barmy Phipps's cousin Egbert from Harrow,' said Catsmeat. 'Most remarkable chap. You see that catapult he's showing those birds. Well, he puts a Brazil nut in it and whangs off at things and hits them every time. It's a great gift, and you might think it would make him conceited. But no, success has not spoiled him. He is still quite simple and unaffected. Would you like his autograph?'

Freddie frankly did not believe the story. The whole nature of a Brazil nut, it being nobbly and of a rummy semicircular shape, unfits it to act as a projectile. The thing, he felt, might be just barely credible, perhaps, of one who was receiving his education at Eton, but Catsmeat had specifically stated that this lad was at Harrow, and his reason revolted at the idea of a Harrovian being capable of such a feat.

'What rot,' he said.

'It isn't rot,' said Catsmeat Potter-Pirbright, stung. 'Only just now he picked off a passing errand-boy as clean as a whistle.'

'Pure fluke.'

'Well, what'll you bet he can't do it again?'

A thrill ran through Freddie. He had found the way.

'A fiver!' he cried.

Well, of course, Catsmeat hadn't got a fiver, but he swiftly formed a syndicate to cover Freddie's money, and the stakes were deposited with the chap behind the bar and a Brazil nut provided for the boy Egbert at the club's expense. And it was as he fitted nut to elastic that Catsmeat Potter-Pirbright said, 'Look.'

'Look,' said Catsmeat Potter-Pirbright. 'There's a taxi just drawing up with a stout buffer in it. Will you make this stout buffer the test? Will you bet that Egbert here doesn't knock off his topper as he pays the cabby?'

'Certainly,' said Freddie.

The cab stopped. The buffer alighted, his top hat gleaming in the sunshine. The child Egbert with incredible nonchalance drew his bead. The Brazil nut sang through the air. And the next moment Freddie was staggering back with his hands to his eyes, a broken man. For the hat, struck squarely abaft the binnacle, had leaped heavenwards and he was down five quid.

And the worst was yet to come. About a minute later he was informed that Lord Blicester had called to see him. He went to the small smoking-room and found his uncle standing on the hearth-rug. He was staring in a puzzled sort of way at a battered top hat which he held in his hand.

'Most extraordinary thing,' he said. 'As I was getting out of my cab just now, something suddenly came whizzing out of the void and knocked my hat off. I think it must have been a small meteor. I am going to write to *The Times* about it. But never mind that. What I came for was to get fifty shillings from you.'

Freddie had already tottered on discovering that it was old Blicester who had been the victim of the boy Egbert's uncanny skill. These words made him totter again. That his uncle should be touching him instead of him touching his uncle gave him a sort of goose-fleshy feeling as if he were rubbing velvet the wrong way.

'Fifty shillings?' he bleated.

'Two pounds ten,' said old Blicester, making it clear to the meanest intelligence. 'After you left me, I was dissatisfied with your figures, so I went and consulted my cook, a most capable woman, as to the market price of buns and cocoa, and what she told me convinces me that you can do the whole thing comfortably on seven pounds ten. So I hurried here to recover the fifty shillings which I overpaid you. I can give you change.'

Five minutes later, Freddie was at a writing-table with pen and paper, trying to work out how he stood. Of his original capital, two pounds ten shillings remained. According to his uncle, who had it straight from the cook's mouth, buns and cocoa could be provided for four hundred at a little over fourpence a head. It seemed incredible, but he knew that his uncle's cook, a level-headed woman named Bessemer, was to be trusted implicitly on points of this kind. No doubt the explanation was that a considerable reduction was given for quantity. When you buy your buns by the ton, you get them cheaper.

Very well then. The deficit to be made up appeared still to be five pounds. And where he was to get it was more than he could say. He couldn't very well go back to old Blicester and ask for a further donation, giving as his reason the fact that he had lost a fiver betting that a kid with wind-jammer ears wouldn't knock his, old Blicester's, hat off with a Brazil nut.

Then what to do? It was all pretty complex, and I am not surprised that for the next two or three days Freddie was at a loss.

During these days he continued to haunt Notting Hill. But though he was constantly in the society of the girl Dora, and though he was treated on all sides as the young Lord Bountiful, he could not bring himself to buck up and be fizzy. Wherever he went, the talk was all of this forthcoming beano of his, and it filled him with a haunting dread. Notting Hill was plainly planning to go for the buns and cocoa in a big way, and who – this was what he asked himself – who was going to foot the bill?

The ironical thing, he saw now, was that his original capital would have seen him through. There had been no need whatsoever for him to go plunging like that in the endeavour to bump up the kitty. When he reflected that, but for getting his figures twisted, he would now have been striding through Notting Hill with his chin up and his chest out and not a care on his mind, he groaned in spirit. He told me so himself. 'I groaned in spirit,' he said.

And then one afternoon, after he had explored every possible avenue, as he thought, without getting a bite, he suddenly stumbled on one that promised to bring home the gravy. Other avenues had let him down with a bump, but this one really did look the goods.

For what happened was that he learned that on that very evening the East Bottleton Palace of Varieties was holding its monthly Amateur Night and that the prize of victory – he reeled as he read the words – was a handsome five-pound note.

At the moment when he made this discovery, things had

been looking their darkest. Freddie, in fact, was so up against it that he had come to the conclusion that the only thing to do, if he was to fulfil his honourable obligations, was to go to his uncle, confess all, and try to tap him again.

The old boy, apprised of the facts in the matter of his ruined topper, would unquestionably want to disembowel him, but he was so keen on the wedding coming off that it might just conceivably happen that he would confine himself to harsh words and at the end of a powerful harangue spring the much-needed.

Anyway, it was his only chance. He rang up the Blicester residence and was informed that the big chief was again down at Bottleton East presiding at one of those political meetings. At the Bottleton Palace of Varieties, said the butler. So, though he would much have preferred to go to Whipsnade and try to take a mutton chop away from a tiger, Freddie had a couple of quick ones, ate a clove and set off.

I don't suppose you are familiar with Bottleton East, except by name. It is a pretty tough sort of neighbourhood, rather like Limehouse only with fewer mysterious Chinamen. The houses are small and grey, cats abound, and anyone who has a bit of old paper or a piece of orange peel throws it on the pavement. It depressed Freddie a good deal, and he was feeling pretty well down among the wines and spirits when a burst of muffled cheering came to his ears, and he found that he was approaching the Bottleton Palace of Varieties.

And he was just toddling round to send in his name to old Blicester when he saw on the wall this poster announcing the Grand Amateur Night and the glittering reward offered to the performer who clicked.

It altered the whole aspect of things in a flash. What it meant was that that distressing interview with Lord Blicester could now be pigeonholed indefinitely. Here was the five he needed, as good as in his pocket.

This gay confidence on his part may surprise you. But you must remember that it was only a day or two since he had burned up the Notting Hill mothers with his crooning. A man who could put over a socko like that had little to fear, he felt, from any opposition a place like Bottleton East could bring against him.

There was just one small initial difficulty. He would require an accompanist, and it was rather a problem to see where he was to get one. At Notting Hill, you will recall, the girl Dora had tinkled the ivories on his behalf, but he could scarcely ask her to officiate on the present occasion, for – apart from anything else – secrecy was of the essence. For the same reason he could not get anyone from the Drones. The world must never know that Frederick Widgeon had been raising the wind by performing at Amateur Nights in the East End of London.

He walked on, musing. It was an annoying little snag to crop up just as everything looked nice and smooth.

However, his luck was in. Half-way down a grubby little street he saw a card in a window announcing that Jos. Waterbury gave piano lessons on those premises: and rightly reasoning that a bloke who could teach the piano would also know how to accompany, he knocked at the door. And after he had been subjected to a keen scrutiny by a mysterious eye through the keyhole, the door opened and he found himself *vis-à-vis* with the greasy bird whom you saw outside there just now.

The first few minutes of the interview were given up to mutual explanations. Freddie handed the greasy bird his card. The greasy bird said that he would not have kept Freddie waiting only something in the timbre of his knock had given him the idea that he was Ginger Murphy, a gentleman friend of his with whom he had had a slight difference and who had expressed himself desirous of seeing the colour of his insides. Freddie explained that he wanted the greasy bird to accompany him on the piano at Amateur Night. And the greasy bird said that Freddie couldn't have made a wiser move, because he was an expert accompanist and having him with you on such an occasion was half the battle.

After this, there was a bit of haggling about terms, but in the end it was arranged that Freddie should pay the greasy bird five bob – half a crown down and the rest that night, and that they should meet at the stage door at eight sharp.

'If I'm not there,' said the greasy bird, 'you'll find me in the public bar of the Green Goose round the corner.'

'Right ho,' said Freddie. 'I shall sing "When the Silver of the Moonlight Meets the Lovelight in Your Eyes".'

'Ah, well,' said the greasy bird, who seemed a bit of a philosopher, 'I expect worse things happen at sea.'

Freddie then pushed off, on the whole satisfied with the deal. He hadn't liked this Jos. Waterbury much. Not quite the accompanist of his dreams. He would have felt kindlier towards him if he had bathed more recently and had smelled less strongly of unsweetened gin. Still, he was no doubt as good as could be had at the price. Freddie was not prepared to go higher than five bob, and that ruled out the chaps who play at Queen's Hall.

Having completed the major preliminary arrangements, Freddie now gave thought to make-up and appearance. The other competitors, he presumed, would present themselves to their public more or less aziz, but their circumstances were rather different from his own. In his case, a certain caution was indicated. His uncle appeared to be making quite a stamping ground of Bottleton East just now, and it would be disastrous if he happened to come along and see him doing his stuff. So, though it was not likely that Lord Bicester would attend Amateur Night at the Palace of Varieties, he thought it best to be on the safe side and adopt some rude disguise.

After some meditation, he decided to conceal his features behind a strip of velvet and have himself announced as The Masked Troubadour.

He dined lightly at the club off oysters and a pint of stout, and at eight o'clock, after an afternoon spent in gargling throat tonic and saying 'Mi-mi-mi' to limber up the larynx, he arrived at the stage door.

Jos. Waterbury was there, wearing the unmistakable air of a man who has been more or less submerged in unsweetened gin for several hours, and, half a crown having changed hands, they proceeded to the wings together to await their turn.

It was about a quarter of an hour before they were called upon, and during this quarter of an hour Freddie tells me that his spirits soared heavenwards. It was so patently absurd, he felt, as he watched the local talent perform, to suppose that there could be any question of his ability to cop the gage of victory. He didn't know how these things were decided – by popular acclamation, presumably – but whatever system of marking might prevail it must inevitably land him at the head of the poll.

These Bottleton song-birds were all well-meaning – they spared no pains and gave of their best – but they had nothing that could by the remotest stretch of the word be described as Class. Five of them preceded him, and not one of the five could have held those Notting Hill mothers for a minute – let alone have wowed them as he had wowed them. These things are a matter of personality and technique. Either you have got personality and technique or you haven't. These chaps hadn't. He had. His position, he saw, was rather that of a classic horse put up against a lot of selling platers.

So, as I say, he stood there for a quarter of an hour, muttering 'Mi-mi-mi' and getting more and more above himself: and finally, after a cove who looked like a plumber's mate had finished singing 'Just Break the News to Mother' and had gone off to sporadic applause, he saw the announcer jerking his thumb at him and realized that the moment had come.

He was not a bit nervous, he tells me. From what he had heard of these Amateur Nights, he had rather supposed that he might for the first minute or so have to quell and dominate a pretty tough audience. But the house seemed in friendly mood, and he walked on to the stage, adjusting his mask, with a firm and confident tread.

The first jarring note was struck when the announcer turned to inquire his name. He was a stout, puffy man with bags under his eyes and a face the colour of damson, and on seeing Freddie he shied like a horse. He backed a step or two, throwing up his arms, as he did so, in a defensive sort of way.

'It's all right,' said Freddie.

The man seemed reassured. He gulped once or twice, but became calmer.

'What's all this? he asked.

'It's quite all right,' said Freddie. 'Just announce me as The Masked Troubadour.'

'Coo! You gave me a nasty shock. Masked what?'

'Troubadour,' said Freddie, spacing the syllables carefully.

He walked over to the piano, where Jos. Waterbury had seated himself and was playing chords.

'Ready?' he said.

Jos. Waterbury looked up, and a slow look of horror began to spread itself over his face. He shut his eyes, and his lips moved silently. Freddie thinks he was praying.

'Buck up,' said Freddie sharply. 'We're just going to kick off.'

Jos. Waterbury opened his eyes.

'Gawd?' he said. 'Is that you?'

'Of course it's me.'

'What have you done to your face?'

This was a point which the audience, also, seemed to wish thrashed out. Interested voices made themselves heard from the gallery.

'Wot's all this, Bill?'

'It's a masked trebudder,' said the announcer.

'Wot's a trebudder?'

'This is.' The damson-faced man seemed to wash his hands of the whole unpleasant affair. 'Don't blame me, boys,' he begged. 'That's what he says he is.'

Jos. Waterbury bobbed up again. For the last few moments he had just been sitting muttering to himself.

'It isn't right,' said Jos. Waterbury. 'It isn't British. It isn't fair to lead a man on and then suddenly turn round on him –'

'Shut up!' hissed Freddie. All this, he felt, was subversive. Getting the audience into a wrong mood. Already the patrons' geniality was beginning to ebb. He could sense a distinct lessening of that all-pals-together spirit. One or two children were crying.

'Ladyeezun-gennelmun,' bellowed the damson-faced man, 'less blinking noise, if you please. I claim your kind indulgence for this 'ere trebudder.'

'That's all right,' said Jos. Waterbury, leaving the piano and coming downstage. 'He may be a trebudder or he may not, but I appeal to this fair-minded audience – is it just, is it ethical, for a man suddenly to pop out on a fellow who's had a couple –'

'Come on,' cried the patrons. 'Less of it.' And a voice from the gallery urged Jos. Waterbury to put his head in a bucket.

'All right,' said Jos. Waterbury, who was plainly in dark mood. 'All right. But you haven't heard the last of this by any means.'

He reseated himself at the piano, and Freddie began to sing 'When the Silver of the Moonlight Meets the Lovelight in Your Eyes'.

The instant he got going, he knew that he had never been in better voice in his life. Whether it was the oysters or the stout or the throat tonic, he didn't know, but the notes were floating out as smooth as syrup. It made him feel a better man to listen to himself.

And yet there was something wrong. He spotted it almost from the start. For some reason he was falling short of perfection. And then suddenly he got on to it. In order to make a song a smash, it is not enough for the singer to be on top of his form. The accompanist, also, must do his bit. And the primary thing a singer expects from his accompanist is that he shall play the accompaniment of the song he is singing.

This Jos. Waterbury was not doing, and it was this that was causing the sweet-bells-jangled effect which Freddie had observed. What the greasy bird was actually playing, he could not say, but it was not the twiddly-bits to 'When the Silver of the Moonlight Meets the Lovelight in Your Eyes'.

It was obviously a case for calling a conference. A bit of that inter-office communication stuff was required. He made a sideways leap to the piano, encouraging some of the audience to suppose that he was going into his dance.

'*There is silver in the moonlight* . . . What the hell are you playing?' sang Freddie.

'Eh?' said Jos. Waterbury.

'*But its silver tarnished seems* . . . You're playing the wrong song.'

'What are you singing?'

'*When it meets the golden lovelight* . . . *I*'m singing "When the Silver of the Moonlight Meets the Lovelight in Your Eyes", you silly ass.'

'Cool!' said Jos. Waterbury. 'I thought you told me "Top Hat, White Tie and Tails". All right, cocky, now we're off.'

He switched nimbly into the correct channels, and Freddie was able to sing '*In your eyes that softly beams*' without that set-your-teeth-on-edge feeling that he had sometimes experienced when changing gears unskilfully in his two-seater. But the mischief had been done. His grip on his audience had weakened. The better element on the lower floor were still sticking it out like men, but up in the gallery a certain liveliness had begun to manifest itself. The raspberry was not actually present, but he seemed to hear the beating of its wings.

To stave it off, he threw himself into his warbling with renewed energy. And such was his magnetism and technique that he very nearly put it over. The muttering died away. One of the crying children stopped crying. And though another was sick Freddie thinks this must have been due to something it had eaten. He sang like one inspired.

> '*Oh, the moon is bright and radiant,*
> *But its radiance fades and dies*
> *When the silver of the moonlight*
> *Meets the lovelight in your eyes.*'

It was when he had reached this point, with that sort of lingering, caressing, treacly tremolo on the 'eyes' which makes all the difference, that the mothers of Notting Hill, unable to restrain themselves any longer, had started whooping and stamping and whistling through their fingers. And there is little doubt, he tells me, that ere long these Bottletonians would have begun expressing themselves in similar fashion, had not Jos. Waterbury, who since the recent conference had been as good as gold, at this moment recognized an acquaintance in the front row of the stalls.

This was a large, red-haired man in a sweater and corduroy trousers who looked as if he might be in some way connected with the jellied eel industry. His name was Murphy, and it was he who, as Jos. Waterbury had informed Freddie at their first meeting, wished to ascertain the colour of the accompanist's insides.

What drew Jos. Waterbury's attention to this eel-jellier – if eel-jellier he was – was the circumstance of the latter, at this juncture, throwing an egg at him. It missed its mark, but it had the effect of causing the pianist to stop playing and rise and advance to the footlights. There was a cold look of dislike in his eyes. It was plain that there was imperfect communion of spirit between these two men. He bent over and asked:

'Did you throw that egg?'

To which the red-haired man's reply was:

'R.'

'You did, did you?' said Jos. Waterbury. 'Well, what price sausage and mashed?'

Freddie says he cannot understand these East End blokes. Their psychology is a sealed book to him. It is true that Jos. Waterbury had spoken in an unpleasant sneering manner, but even so he could see nothing in his words to stir the passions and cause a human being to lose his kinship with the divine. Personally, I am inclined to think that there must have been some hidden significance in them, wounding the eel-jellier's pride, so that when Jos. Waterbury said 'What price sausage and mashed?' the phrase did not mean to him what it would to you or me, but something deeper. Be that as it may, it brought the red-haired chap to his feet, howling like a gorilla.

The position of affairs was now as follows: The red-haired chap was saying wait till he got Jos. Waterbury outside. Jos. Waterbury was saying that he could eat the red-haired chap for a relish with his tea. Three more children had begun to cry, and the one who had stopped crying had begun again. Forty, perhaps – or it may have been fifty voices were shouting 'Oy!' The announcer was bellowing 'Order, please, order!' Another infant in the gallery was being sick. And Freddie was singing verse two of 'When the Silver of the Moonlight Meets the Lovelight in Your Eyes'.

Even at Queen's Hall I don't suppose this sort of thing could have gone on long. At the Bottleton Palace of Varieties the pause before the actual outbreak of Armageddon was only of a few seconds' duration. Bottleton East is crammed from end to end with costermongers dealing in tomatoes, potatoes, Brussels sprouts and fruits in their season, and it is a very negligent audience there that forgets to attend a place of entertainment with full pockets.

Vegetables of all kinds now began to fill the air, and Freddie, abandoning his Art as a wash-out, sought refuge behind the piano. But this move, though shrewd, brought him only a temporary respite. No doubt this audience had had to deal before with singers who hid behind pianos. It took them perhaps a minute to find the range, and then some kind of a dried fish came dropping from the gallery and caught him in the eye. Very much the same thing, if you remember, happened to King Harold at the battle of Hastings.

Forty seconds later, he was in the wings, brushing a tomato off his coat.

In circumstances like these, you might suppose that Freddie's soul would have been a maelstrom of mixed emotions. This, however, was not the case. One emotion only gripped him. He had never been more single-minded in his life. He wanted to get hold of Jos. Waterbury and twist his head off and stuff it down his throat. It is true that the red-haired chap had started the final mix-up by throwing an egg, but an accompanist worth his salt, felt Freddie, should have treated a mere egg with silent disdain, not deserted his post in order to argue about the thing. Rightly or wrongly, he considered that it was to Jos. Waterbury that his downfall was due. But for that sozzled pianist, he held, a triumph might have been his as outstanding as his furore at Notting Hill.

Jos. Waterbury had disappeared, but fortunately Freddie was now not unfamiliar with his habits. His first act, on reaching the stage door and taking a Brussels sprout out of his hair, was to ask to be directed to the Green Goose. And there, a few moments later, he came upon the man he sought. He was standing at the counter drinking an unsweetened gin.

Now, just before the tiger of the jungle springs upon its prey, I am told by chaps who know tigers of the jungle, there is always a moment when it pauses, flexing its muscles and rubbing its feet in the resin. It was so with Freddie at this point. He did not immediately leap upon Jos. Waterbury, but stood clenching and unclenching his fists, while his protruding eyes sought out soft spots in the man. His ears were red and he breathed heavily.

The delay was fatal. Other people were familiar with Jos. Waterbury's habits. Just as he was about to take off, the swing door flew open violently, disclosing the red-haired man. And a moment later the red-haired man, pausing only to spit on his hands, had gone into action.

The words we speak in our heat seldom stand the acid test.

In the very first seconds of the encounter it would have become plain to the poorest judge of form that in stating that he could eat the red-haired man for a relish with his tea. Jos. Waterbury had over-estimated his powers. He put up the rottenest kind of show, being as chaff before the red-haired bloke's sickle. Almost before the proceedings had begun, he had stopped a stinker with his chin and was on the sawdust.

In places like Bottleton East, when you are having a scrap and your antagonist falls, you don't wait for anyone to count ten – you kick him in the slats. This is a local rule. And it was so obvious to Freddie that this was what the red-haired bird was planning to do that he did not hesitate, but with a passionate cry rushed into the fray. He isn't a chap who goes out of his way to get mixed up in bar-room brawls, but the sight of this red-haired fellow murdering the bounder he wanted to murder himself seemed to him to give him no option. He felt that his claim was being jumped, and his generous spirit resented it.

And so moved was he by the thought of being done out of his rights, that he might have put up a very pretty fight indeed had not the chucker-out attached to the premises intervened.

When the summons for his professional services reached him, the honest fellow had been enjoying a pint and a bit of bread and cheese in a back room. He now came in, wiping his mouth.

These chuckers-out are no fools. A glance showed this one that a big, beefy, dangerous-looking chap was having a spot of unpleasantness with a slim, slight, slender chap, and with swift intelligence and sturdy common sense he grabbed the slim, slender chap. To pick Freddie up like a sack of coals and carry him to the door and hurl him out into the great open spaces was with him the work of a moment.

And so it came about that Lord Blicester, who was driving home after one of his meetings in the Conservative interest, became aware of stirrings afoot off-stage left, and the next moment perceived his nephew Frederick coming through the air like a shooting star.

He signalled to the chauffeur to stop and poked his head out of the window.

'Frederick!' he called – not, as you may well suppose, quite grasping the gist.

Freddie did not reply. Already he was re-entering the swing door in order to take up the argument at the point where it had been broken off. He was by now a bit stirred. Originally he had wanted to assassinate Jos. Waterbury, but since then his conception had broadened, if you know what I mean. He now wished to blot out the red-haired chap as well – also the chucker-out and anybody else who crossed his path.

Old Blicester emerged from the car, just in time to see his flesh and blood popping out again.

'Frederick!' he cried. 'What is the meaning of this?' And he seized him by the arm.

Well, anybody could have told him he was asking for it. This was no time to seize Freddie by the arm. There was an arm left over which old Blicester hadn't seized, and with this Freddie smote him a snappy one in the midriff. Then, passing a weary hand over his brow, he made for the swing door again.

The catch about all this sort of thing – running amuck, I mean, and going berserk, or whatever they call it – is that there inevitably comes a morning after. The following morning found Freddie in bed, and so did old Blicester. He appeared as early as nine a.m., rousing Freddie from a troubled sleep, and what he wanted, it seemed, was a full explanation. And when Freddie, who was too weak for polished subterfuge, had given him a full explanation, not omitting the incident of the Brazil nut and the top hat, he put on the black cap.

He had changed his mind about that marriage. It was not right, he said – it was not human – to inflict a fool like Freddie on so sweet a girl, or on any girl, for that matter. After a powerful passage, in which he pointed this out, he delivered sentence. Freddie was to take the afternoon train to Blicester Regis, repair by the station cab to Blicester Towers, and at Blicester Towers to remain secluded till further notice. Only thus, in his opinion, could the world be rendered safe for the human race. So there was nothing for Freddie to do but ring up the girl, Dora, and inform her that the big binge was off.

The statement was not very well received.

'Oh, dear,' she said, and Freddie, reading between the lines, could see that what she really meant was 'Oh hell.' 'Why?'

Freddie explained that he had got to go down to the country

that afternoon till further notice. The girl's manner changed. Her voice, which had been sniffy, brightened.

'Oh, but that's all right,' she said. 'We shall all miss you, of course, but I can send you the bill.'

'Something in that,' said Freddie. 'Only the trouble is, you see, I can't pay it.'

'Why not?'

'I haven't any money.'

'Why haven't you any money?'

Freddie braced himself.

'Well, the fact is that in a mistaken moment of enthusiasm, thinking – wrongly, as it turned out – that I was on a pinch, I betted –'

And in broken accents he told her the whole story. Wasted, of course, because she had hung up with a sharp cry at the word 'betted'. And about ten minutes later, after saying 'Hullo, hullo' a good many times, he, too, hung up – sombrely, because something told him that one more girl whom he had loved had gone out of his life.

And no sooner had he left his rooms and tottered into the street, his intention – and a very sound one – being to make his way to the club and have a few before it was too late, something small and greasy nipped out from the shadows. To cut a long story short, Jos. Waterbury.

And Freddie was just about to summon up all that remained of his frail strength after last night's doir.gs and let him have it right in the eyeball, when Jos. Waterbury began to thank him for saving his life.

Well, you can't swat a man who is thanking you for saving his life, not if your own is ruled by the *noblesse oblige* code of the Widgeons. And when he tells you that times are hard and moots the possibility of your being able to spare a trifle, you cannot pass on unheeding. It was a bob that time, and on Freddie's return to London some three weeks later – the very day, oddly enough, when he read in the *Morning Post* that a marriage had been arranged and would shortly take place between Percival Alexander, eldest son of Gregory Hotchkiss, Esq., and Mrs Hotchkiss, and Dora, only daughter of the late Sir Ramsworthy Pinfold and Lady Pinfold – it was two,

Freddie not having anything smaller on him. And there you are.

There was a thoughtful silence.

'And so it goes on,' said the Crumpet.

'So it goes on,' said the Senior Bean.

The Junior Bean agreed that so it went on.

Chapter Seven
Ukridge and the Home from Home

Somebody tapped on my door. I sat up in bed, electrified. Except for Macbeth, I should imagine that few people have ever been quite so startled by a nightly knocking. The hour was three in the morning, and in London lodgings the sleeper is rarely awakened at such a time in such a manner.

The door was now open, and I perceived, illuminated by a candle, the Roman Emperor features of Bowles, my landlord. Bowles, like all proprietors of furnished rooms in the Sloane Square neighbourhood, is an ex-butler, and even in a plaid dressing-gown he retained much of the cold majesty which so intimidated me by day.

'Excuse me, sir,' he said, in the reserved voice in which he always addresses me. 'Do you happen to have the sum of eight shilling and sixpence?'

'Eight shillings?'

'And sixpence, sir. It is for Mr Ukridge.'

As he mentioned the name, his tone seemed to take on a sort of respectful affection. One of the mysteries of my life is why this godlike man, while treating me, who pay my rent regularly, with a distant *hauteur*, as if I were something very young and callow in baggy trousers whom he had just caught eating the *entrée* with a fish-knife, should positively fawn on Stanley Featherstonehaugh Ukridge, who is – and has been for years – a recognized blot on Society.

'For Mr Ukridge?'

'Yes, sir.'

'What does Mr Ukridge want eight and six for?'

'To pay his cab, sir.'

'You mean he's here?'

'Yes, sir.'

'In a cab?'

'Yes, sir.'

'At three in the morning?'

'Yes, sir.'

I could make nothing of this. As a matter of fact, mystery had enveloped all Ukridge's movements of late. I had not seen him for months, though I knew that, in the absence of his Aunt Julia, the well-known novelist, he was residing at her house on Wimbledon Common as a sort of caretaker. The most mysterious thing of all was that I had received a letter from him one morning, enclosing ten pounds in bank-notes – part-payment, he explained, of loans floated by me in the past, for which, he said, he could never be sufficiently grateful. Of this miracle he had given no other explanation than that his genius and opportunism had at last found the road to wealth.

'There's some money on the dressing-table.'

'Thank you, sir.'

'Did Mr Ukridge mention what he thought he was doing, dashing about London in cabs at this time of night?'

'No, sir. He merely inquired if I had a spare room, and desired me to set out the whisky and soda. I have done this.'

'He's come to stay, then?'

'Yes, sir,' said Bowles, with marked gratification. He looked like the father of the Prodigal Son.

I put on a dressing-gown and went into the sitting-room. There, as Bowles had foreshadowed, was the whisky and soda. I am not a great drinker in the small hours, but I felt it prudent to mix myself a glassful. I have generally found that on the occasions when S. F. Ukridge descends on me out of the void it is best to be ready.

The next moment the stairs shook beneath the clumping of heavy feet, and the man of wrath entered in person.

'What on earth –!' I exclaimed.

My emotion was not unjustified. For the appearance of Ukridge I had been prepared, but not for his appearance in his present costume. Never a natty dresser, he had sunk now to hitherto unimagined depths. Above a suit of striped pyjamas he was wearing the yellow mackintosh which has been his companion through so many discreditable adventures. On

160

his feet were bedroom slippers. He had no socks. His whole appearance was that of one who has recently been caught in a fire.

In answer to my exclamation, he waved a hand in silent greeting. Then, having adjusted the pince-nez which were attached to his outstanding ears by ginger-beer wire, he plunged forcefully at the decanter.

'Ah!' he said, putting down his glass.

'What on earth are you doing,' I asked, 'roaming about London in that costume?'

He shook his head.

'No roaming, Corky, old horse. I came straight as the taxi flies from Wimbledon Common. And why, laddie? Because I knew that a true friend like you would be sure to have the latch-string hanging out and the lighted candle in the window. How are you off for socks these days?'

'I have a sock,' I replied guardedly.

'I shall need some tomorrow. Also shirts, underlinen, cravats, a suit, a hat, boots, and a pair of braces. You see before you, Corky, a destitute man. Starting life all over again, you might say.'

'What are you wearing those pyjamas for?'

'The ordinary slumber-wear of an English gentleman.'

'But you're not slumbering.'

'I was,' said Ukridge, and it seemed to me that a look of pain flitted across his face. 'An hour ago, Corky – or perhaps nearer an hour and a half – I was slumbering like the dickens. And then –'

He reached for the cigar-box, and smoked for a while in a rather brooding manner.

'Ah, well!' he said.

He emitted what I suppose was intended to be a mirthless laugh.

'Life!' he said. 'Life! That's what it is – just Life. Did you get that tenner I sent you, Corky?'

'Yes.'

'I dare say it came as a bit of a surprise?'

'It did.'

'When I coughed up that tenner, do you know what it was to

me? A nothing. A mere nothing. A bagatelle. An inconsiderable trifle out of my income.'

'Your what?'

'My income, old horse. A mere segment of my steady income.'

'Where did you get a steady income?'

'In the hotel business.'

'What business?'

'Hotel business. From my share of the proceeds of Ukridge's Home From Home. I didn't actually call it that, but that was how I thought of it. The Home From Home.'

Once more a cloud passed over his expressive face.

'What a bonanza it was, while it lasted! While,' he repeated sadly, 'it lasted. That's the trouble with these good things – they do not last. They come to an end.'

'How did this one come to a beginning?'

'My aunt suggested it. At least, when I say suggested it – It was like this, Corky. You know that, now these talking pictures have come in, the studio people are scouring the world for blokes of either sex, capable of writing dialogue? It was but a question of time before my aunt was approached. She signed a contract to go to Hollywood for a year. And her last words, as she poked her head out of the boat-train at Waterloo, consisted of instructions to me on no account to let the house in her absence. I dare say you know she had a horror of strangers in the home?'

'I noticed it that time I was dining with you there and she came in.'

'Well, I give you my honest word, Corky, that up to that moment I had had not the slightest idea of doing anything but stay in the house and bark at burglars. I anticipated a quiet and reposeful year, during which I could look about me and try to find my niche. The butler and the rest of the servants were on board wages. I was assured of three square meals a day. The future, if placid, looked rosy. I was content.

'And then my aunt spoke those ill-judged words.

'I don't know if you are a student of history, Corky, but if you are you'll agree with me that half the trouble in this world has come from women speaking ill-judged words. Everything is set and looks nice and smooth, and then along comes some woman with a few ill-judged words, and there you are. Upon my solemn Sam, until my Aunt Julia delivered that parting speech with one elbow in the eye of a fellow-passenger and the other arm waving authoritatively in my direction, the idea of turning The Cedars, Wimbledon Common, into a residential hotel had never so much as crossed my mind.'

This seemed to me to be on a major scale. I gasped reverently.

'You turned your aunt's house into an hotel?'

'It would have been flouting Providence not to. There was big money in the scheme. If you are acquainted with the suburbs, you are aware that these residential hotels are springing up on every side. There is an ever-increasing demand for them. Owners of large private houses find it's too much of a sweat to keep them up, so they hire a couple of Swiss waiters with colds in their heads and advertise in the papers that here is the ideal home for the City man.

'But mark the difference between joints like those and the Maison Ukridge. On the one hand, comparative squalor. On the other, luxury. You may not look on my Aunt Julia as a personal friend, Corky, but even you can't deny that she knows how to furnish a house. Taste. Elegance. The *dernier cri* in refinement.

'And then the staff! No Swiss waiters here, but a butler, alone worth price of admission. Parlourmaids trained to the last ounce. A cook in a million. Outstanding housemaids. A tweeny renowned throughout Wimbledon. I tell you that, as I tottered out of Waterloo Station to go to the nearest newspaper office and insert my advertisement, I sang. Not for long, because people began to look at me. But nevertheless, I sang.

'You would have been surprised, Corky – I will go further, you would have been astounded at the number of replies I got. I had planned the terms on a liberal scale, for of course before floating an enterprise of this kind it had been necessary to square a butler, two parlourmaids, two housemaids, a cook, a tweeny, and the boy who cleaned the boots – bloodsuckers to a man and woman ; but, in spite of that, half the population of London seemed anxious to chip in.

'The fact is, you see, Wimbledon Common is a good address. It means something, lends a lustre. The cognoscenti, hearing it, are impressed. You are one of these City blokes, and you meet another City bloke and say to him casually, "Drop in and see me some time, old man. I am always to be found at The Cedars, Wimbledon Common," and he fawns on you and probably stands you lunch.

'So, as I say, I was flooded, positively inundated with requests to be allowed to sit in. All that remained to do was to throw the handkerchief. I bunged it eventually to a well-chosen six, headed by Lieutenant-Colonel B. B. Bagnew, late of the Fourth Loyal Lincolnshires, and Lady Bastable, widow of one of those birds who get knighted up North. The rest were good, solid fellows who were busy being the backbone of England, but not so busy as to forget to settle up regularly every Friday night.

'They came trooping in, one by one, and presently the nest was full and the venture a going concern.'

Well, it couldn't have been a bigger success (continued Ukridge). Everything from the start was one grand, sweet song. It was idyllic, Corky, that's what it was. I am not a man who speaks hastily. I weigh my words. And I tell you it was idyllic. We were just a great, big, happy family.

Too often in the past it has happened that circumstances have compelled me to appear in the *rôle* of guest, but you can take it from me that Nature really intended me for a host. I have the manner, the air. I wish you could have seen me presiding over the dinner-table of a night. Suave, genial, beloved by all. A kind word here, a quick smile there. The aristocrat of the old school, nothing less.

Talk about feasts of Reason and flows of Soul. A pretty high level the conversation round the board invariably touched. The Colonel had his anecdotes of India, where he had served his country faithfully and well. Lady Bastable could tell you some good things about Blackpool in August, though sometimes – in a graver vein – she spoke of the clique-i-ness of Huddersfield. And the others were all intelligent, active-minded men who read their evening papers in the train and were never without something sparkling to say about Brighton's A's and the weather.

And after dinner. The quiet rubber. The wireless. The murmur of pleasant talk. The occasional spot of music.

Did I say it was idyllic? Well, it was.

Here Ukridge helped himself to another whisky and soda, and sat for a space, brooding.

My Aunt Julia (he resumed), on these occasional absences of hers from the fireside, is never a great correspondent. At least, she very seldom writes to me. The fact that I did not hear from her, therefore, occasioned me no concern. I assumed that she was doing her bit in Hollywood, basking in the pleasant sunshine and being the curse of such parties as she might attend; and, apart from wishing that she had had the vision and enterprise to sign up for three years instead of one, I scarcely gave her a thought.

And then, one afternoon, when I had run into London to lay in a fresh supply of cigars, I happened to meet her friend, Angelica Vining, the poetess, in Bond Street. You may remember this bird, Corky? She was the one who wanted to borrow my aunt's brooch on a certain memorable occasion, but I was firm and wouldn't let her have it – partly on principle and partly because I had pawned it the day before.

Since that episode a certain coldness had existed, but she seemed to have got over it. She now beamed upon me, not without a toothy geniality.

'I suppose you were delighted to hear the news?' she said, after we had exchanged the customary civilities.

'News?' I said, for she had me fogged.

'About your aunt coming home,' said the Vining.

Have you ever, Corky, during a friendly political discussion in a pub, been punched squarely on the nose? Well, that's how I felt when I heard those words, so casually uttered in the heart of Bond Street. We were standing outside the dog-shop at the moment, and I give you my word that the two Scotties and the bulldog pup in the window suddenly seemed to become four

Scotties and two bulldog pups, all shimmering. The ground rocked beneath my feet.

'Coming home?' I gurgled.

'Hasn't she written and told you? Yes, she's sailing home almost immediately.'

And, as in a trance, Corky, I heard the woman relating the events which led up to the tragedy. And the longer I listened, the more solid did my conviction become that my Aunt Julia ought to have been chloroformed at birth.

In that particular studio which had engaged her services, it seems a good deal of latitude is granted to the distinguished authors on the pay-roll. The kindly powers-that-be recognize the existence of the artist temperament and make allowances for it. If, therefore, my aunt had confined herself to snootering directions, harrying camera-men, and chasing supervisors up trees, nothing would have been said. But there is one thing the artist soul must not do at the Colossal-Superfine, and that is swat the Main Boss with a jewelled hand over the ear-hole.

And this, in a moment of emotion due to the fact that he had described some dialogue submitted by her as a lot of boloney that didn't mean a thing, my Aunt Julia had done.

And, as a consequence, she was now headed eastward and, according to the Vining, expected home at any moment.

Well, Corky, you have seen me in some tight places. You have observed your old friend – not once but many times – with his back to the wall and the grim, set smile on his face, and you have come, no doubt, to the conclusion that he is a hard man to beat. And so I am. But here was one occasion when, frankly, I confess, I could not discern the happy ending.

My course, you may say, was obvious. Frightful though the thought might be of closing down what was nothing more or less than a gold-mine, there was nothing for it but to sling my guests out of The Cedars without delay, so that my aunt, returning to the old home, should find it swept and garnished and with no signs of alien occupation.

I saw that, of course, myself. I saw it in a flash. But the difficulty was, how the dickens was it to be done? You see, all my little group of squatters had watertight agreements and were legally entitled to stick on for six months, of which only three had expired. It wasn't a case of just walking in and saying: 'Out you get, all of you!'

A problem of the trickiest. I didn't shine at the dinner-table that night. Many were the comments on my preoccupation For the first time, the genial Squire of The Cedars was to be observed sitting distrait and silent and contributing nothing to the quips and cranks that flashed like lightning to and from across the board.

After dinner I withdrew into my aunt's study to do some more thinking. And then it occurred to me that, if two heads were better than one, nine would be better still. I was not alone in this enterprise, you will remember. The proceeds of the venture had been split up from the first – in proportions decided upon at a preliminary conference – between myself, the butler, the two parlourmaids, the two housemaids, the cook, the tweeny, and the boy who cleaned the boots. I rang the bell and instructed the butler to summon the shareholders for an extraordinary meeting.

And presently in they filed – the boy who cleaned the boots, the tweeny, the cook, the two housemaids, the two parlourmaids, and the butler. The females got chairs, the males stood against the wall, and I sat on the desk, and, after a few formalities, rose and explained the situation which had arisen.

Considering what a bolt from the blue it was, I must admit that they all took it very well. True the cook burst into tears and said something about the Wrath of the Lord and the Cities of the Plain – she being a bit on the Biblical side ; and one of the housemaids had hysterics. But you have to expect that sort of thing at a critical meeting of shareholders. Somebody lent the cook a handkerchief, and the tweeny soothed the housemaid, and then we settled down to bend our brains to it.

Of course, in a mixed gathering like that, it was to be foreseen that there would be a certain amount of dithering. Some of the suggestions offered were, frankly, goofy. And in saying this I have in mind principally the boy who cleaned the boots.

This stripling was a small, freckled lad who, after being dropped on the head when a baby, appeared to have spent the formative years of his life reading sensational fiction. You will scarcely credit it, Corky, but his idea of solving the problem

167

was that we should all dress up as ghosts and scare the cash customers out of the place. And it will give you some inkling of the state to which I had been reduced by much thinking, that for a moment I actually toyed with the notion. Then the impracticability of the scheme of having a mob of nine spectres of mixed sexes surging about the house swept over me, and I asked him to try again.

This time he advised appointing a quorum to meet my aunt at Southampton and kidnap her and keep her imprisoned in a cellar somewhere till further notice. An attractive by-product of this course of action, he pointed out, was that, if you cut a toe or a finger off from time to time, she could be induced to sign large cheques which would do us all a bit of good.

At this point the butler very properly took the child by the ear and slung him out. And after that things began to clarify. And finally it was agreed upon that a friend of the butler's should come to the house, posing as an inspector of drains, and condemn the system of The Cedars as unfit for human consumption. He had generally found, the butler said, that ladies and gentlemen were sensitive to adverse criticism directed at the drainage systems of the houses which they occupied; and his friend, he thought, would be happy to undertake the job for a pound down, his expenses both ways from Putney, and a glass of beer. And, nobody having anything better to suggest, this ruse was decided upon.

On the following morning, accordingly, I went about sniffing in a suggestive manner and asking my guests if they hadn't noticed an odd smell; and in the afternoon the butler's pal rolled up and got down to the agenda.

I must pay a marked tribute to the butler's pal. In my opinion, he did his work well. There were moments when even I was almost deceived. He had just that rather dingy look and that drooping moustache which seem somehow to go with drains-inspecting. Add a black note-book and a peaked cap of vaguely official aspect, and you have a convincing picture.

But the trouble in this life, Corky, is that you can never be sure when you won't come up against the Man Who Knows, the nib, the specialist, the fellow who has studied the subject and has no illusions. By seven o'clock, when our chap left, sniffing to the last, five of my six guests had been reduced to so admirable a state of mental collapse that it was plainly only a matter of moments before they started packing. And it was at this juncture that the sixth guest, a fellow of the name of Wapshott, returned to the fold. He had been spending the afternoon at the Oval, watching a cricket match.

Now, in assembling my little family, Corky, I had taken no steps to ascertain their particular walks in life, contenting myself with bankers' references and the like. Imagine my concern, then, when this bloke Wapshott, on learning what had occurred, flung up his head like a war-horse at the note of a bugle, and announced with flashing eyes, that, until his retirement from business six months before, he himself had been an inspector of drains and, what is more, well-known as one of the keenest minds in the profession.

Opening his remarks by relating a striking compliment which had been paid to his acumen and intuition by somebody high up in the drains world in the summer of the year '26, he said with considerable heat that, if anyone was going to tell him there was anything wrong with the system at The Cedars, he would eat his hat. He exhibited the hat – a plush Fedora.

'Show me the man,' he said warmly, 'who says I have been living three months in a house without knowing if the drains were all right, and I will give him the lie in his teeth.'

And he went on to speak for a while of drains he had met, of drains which had tried to deceive him, and of the pitiful lack of success which such drains had enjoyed.

Well, we couldn't show him the man, because he had had his glass of beer, trousered his quid, and left on a west-bound bus an hour ago. But eager voices described his methods of procedure, and Wapshott simply scoffed. He absolutely scoffed, Corky.

Apparently there is a technique in drains-inspecting. The expert can recognize the touch. For all his peaked cap, for all his note-book and drooping moustache, it was now plain that the butler's pal had betrayed his amateurishness in a dozen ways. He had done the wrong things. He had asked the wrong questions. Even his sniffing came in for criticism.

'The fellow was an impostor,' said Wapshott.

169

'But what could his motive have been?' asked Lady Bastable. 'Such a nice, respectable-looking man, too. He reminded me of one of the Mayors of Huddersfield.'

Colonel Bagnew gave tongue. I have wondered since if he could have been any relation of the boy who cleaned the boots. Both their minds ran on the same lurid, imaginative lines.

'Advance man of a gang of burglars,' said the Colonel. 'Regular thing with these fellows. They send a chap on first to spy out the land, and then they come charging in, having been thoroughly informed of the topography of the house.'

For a moment, Corky, it seemed as if this suggestion were about to solve everything. The company reacted noticeably. Two of the City blokes looked at one another in a sickly sort of way, and Lady Bastable turned definitely green at the gills.

'Burglars!' she cried. 'I shall leave immediately.'

And the two City blokes began to mumble something about how lonely and remote these houses on Wimbledon Common were, and how difficult it would be to find a policeman if you wanted one.

And then the Colonel – silly ass – went and spoiled the whole thing.

'Madam,' he said, 'be British! Gentlemen, be men! Are we to be scared from our comfortable home by a few paltry burglars?'

Lady Bastable said she didn't want to be murdered in her bed. The City blokes said nor did they – in their own beds, that was to say – and I tried to push the good work along by saying that I couldn't imagine anything rottener than being murdered in your bed. But the Colonel had now got it thoroughly up his nose. You can never trust these old Indian Army men, Corky. Heroes all of them, and it gets them greatly disliked.

'You little know these scoundrels if you think such a thing possible,' he said. 'A craven crew. Show them a good old Army revolver, and they run like rabbits.'

Lady Bastable said she hadn't got an Army revolver.

'I have,' said the Colonel. 'And my bedroom door is down the passage from yours. Rely on me, madam. At the first cry from you, I shall be out of my door and blazing away like billy-o.'

That turned the scale. The company decided to stay on. And there was I, with all the weary work to do over again.

But it is at just these times, when the ordinary man would be nonplussed, Corky, that your old friend comes out strongest. Peril seems to sharpen his intellect. Of course, you may say that I ought to have thought of it from the first, and I admit the criticism is justified. Still, it wasn't an hour after the discussion I have just outlined before I got the idea which seemed to solve the whole problem.

I saw now that, by fooling about and planning elaborate schemes to cast discredit on the drainage system of The Cedars, I had merely been scratching the surface. What I needed was to go right to the root of the things. I've studied human nature pretty closely, and I know one thing – viz., that, however firmly he may be settled in, you can always dislodge the stoutest limpet by telling him there is infectious illness in the house.

Colonel Bagnew might brandish his Army revolvers and speak sneeringly of burglars, but I was prepared to bet that, if informed that the tweeny was down with scarlet fever, he would be out of the place so quick that you would only see a sort of blur going down the drive.

I put this to the butler, as a knowledgeable man, and after myself the heaviest shareholder, and he agreed with me *in toto*. He recalled to my mind the occasion when my Aunt Julia, woman of chilled steel though she is, had left the home on learning that one of the housemaids had mumps, and kept on going till she reached Bingley-on-Sea, where she remained three weeks.

It was arranged, therefore, that the tweeny should steal off privately to her mother's next morning and that the butler, after going about looking grave and shaking his head ominously for a day or two, should come to me at a moment when I was surrounded by my little flock and spring the big news.

I previewed the scene over and over again, and could find no flaw in it.

'Might I have a word with you, sir?'

'Yes, Barter? What is it?'

'I regret to have to inform you, sir, that Jane is far from well.'

'Jane? Jane? Our worthy tweeny? Indeed, Barter? This is certainly most regrettable. Nothing serious, I trust?'

'Yes, sir. I am afraid so, sir.'

'Speak out, Barter. What is it?'

'Scarlet fever, sir, the doctor informs me.'

Sensation followed by immediate stampede of all. I didn't see how it could fail.

However, it is always the unforeseen that pops up and upsets things. At tea time on the following day, just as Barter had dished up the crumpets and withdrawn, shaking his head ominously, a wireless came from my aunt, dispatched in mid-ocean. And I want you to note this wireless very carefully, Corky, and to tell me if it did not justify me in doing what I did.

It ran as follows:

'Arriving in Paris Tuesday.'

That was all. 'Arriving in Paris Tuesday.' But it was sufficient to cause me to alter my entire plan of campaign.

Up to this point my every nerve had been strained to the task of dislodging the *clientèle*. I now saw that to do so would be a grave blunder.

Consider the facts, Corky. After deducting expenses and paying off my fellow shareholders, every extra week these people remained at The Cedars meant a matter of thirty-odd quid in my kick. It would be madness to hoof them out until the moment arrived. And this wireless showed that the moment was far distant.

You see, when my Aunt Julia goes to Paris, she always stays there at least a couple of weeks. This even at normal times, with the home she loves beckoning to her to return. How long, therefore, would she stay, if she received a telegram informing her that The Cedars was ravaged with scarlet fever? I was convinced that I could reckon on being able to run my Home From Home for at least another month. Which month would bring me in the colossal sum of about a hundred and twenty solid o'goblins.

There seemed to be no alternative. I went round to the local post office next morning, and wired her at the Hôtel Crillon, where she always stayed, and came back, feeling at peace with all the world. The wire had run into money, for I had spared no words to make my meaning clear, but if you don't speculate you can't accumulate.

At dinner that night, no one had occasion to rally me on my preoccupation. It had just occurred to me that, when the time came to announce the scarlet fever, I could not only send these birds racing out of the house, but would probably be in a position to mulct them in heavy damages for breaking their legal agreements. The result was that I sparkled as never before. I had instructed Barter, in view of the changed conditions, to stop looking grave and to lay off the ominous head-shaking till I gave the word, so that there was not an unsmiling face about the board. The evening was voted by all one of our best and jolliest.

The following day passed off equally well. Dinner was a perfect joy-feast. And, the others having retired to rest and not feeling particularly sleepy myself, I fished out a cigar and mixed myself a drink and went and sat in the study, trying to estimate how far ahead I should be when at length the good thing had to be closed down.

And I may tell you, Corky, that I was in extremely sunny mood, as a man may well be who has snatched victory from the jaws of defeat and by his level head and vision has placed himself in a position to amass enormous wealth.

Such were my meditations, old horse, and they were getting juicier and juicier every moment, when suddenly from somewhere upstairs there came the sound of a shot. And then another. Two shots in all. And something seemed to tell me that they were to be chalked up to the credit of Lieutenant-Colonel B. B. Bagnew's Army revolver.

And, sure enough, after a while, as I stood at the door listening for further manifestations, along came the Colonel, waving the weapon.

'What was all the shooting for?' I asked.

The Colonel was looking pretty pleased with himself. He followed me into the study and took a chair.

'Didn't I tell you,' he said, 'that that chap who pretended to inspect the drains was the advance-man of a gang of burglars? I was just dropping off to sleep when I thought I heard a

173

noise on the stairs. I took my revolver and, stepping softly like a leopard, went out into the passage. And there, at the head of the stairs, was a shadowy figure, creeping along. It was too dark to distinguish anything but a dim outline, but I blazed away.'

'Yes?' I said. 'Yes?'

The Colonel clicked his tongue, annoyed.

'I must have missed,' he said. 'When I switched on the lights, there was no corpse.'

'No corpse?' I said.

'No corpse,' said the Colonel. 'I attribute it to the fact that the visibility was not good. In fact, we were in almost total darkness. I had the same experience once in Purundapore. Well, I looked around for a while, but I could see it was no use. The passage window was open, and I have no doubt the miscreant made good his escape that way. There is ivy on the walls, and he could have scrambled down without difficulty.'

'Did the fellow say anything?'

'Yes,' said the Colonel. 'Odd that you should ask that. Just after I had fired the first shot, he said something that sounded like "Bah! Bah!" speaking in a curious, high-pitched voice.'

'Bah, bah?' I said, a bit puzzled. It didn't seem to me to make sense.

'That is what it sounded like.'

'A loony burglar.'

'He may have been snarling.'

'Do burglars snarl?'

'Frequently,' said the Colonel.

He helped himself to a liberal spot and sucked it down with the air of a man who has borne himself in a fashion well befitting an ex-officer of a proud regiment.

It struck me that it was strange that the house was so quiet. I should have thought my lodgers, hearing shots in the night, would have been buzzing about a bit, making inquiries.

'Where are all the others?' I asked.

The Colonel chuckled tolerantly.

'Lying deuced low. Well, well,' he said, 'I suppose we mustn't blame them. Physical courage is a thing that comes naturally to some, not so readily to others. I was surprised myself that nobody seemed to have taken any notice of the little affair, so I went the rounds and found them all snug in bed. The bed-clothes weren't actually over their heads, I admit, but it was a very near thing in one or two cases. Poor Lady Bastable was particularly upset. Apparently she has mislaid the key to her door. And now what? Shall we search the house?'

'There doesn't seem much sense in that, does there? You say the bird escaped by the passage window.'

'I think he must have done. Certainly he disappeared with the most extraordinary rapidity. One moment he was there, the next he had vanished.'

'Well, I think one last spot, then, and to bed.'

'Perhaps you're right,' said the Colonel.

So we had a final one and then parted for the night. At least we didn't part immediately, because we were sleeping on the same floor. My room was at the head of the stairs next to Lady Bastable's, and the Colonel dossed at the end of the passage.

I thought it only courteous as a host to tap at Lady Bastable's door as I passed, with a view to inquiring how she was making out. But there was such a frightful yelp of anguished fear from within at the first impact of my knuckles on the wood that I didn't proceed further in the matter. The Colonel had passed on to his well-earned slumber, so I went into my room and, donning my pyjamas, turned in. I was a little disturbed, of course, at the thought that burglars had been busting into The Cedars, but it didn't seem likely that they would come back as long as they thought the good old Colonel's ammunition was holding out; so, dismissing the matter from my mind, I switched off the light and was soon in a dreamless sleep.

And there, Corky, if there was any justice in the world, if Providence really looked after the deserving as it ought to, the story should have ended. But did it? Laddie, not by a jugful.

How long I slept I couldn't tell you. Possibly an hour it may have been. Possibly more. I was aroused by a hand shaking my shoulder, and, sitting up, perceived that there was a female in my room. I couldn't see her distinctly, and I was just going to express my opinion of this lax and Bohemian behaviour in a respectable house, when she spoke.

'Shush!' she said.

'Less of the "Shush!"' I replied, a little warmly. 'What are you doing in my room?'

'It is I, Stanley,' she said.

Corky, it was my aunt!! And I don't mind telling you that for an instant Reason rocked on its throne.

'Aunt Julia!'

'Don't make a noise.'

'But listen,' I said, and I dare say my voice was a bit peevish, for the injustice of the whole thing was rankling very considerably. 'You said in your wireless that you were going to Paris. "Arriving in Paris Tuesday," you said.'

'I said "Arriving *on* Paris." The *Paris* was the boat I travelled by. And what does it matter?'

What did it matter! I'll trouble you, Corky! I ask you, old horse. Here was I, right up against it, with all my nicely reasoned plans gone phut, purely and simply because this woman hadn't taken the trouble to write distinctly. From time to time in the course of my life I have occasion to think some bitter things about women as a sex, but never had my reflections been bitterer than then.

'Stanley,' said my aunt, 'Barter has gone mad.'

'Eh?' I said. 'Who has?'

'Barter. I arrived late at Southampton, but I was anxious to sleep in my own bed, so I hired a motor and drove here from the docks. I let myself in with my latchkey and crept upstairs as quietly as possible, so as not to disturb anyone, and I had just got to the top of the stairs when Barter suddenly appeared and shot a pistol at me. I called out "Barter! Barter!" and he must have recognized my voice, but he paid no attention whatever. He shot at me again, and I ran into your room and hid in the cupboard. Mercifully, he did not follow me. He must be off his head. Have you noticed anything odd, Stanley, about Barter, while I have been away?'

Corky, you have often expressed admiration of my ingenuity and resource. What? Well, if it wasn't you, it was somebody else. At any rate, I have frequently received unstinted compliments for those qualities. But I can tell you I never deserved them so much as at that moment.

For, hanging on the very brink of destruction, as it were; faced by the fact that my aunt was actually on the premises and that those premises housed a retired Colonel, the widow of a knight from Huddersfield, and four assorted City blokes, I nevertheless kept my head and saw the way out.

'Yes, Aunt Julia,' I said. 'I have noticed something odd about Barter. He has been going round looking grave, and shaking his head in an ominous way, as if he were brooding on something. The man is unquestionably potty. And this, Aunt Julia,' I said, 'is what you must do. This house is obviously not safe for you while he remains on the premises. You must leg it, and instantly. Don't wait. Don't linger. Steal out now on tiptoe and execute a noiseless sneak downstairs and out of the front door. There are taxis at all hours of the night on the corner of the road. Take one and go to a hotel. Meanwhile, I will be dealing with Barter,'

'But, Stanley,' she said. And she spoke in a quavering, startled-fawn sort of voice which was music to my ears. I could see that she was deeply impressed by my intrepid courage, and it seemed to me that the whole episode might very well end in my not only escaping disaster, but actually making a most substantial touch. There is nothing that appeals to women more than the old bulldog grit in the male.

'Leave the whole thing to me,' I said. 'This is man's work, Aunt Julia. The great thing is to get you away in safety, immediately.'

'But how will you manage, Stanley? What will you do? He has a pistol.'

'That'll be all right, Aunt Julia,' I said heartily. 'I have the situation well in hand. I shall send for him in the morning, apparently to discuss some trivial domestic matter connected with his butling. "Ah, Barter," I shall say, nonchalantly, "come in, Barter." And then, when his attention is diverted, I shall make a sudden spring and overpower him. Quite simple. You may leave it all to me.'

Well, it was too dark to see the worshipping look in her eyes, but I knew it was there. I went to the door and peeped out. All was quiet in the passage. I took her hand, pressed it in an encouraging sort of way, and led her out.

And then, just as we were moving nicely, Corky, what do you think?

'I can't go to an hotel without a suit-case,' she said. 'There should be one in the cupboard in my room. And I can probably find some things to put in it.'

Corky, my heart stopped. Your old friend's heart stopped. You see, naturally, she being the only female in my troupe, I had given Lady Bastable the best bedroom. My aunt's bedroom, in fact – the very one which my aunt was now reaching for the door-knob of. Her clutching fingers were within half an inch of the handle.

Well, I did my best.

'You don't want a suit-case, Aunt Julia,' I said. 'You don't *need* a suit-case.'

But it was no good. For the first time there crept into her manner something of the old austerity.

'Don't be a fool,' she said. 'I am certainly not going to sleep in my clothes.'

And with these words she turned the handle and shoved her arm in and found the electric-light switch and bunged it on. And simultaneously from within there came the scream of a lost soul. Lady Bastable taking it big. And immediately after that there was a sound like a mighty, rushing wind, and out came the Colonel from the room down the way and resumed his revolver practice where he had left off.

The whole thing was extraordinarily like the big scene in one of those mystery plays.

Well, Corky, I came away. I didn't wait. I could see no profit to be derived from lingering on. I nipped into my room, brushing aside the bullets, reached hastily for my mackintosh, and legged it down the stairs, leaving them to settle things among themselves. I got out of the house. I found a cab. I took the cab. I came here. And here I am.

And one thing, Corky, I want to say to you very seriously, as a man who has been through the mill and knows what he is talking about. Be very wary, old horse, of these opportunities of making easy money. As in the case I have just related, they too often have strings tied to them. You are a young fellow in the spring-time of life; eager, sanguine, alert for every chance of getting something for nothing. When that chance comes, Corky, examine it well. Walk round it. Pat it with your paws. Sniff at it. And if on inspection it shows the slightest indication of not being all you had thought it, if you spot any possible way in which it can blow a fuse and land you eventually waist-high in the soup, leave it alone and run like a hare.

Chapter Eight
The Come-back of Battling Billson

'I like 'em,' said Ukridge.

'You can't.'

'Yes, I do. God bless every adenoid in their system, say I. They have my support.'

We were speaking of the Talking Films. The negotiations for the motion-picture sale of a novel of mine had broken down that morning, and I had been saying to Ukridge, my guest at luncheon, that while one didn't, of course, care two-pence personally, it did seem a pity – taking the broad, general view – that some effort was not made to raise the things to a rather higher artistic level. Thanks, I pointed out, to this short-sighted policy of not acquiring the best material available, Talking Films were, as you might say, wallowing in the depths and in a fair way to becoming a hissing and a byword. In fact . . .

It was at this point that Ukridge said he liked them, and I felt aggrieved. The Etiquette books are silent on the subject, but there is surely an unwritten Gentleman's Agreement that a fellow who is bursting with another fellow's meat shall receive his host's dicta in a spirit of tactful acquiescence.

'Yes, Corky, old man, I know you're feeling sore . . .'

'Nothing of the kind. It is a matter of complete indifference to one whether these people buy one's stuff or not. It is merely . . .'

'. . . . . but I have a soft spot in my heart for the Talkies. They got me out of a very nasty hole some years ago.'

'It couldn't have been very many years ago. The beastly things only started the other day.'

'The one that got me out of the hole was about the first that was produced. It wasn't all-talking, I recollect. Just a patch of sound-effects in the middle somewhere.'

'That must have been "The Jazz Singer".'

'I dare say. I can't remember the name. I wasn't paying much attention to anything at the time, being deeply exercised in my mind about that blighter Battling Billson. You have not forgotten Battling Billson, Corky?'

I certainly had not. The Battler was a heavyweight pugilist whom Ukridge had dug up from somewhere and managed intermittently over a period of a year or so. In which enterprise he had been considerably hampered by the other's unfortunate temperament. A peerless scrapper, this Billson, with muscles strong as iron bands, but of the very maximum boneheadedness. An eccentric soul. He had a habit of developing a sentimental pity for his opponent towards the middle of the second round, or else he would get religion on the eve of battle and refuse to enter the ring. It complicated things a good deal for his manager.

'I've often wondered what became of him,' I said.

'Oh, he married that girl of his – Flossie, the barmaid. I believe they are doing well in the jellied eel line down Whitechapel way. All this happened when he was still a bachelor. I was living with my aunt at the moment, she having recently taken me back after chucking me out. That was how I came to be in a position to let her garden for the afternoon to those Folk Dance people.'

'To do what?'

'I happened to see their advertisement in the paper one morning. The North Kensington Folk Dance Society they called themselves, and they were offering spot cash for some place, not too far from the centre of things, where they could hold their annual beano. I dare say you've heard of these birds, Corky? They tie bells to their trousers and dance old rustic dances, showing that it takes all sorts to make a world. Most of the time, it seems, they do this in decent privacy, but once a year, apparently, they break out and require something in the nature of an open-air arena. And what more suitable, I asked myself, being a bit strapped for money at the time, than the picturesque garden of The Cedars, Wimbledon Common?'

'But what about your aunt?'

'You mean, her views regarding having a platoon of North

Kensington hoofers prancing about on her carefully-tended lawns? There, laddie, with your customary clear-sightedness, you have put your fingers on the very nub of the thing. Aunt Julia would have had a fit at the mere idea. Most fortunately, however, she was scheduled to go off on a lecture-tour. So, taking this fact into consideration, I felt justified in nipping round to the headquarters of these St Vitus's patients and negotiating the deal. I found the Hon. Sec. a little less open-handed than I could have wished, but eventually we came to terms, and I left with the cash in my pocket. Ten quid it was, and as sorely needed a ten quid as I have ever pouched. The future seemed bright.'

'And then, of course, your aunt returned unexpectedly?'

'No. She did not return. And why? Because she never went, curse her. There was some confusion of dates and her tour was postponed. I have had this happen to me before. One of the things that poison this age of ours, Corky, is the beastly slipshod way these lecture bureaux run their affairs. No system. Nothing clean-cut. I was placed in the distressing position of having to inform the Hon. Sec. that the deal was off and that he and his fellow-sufferers must do their bally sarabands elsewhere.'

'How did he take that?'

'None too well. You see, in order to secure the cash, I had rather piled it on about the scenic beauties of my aunt's grounds, and I suppose the disappointment was severe. He beefed quite a good deal. However, there was nothing he could do about it. The real trouble was that I was now, naturally, in common honesty, under an obligation to return him his money.'

'You mean, he threatened to jug you if you didn't?'

'Well, yes, there was some informal talk of it. And what made my position one of some embarrassment was that I had spent it all.'

'Tell me,' I said, 'has this story got a happy ending?'

'Oh, yes, it ended happily.'

'You did go to prison, then?'

'Prison? What do you mean? Of course I didn't go to prison. A man of my vision and resource doesn't go to prison.

Though I'm not saying the shadow of the cell didn't loom to a certain extent during the next few days. You see, for a colossal sum like ten quid, there was absolutely nobody I could touch. George Tupper, always my best prospect, is never good for more than a fiver, and to extract that one is too often compelled to use chloroform and the forceps. As for the rest, like yourself – mere half-crowners and two-bobbists. No, it seemed impossible that I could float the necessary loan. But how about my flesh and blood, my Aunt Julia, you ask.'

'No, I don't.'

'And you are quite right not to. To have tried to bite Aunt Julia's ear would have been to be obliged to reveal all, which would have resulted in the instant boot. Besides, the trouble about having a female novelist for an aunt is that her attitude on these occasions tends to be shoppy. Inform her that unless she coughs up you will be incarcerated in Wormwood Scrubs, and she merely tells you to be sure to take careful notes while doing your little bit of time, so that she can work them up into *Alistair Simms, Convict,* or *They That Are Without Hope,* or something. No sympathy, I mean. The professional outlook. Remind me to tell you some time – no, I won't go into that now. Where was I?'

'On your way to prison.'

'Not at all. I was on my way to a little pub in the Strand where I have always found I can do my best thinking. And thinking of the tensest was certainly needed now. And I had scarcely ordered my modest pint when I saw Wall-Eyed Dixon.'

'Who was he?'

'A fellow who ran a big boxing-place down in the East End. I had made his acquaintance while managing the Battler, who had frequently fought under his auspices. He asked me to come over and join him, and I went. I remember feeling that this looked very much as if my luck might be turning, because if he had come in ten minutes later I should have paid for my pint out of my own straitened means.

'"Listen," said this Dixon, after we had exchanged the usual civilities. "Are you still managing that Billson fellow?"

'Now, as a matter of fact, I hadn't seen the old Battler for nearly a year and hadn't the remotest notion where he was, if still alive, but you know me, Corky. The quick brain. The ready intelligence.

' "Yes," I said. "I am."

' "How is he these days?"

' "Fine. Never better."

' "Well, listen. One-Round Peebles is fighting Teddy Banks at my place next month, and Teddy's broken his leg. So Billson can have the match, if he likes."

' "I'll sign the articles now," I said.

'So we called for paper and ink and drafted a rough agreement. And after a brief chat we parted – he to remain and fill himself with double whiskies, I, with ten quid in advance in my pocket, to trot round to the North Kensington Hon. Sec. and give him his money and then start combing the town for Billson.'

Well, I won't go into all the trouble and anguish I had finding the fellow (continued Ukridge), it involved incessant inquiry in pubs and places, and a dashed sight more walking than I could have wished, but eventually I ran him to earth and, what was more, found him in malleable mood.

It seemed that just what he was needing at the moment was the chance of picking up a little easy money. This barmaid of his, this Flossie, had apparently been kicking to some extent because the wedding-day didn't come along a bit quicker, and his idea was to collect his share of the winner's end of the purse and then chance his arm at the nearest registrar's. He signed up. And there I was, on velvet.

And yet not so entirely on velvet as I had supposed in the first flush of getting the man pinned down. The snag was, you see, this matter of training. If the Battler had a defect, it was that he treated training in rather an airy and offhand way. Left to himself, he would have prepared for this vitally important contest by drinking mixed ale and smoking twopenny cigars. And the problem was, how could I, residing at Wimbledon Common, exercise watchful and incessant care over a bloke in a back-floor bed-sitting-room in Limehouse?

It was a matter that called for a good deal of thought. And I was bending my mind to it when this streak of luck of mine

184

cropped up again. It's odd about luck. You don't see a sight of it for months, and then it suddenly comes frisking after you like a friendly dog and won't leave you. At this difficult point in my affairs, what should happen but out of a blue sky the odd-job man at The Cedars handed in his portfolio for some reason or other, and my aunt told me to go to the Employment agency and enrol a successor.

It solved the whole thing. On the following morning, Battling Billson was on the premises, odd-jobbing away like the dickens, and it really did seem to me at last that all my troubles were at an end.

Because there is no getting away from it, the house of a maiden lady of studious tastes on Wimbledon Common is absolutely the ideal training-camp for a heavyweight pugilist with a big match in prospect. Nowhere is the air more fresh and bracing than that which sweeps across those great open spaces. And where, again, could you find a place more suitable than Wimbledon Common for roadwork? The vast expanse of it simply invites a fighter to pick his feet up and trot out into the sunset. Add a large garden, full of nooks where a punching bag may be suspended from a handy bough, and you will see that as far as exercise was concerned the conditions could scarcely have been bettered.

Then again, The Cedars was a quiet house. Early to bed and early to rise was our motto. None of those big dinners lasting into the small hours, with the staff waiting in the kitchen till dawn to dig into the remains. It looked to me as if everything was rosy. The only flaw was that I couldn't quite see how my man was to get any sparring.

And then, on the second night, my aunt, who had been looking thoughtful during dinner, touched on a point which had evidently been causing her perplexity.

'Stanley,' she said. 'That new odd-job man. When you engaged him at the agency, did you examine his references?'

I didn't care for the turn the conversation was taking, but I maintained a nonchalant front.

'Oh, yes,' I said. 'They were terrific. Why?'

'He seems so eccentric. I was walking on the Common yesterday, and he suddenly came past me, running. He had on an old sweater and a cap. I stared at him, and he touched the cap and went on running.'

'Odd,' I said, swallowing a beaker of port, of which I had some need. 'Very strange.'

'And this morning I looked out of my window, and there he was, skipping with a skipping rope, like a child. And after that he suddenly began jumping about and striking out with hands at nothing, as if he were having some sort of seizure. I wonder if he can be quite right in the head.'

I could read her thought. She was debating within herself the advisability of continuing to employ a loony odd-job man. I saw that a strong effort was called for.

'I expect it's just this modern craze for exercise, Aunt Julia,' I said. 'You see it everywhere nowadays. I should have thought it was rather a good thing myself. The healthy mind in the healthy body, what? I mean, if an odd-job man prefers to fill in his hours of leisure with a skipping-rope, jacking up his liver, instead of hanging round the kitchen with a mug of beer, isn't that, from the employer's view-point, so much goose?'

'Perhaps you are right,' she said thoughtfully. Then, for her table-talk always tends to get a bit personal: 'It would be better if you took more exercise yourself, Stanley. You are getting a sort of puffy look.'

I seized the opening with the quickness of a lightning-flash. Napoleon used to do the same thing.

'You're quite right, Aunt Julia,' I said cordially. 'From now on, I'll do a bit of boxing every day with the odd-job man.'

'Perhaps he does not box.'

'I'll teach him.'

'And I am not sure that I quite approve of my nephew hob-nobbing with the odd-job man.'

'Oh, it isn't hobnobbing, Aunt Julia. Between the act of hobnobbing and that of pasting a man on the nose there is a wide and substantial difference.'

'Very well. I dare say it will do no harm. Oakshott tells me he is a very civil and respectful young man, so perhaps there will be no objection to your boxing with him. Certainly you ought to do something without delay. You are getting positively stout.'

So that was that. A little diplomacy, Corky, a touch of the old Machiavelli method, and there I was with the major problem of the Battler's training solved.

Every morning, accordingly, at ten on the dot, I would repair to the back garden and we would put in two or three nice rounds together. And once more I felt that Providence was doing the square thing by one who deserved it. It looked to me as if my share of the winner's end of the handsome purse offered by the management of the Whitechapel Stadium was as good as in my pocket.

And so the happy days went on.

But a cloud was gathering in the blue, Corky, the skies were soon to grow dark and overcast. Little as I had suspected it, the Eden of The Cedars, Wimbledon Common, contained a serpent, and a Grade A serpent at that.

I allude to Oakshott, the butler.

It was not immediately that I discovered this. In fact, up to the middle of the second week I don't suppose I had given Oakshott a thought, except that I was relieved to hear that he approved of the Battler. I mean, a butler can do so much to mar the destinies of the humbler members of the entourage. A word from Oakshott, for instance, to the effect that in his opinion the Battler was unfitted for his odd-job-manly duties would have been enough to cause my aunt to sack him on the spot. But Oakshott thought him civil and respectful, and Oakshott was an honourable man. Or so I thought then. I little knew.

Well, as I say, Corky, the happy days wore on. But gradually there began to creep over me a sort of uneasy feeling. And I'll tell you why. It was because, as I sparred with Battler, I grew conscious of a subtle change in the man.

You have seen Battling Billson in action, Corky, and you know what he was like at his best. Of course, I wasn't expecting him to give of his best in a friendly training bout with a fellow like myself whom he could have wiped out with a single blow, but I did expect a certain something – a certain zip, as it were ;

a shadowy modicum of the old pep. And this, beyond a question, was lacking.

I'm fairly useful with the gloves, but, after all, I'm only an amateur and, as such, I had no right to land on the man quite so often. Still less had he the right, when I landed, to gurgle like a leaking cistern. And I didn't like the feel of that tummy of his when I hit it. Squashy. The tummy of a man who has been living a dashed sight too high. I am a pretty penetrating chap, Corky, and it didn't take me long to realize that something was going wrong with the training schedule. I decided to make inquiries.

Well, it was no good asking the fellow himself, of course. I don't know how vividly you remember this Billson, but perhaps you recall his peculiar conversational method. You would say something to him and pause for a reply, and he would stand there with his face, if you could call it a face, a perfect blank for possibly thirty seconds. Not a muscle stirring while the words gradually got themselves assembled under that concrete skull. Then a ripple – something coming to the surface. Then a sort of dull gleam in the eye. Then a twitching of the lips. And finally the 'Ah' or the 'Oh' or the 'Ur' or whatever it might be. To have got anything like the facts from him at this juncture would have taken hours.

So I forbore to question the poor dumb brick in person, and went straight to the cook, a woman with her fingers always on the pulse of life at The Cedars. Remember that, Corky. If you ever want to know anything, consult the cook. A cook's tentacles reach everywhere. Nothing in the line of gossip that doesn't come her way sooner or later. It was so in the present case. I found her well abreast of the state of affairs.

The whole trouble, she informed me, was that Mr Oakshott had made a sort of pet of this odd-job man. Kept taking him into his pantry for port and cigars. Pressed tit-bits on him at the table. Saw to it that he wallowed in beer. Pretty mordant she was about the whole thing, she being one of the old school with rather a nice sense of social values and feeling that a butler lowered his prestige by chumming with an odd-job man.

And, as for the Battler, his better self appeared to be entirely dead. Reckless of the fact that his waistline was increasing at the rate of a quarter of an inch a day, he followed Oakshott about like a dog and swilled his port without a pang.

You see what had happened, Corky? It was a contingency I ought to have taken into my calculations right from the beginning. But somehow I had overlooked it. I mean to say, the one objection to training a boxer at your aunt's house is that he must inevitably be thrown into the society of the butler, and what more likely than that the latter should lead him astray?

Have you ever stopped to consider what the impact of a butler on a boneheaded proletarian of the Billson type must be like? It can scarcely fail to be unsettling. And Oakshott was one of those stout, impressive, ecclesiastical butlers. A man with a presence. Meeting him in the street and ignoring the foul bowler hat he wore on his walks abroad, you would have put him down as a Bishop in mufti or, at the least, a plenipotentiary at one of the better courts.

Personally, having run into him one afternoon at Ally Pally just after the second race, and having found him a bloke with a distinctly sporting vein in his composition, I had never felt for him the reverence he excited in others. More one of the boys than a butler was the way I had always regarded him. But I could see that to Battling Billson, a chap brought up in the cruder surroundings of the Wapping water-front, and accustomed all his life to look upon a Silver Ring bookie as the highest thing in the social scale, he must have seemed like a being from another and more rarefied world. Anyway, be that as it may, there was no room for doubt that he had fallen under this butler's glamorous spell, and something had got to be done to switch off the other's heady influence before it was too late.

I went in search of Oakshott immediately, and found him outside my aunt's study, just closing the door.

'A visitor for Miss Ukridge, sir,' he explained.

I was not interested in my aunt's visitors.

'Oakshott,' I said, 'I want a word with you.'

'Very good, sir.'

'In private.'

'If you would care to step into my pantry, sir.'

We headed for the pantry, and I started in.

'It's about the odd-job man, Oakshott.'

'Yes, sir?'

'I hear you've been giving him port.'

'Yes, sir.'

'You oughtn't to do that.'

'It is not the best port, sir.'

'I don't care what port it is. What I'm driving at . . .'

I paused. I could see that this was going to be a bit difficult. The only thing to do seemed to be to lay the cards on the table.

'Look here, Oakshott,' I said. 'I know you're a sportsman –'

'Thank you, sir.'

'– So I'll tell you something I wouldn't care to have generally known. This chap Billson is really a boxer. He's under my management, and I've brought him here to train for a most important fight –'

'– At the Whitechapel Stadium on the sixteenth of next month, versus One-Round Peebles, yes, sir.'

I goggled.

'You know?'

'Yes, sir. I always make a practice of attending the meetings at the Whitechapel Stadium as often as my duties permit. I have frequently seen the young fellow performing there, and I heard that this match was in prospect. Personally, I do not fancy the young man's chances.'

'Well, dash it,' I said, 'nor do I, if you lush him up with port all day long, when he's supposed to be training. How do you think he can win, if you do that?'

'I am not anxious for him to win, sir.'

'What!'

The fact is, I have placed a substantial wager on his antagonist.'

I don't know if you have ever been in a pantry, Corky, and suddenly had it start to rock about you. It's a most unpleasant experience. It happened to me now. There was a sort of singing in my ears, and through it I heard this serpentine butler proceed with his remarks.

'I have never thought highly of the pugilistic gifts of this young man, Billson. He has a nice left hook, but otherwise is almost completely lacking in science and has contrived to achieve success hitherto purely by means of physical strength and fitness. Peebles, on the other hand, is a clever boxer. Now that I am in a position to ensure that the young fellow enters the ring on the sixteenth in poor condition, I feel that the money I have wagered upon Peebles should prove a most satisfactory investment.'

Corky, old horse, I've had some stunning revelations in my time of the depths to which humanity can sink, but I tell you frankly that this topped them all. For some minutes I spoke my mind freely, and this saintly looking blighter stood listening with a courteous and indulgent inclination of the head as if he were an Archdeacon receiving the confidences of a choirboy. Eventually I tottered out to seek some quiet spot where I might brood over the matter and decide what was to be done for the best.

And I was just going through the hall when the door of my aunt's study opened, and I heard her calling to me to come here for a moment in a voice which in my experience has always heralded trouble and a general quivering of hell's foundations. I feared the worst.

Nor had my instinct deceived me. Do you know what had happened, Corky? You remember that when I found Oakshott he had just been showing in a visitor. Who do you think that visitor was? The Hon. Sec., in person. No less. None other than the blighted Hon. Sec. of the North Kensington Hootchy-Kootchers. It appeared that, having failed to secure a suitable pitch for the annual orgy of his half-witted organization, he had called to see if there wasn't some hope of getting the garden of The Cedars after all. Apparently, I had boosted the glories of the place so shrewdly that the man's imagination had become inflamed and he was feeling like somebody who had been excluded from Paradise. So in he had popped, and within two minutes had spilled the entire beans.

Well, the result was a foregone conclusion. When you consider on what trivial grounds my Aunt Julia had so often hurled me out in the past, you can imagine with what swift enthusiasm she spat on her hands and hurled me out now. Five minutes later, after a most painful scene, I was in the hall again with specific instructions to get out of the house immediately and, having got out, to stay out. A maid, it seemed, was even now packing my suit-case.

So there was nothing to be done but to go round to the back premises, collect the Battler, break it to him that the good times among the fleshpots were at an end, and take him off somewhere where he could carry on till the day of battle.

Where that would be, I couldn't, at the moment, say. As far as I could figure it out, it looked as if we should have to share his bed-sitting-room in Limehouse. A fairly bleak prospect it seemed, but, by Jove, it wasn't half as bleak as the one that opened out after I had had a couple of minutes' chat with him. Corky, the man refused to move. He absolutely declined to stir. Here he was, he said, and he liked it. And nothing that I could say would shift him.

So the upshot of it was that I had to leave him there. And you can imagine that it was in sombre mood that I lugged my suit-case to the Tube station, my aunt not having had the common humanity to blow me to a taxi. It seemed to me that all was lost. My whole financial future hung upon the ability of this bloke to knock the stuffing out of a formidable antagonist on the sixteenth *prox.*, and he would take the ring with a couple of double chins and a tummy on him like an alderman. Another two weeks of Oakshott's malign influence, and it would be as much as he would be able to do to climb into the ring at all under his own power. They would have to use derricks and pulleys. And no more chance of getting him away from that malign influence than if he had been trapped in the underground cellar of the Secret Nine.

I don't mind confessing, Corky, that for the better part of two days I was nonplussed. Resourceful though I am, I could see no way out.

But, of course, with a fellow of my extraordinary mental alertness, no impasse lasts indefinitely. The idea was bound to come, and it did so towards the evening of the second day. As I walked away from the Foreign Office after touching George Tupper – not without trouble and anxiety – for a couple of quid, my brain, exploring every avenue, suddenly got a bite. It was as if a voice from heaven had bellowed in my ear the word 'Flossie'. I realized, what I ought to have realized from the

192

start, that what was needed to awaken Battling Billson's better self was the gentle influence of a woman. There was only one person who could reason with him, and that was his betrothed.

This Flossie's interests, I perceived, were identical with mine. To her, as to me, it was all important to get the Battler into the ring, on the sixteenth, in good shape. Already, as I have said, she had been growing a bit hot under the collar at her dream-man's supineness in letting the days slide by and no wedding-cake in sight. The difference between the winner's and the loser's end of the purse would mean to her the difference between the holy state hot off the griddle and all that weary wait-ing once more. Naturally, she would be heart and soul with me in my enterprise. Hailing a passing taxi – which, thanks to Tuppy's munificence, I could now afford – I shot off to the Blue Anchor in Knightsbridge, where Billson had informed me that she had recently accepted office as vice-president in charge of the beer-engine.

I have an idea you didn't like Flossie much, Corky, that time when she came for a brief moment into your life. I seem to remember hearing complaints. Well, of course, she wasn't everybody's girl. The peroxide a bit vivid, I grant you, and the manner perhaps a trifle too hearty for the fastidious. But for a partner in a crisis like this I could have wished no one better. Talk of entering into the spirit of the thing – well, when I tell you that she actually went to the trouble of selecting the heavier of her two parasols in case of anything in the nature of back-chat on the part of her affianced, you will understand that it was not merely moral support that I was getting from her. We set off for Wimbledon together, up and doing with a heart for any fate.

For of course, we both saw that a visit to The Cedars must be paid without delay. What I told her about the Battler had convinced her that the evil had gone so deep that only the promptest measures could avail. It was her purpose to call at the back door, ask for Billson, take him – when he presented himself – by the left ear, and by that ear lead him back on to the straight and narrow path.

'Him and his port!' she kept saying, and there was

something about the way she spoke that thrilled me. I can't remember ever having admired a girl more. She reminded me of Boadicea.

The journey to Wimbledon ran into money, of course, but you can't stop to count the pennies when great issues are at stake. We did it in a taxi, and it will give you some idea of my state of mind when I tell you that the sight of the figures leaping up on the clock occasioned me none of the usual feeling of nausea. I was indifferent to them. I felt like that French general who brought up the reserves to the Battle of the Marne in taxi-cabs. Do you suppose he worried about the way the clock was going up? Of course not.

And presently the old familiar road hove in sight, and we stopped outside The Cedars, and I boosted Flossie out in order that she should go around to the back door and get into action. All things considered, it seemed more prudent that I should remain in the vehicle. My aunt has an unpleasant habit of doing a bit of gardening sometimes in the evenings, and to get soaked with weed-killer or chased off the premises with a trowel would have been foreign to my policy.

There was an interval of waiting, during which the driver chap and I exchanged views on the forthcoming meeting at Hurst Park, and then Flossie came back, empty-handed.

'He's gone to the pictures,' she announced. 'Him and that butler.'

'How long ago?'

'Not long.'

'Then tally-ho!'

And a word to the driver, and we were off to the Wimbledon Rotunda. And the first person we saw in the entrance as we drew up was the Battler. He was standing there with his customary air of thinking hard about absolutely nothing, and Flossie made for him like a peroxided leopardess.

'Wilberforce!' she cried.

And, as she did so, another figure suddenly manifested itself. It was the figure of the snake, Oakshott. And it dished the whole enterprise.

I have spoken of the overwhelming effect of a butler on a thick-skulled proletarian like Billson. I was now to see that such a butler can produce similar reactions in a seasoned barmaid. Before my horrified eyes, Corky, the fire faded out of Flossie as if somebody had turned a tap, and she changed almost in an instant from an avenging goddess to a mere simperer and shoe-shuffler. She had come in like a leopardess and she was now a lambkin. Her whole demeanour, as Oakshott loomed up on the horizon, was that of a schoolgirl confronted by a headmistress.

This entire question of butlers, Corky, is one that wants thoroughly thrashing out. How do they do it? Wherein consists their mystic spell? What is this magnetism in them that subdues the proudest? You would have thought a barmaid, accustomed to mixing whisky-and-splashes for the highest in the land – for the *clientèle* of the Blue Anchor is notoriously exclusive and numbers in its ranks people like shop-walkers from Harrods and sergeants in the Guards – would have been proof against it. But no. One glance from those bulbous eyes had reduced Flossie to a blushing pulp.

'Good evening, sir,' said Oakshott. 'I had not expected to see you in these parts.' He cast a gallant eye at Flossie. 'Will you present me?'

The Battler, who had paled visibly at the sight of his betrothed but was now looking better, jerked a thumb, which is how you do these formal introductions in Limehouse.

'My young lady.'

'Indeed?'

'R.'

'And has the young lady a name?' asked Oakshott indulgently.

'Miss Dalrymple,' said Flossie, wriggling a shoe.

'Dalrymple? Indeed? One of the Sussex Dalrymples, may I ask?'

'Coo!' said Flossie.

'I had the honour to serve the late Sir Gregory Dalrymple some years ago,' said Oakshott suavely. 'A most estimable gentleman. It would be interesting to find that you were some connexion. His daughter – his younger daughter, I should say married a Shropshire Pobleigh. His elder daughter, is, of course, Lady Slythe and Sayle. There had been some talk of an understanding between her and His Grace the Duke of Walmer, but it never came to anything. Dalrymple. Most interesting. No doubt your family, Miss Dalrymple, would be one of the cadet branches? One knows, of course, of the Devonshire Dalrymples – one of whom, I was interested to see in the paper, recently became engaged to Lady Joyce Sproule, the daughter of the Earl of Kidderminster.'

I could hear Flossie breathing like a bull-pup choking over a chicken-bone. Every woman, Corky, has her Achilles heel. She may set out on a punitive expedition as stoutly as any man, but let her encounter a butler who talks Titles at her and speculates on her family being one of the cadet branches, and she falters, hesitates, and is lost. I could see that Flossie as a Force in this matter of leading Billson back to the light had ceased to function.

'My young friend here and myself,' proceeded Oakshott, 'were about to witness the entertainment at this cinema. It is the first of these new Talking Pictures of which the papers have been so full of late. I should be delighted if you would join us, Miss Dalrymple. And you, sir?'

And before we knew where we were, Corky, we were all seated somewhere at the back and the picture had begun.

When you asked me just now if the title of this show was 'The Jazz Singer', I replied that I was unable to tell you, being too greatly exercised in my mind at the moment about the Battler. It was the simple truth. Yes, Corky, it was a heavy-hearted and preoccupied Stanley Featherstonehaugh Ukridge who sat sombrely in his seat and gazed at the screen with a lack-lustre eye. You will appreciate my feelings. This barmaid, this Flossie, my ace of trumps, had proved a broken reed. I had thought her a very present help in time of trouble, and she had turned blue on me.

What made it so poignant was that, even if she threw off this butler's spell on thinking things over quietly in her room that night, it would be too late for her to accomplish anything of practical value. You see, by what had seemed to me at the time the most extraordinary bit of good luck, I had happened to get in touch with her on her evening off – finding her, indeed, not ten minutes before she was about to leave. She didn't get another free evening till next week, which meant that, supposing by a miracle she got herself into fighting trim again and brought herself to defy Oakshott and battle with his dark forces, she would have to wait seven days before she could do it. For my aunt's house is not one you can stroll into any hour of the day you please. No wandering along round about midnight and expecting to be able to interview members of the staff.

And in seven days who knew to what a condition our man might have been reduced?

You will understand, therefore, that I am not a good person to come to for information about this picture. All I can tell you is that it went on and on, and then suddenly we got these sound-effects we had heard so much about. There was a sort of bronchial whirring, and somebody on the screen had begun to speak.

And he had no sooner done so than Battling Billson heaved himself to his feet and said ' 'Ush!'

You see what had happened. Just one of those misunderstandings which are bound to occur when a fellow of the Battler's shape of head is brought up against the marvels of Science. I have no doubt that for days past Oakshott had been preparing him for this moment ; had spoken to him at length of the wonderful new invention which was to revolutionize the motion-picture industry ; had told him, in a word, that the whole point of the thing was that the Screen had now become the Talking Screen.

But it just hadn't penetrated. Ideas didn't with the Battler, unless you used a steam-drill.

' 'Ush!' he said.

Well, you know what the effect of that is on a theatre-full of the citizenry. Eighty-seven voices shouted 'Sit down!'

'There's someone in this 'ouse spoilin' other people's pleasure by talkin',' bellowed the Battler.

'Sit down!' yelled the many-headed.

It was the worst possible policy, of course. Tell a chap of the Battler's mentality to sit down, and he at once suspects a trap and continues to stand more resolutely than ever.

'There's somebody talkin', and I won't 'ave it!'

197

And at this point, just when everything was so tense and it only needed a spark to precipitate the explosion, what should happen but that the laryngitis-patient on the screen suddenly burst into song.

It was the end. I could see the grim look on the Battler's face deepen. There was a little fellow sitting in the row in front, and for some mysterious reason he seemed to think that in him he had found one of the ringleaders. He leaned over and tapped him on the shoulder.

'Is that you makin' that singin' noise?' he demanded. And he scooped the chap out of his seat like a winkle from its shell and held him up. To examine his vocal chords, I suppose.

The next moment, the little man's companion, a woman of the sort that stands no nonsense, was hitting him with her umbrella. Somebody in the row behind jumped on his back. Somebody else grabbed his neck. And in about a quarter of a minute the action had become general. I could see a sort of confused blur, with the voice of the Battler proceeding from the middle of it, and then commissionaires and others began to arrive, and finally policemen in bevies, and all was over.

Next day, the Battler was hauled up before the majesty of the Law, soundly ticked off by the Bench, and sentenced to fourteen days in the coop without the option. On the morning of the fifteenth day I was waiting at the prison gates, and out he came, trained to a hair, without a superfluous ounce on him, and with but one thought in his mind – viz., to get his own back from the human race. And, most fortunately, the idea of starting with One-Round Peebles seemed to enchant him.

The rest is history. One-Round Peebles failed to justify his name by forty-five seconds, it taking the Battler exactly two minutes and a quarter to flatten him. I ran into Oakshott on the way out, and I don't think I have ever seen a sicker butler. He looked like a Bishop who has just discovered Schism and Doubt among the minor clergy. How much he was actually down, I could not say. The hoarded savings of a lifetime, I trust.

So that is what I mean, Corky, when I say I like the Talkies. Those responsible for their production may turn down the tripe you write, and for that I am, of course, sorry – especially as I had been hoping on the strength of the sale to get into your ribs for a trifling sum. But I cannot recede from my opinion. I like 'em. I can never forget that they once saved my life.

'It completes my case against the foul things,' I said.

Chapter Nine
The Level Business Head

'Another beaker of port, laddie?' urged Stanley Featherstone-haugh Ukridge, hospitably.

'Thanks.'

'One more stoup of port for Mr Corcoran, Baxter. You may bring the coffee, cigars and liqueurs to us in the library in about a quarter of an hour.'

The butler filled my glass and melted away. I looked about me dizzily. We were seated in the spacious dining-room of Ukridge's Aunt Julia's house on Wimbledon Common. A magnificent banquet had wound its way to a fitting finish, and the whole thing seemed to be inexplicable.

'I don't understand this,' I said. 'How do I come to be sitting here, bursting with rich food paid for by your aunt?'

'Perfectly simple, laddie. I expressed a desire for your company tonight, and she at once consented.'

'But why? She has never let you invite me here before. She can't stand me.'

Ukridge sipped his port.

'Well, the fact of the matter is, Corky,' he said, in a burst of confidence, 'things have been occurring recently in the home which have resulted in what you might call the dawning of a new life as far as Aunt Julia and I are concerned. It is not too much to say that she now eats out of my hand and is less than the dust beneath my chariot's wheels. I will tell you the story, for it will be of help to you in your journey through the world. It is a story which shows that, be the skies never so black, nothing can harm a man provided that he has a level business head. Tempests may lour –'

'Get on with it. How did all this happen?'

Ukridge mused for a while.

'I suppose the thing really started,' he said, 'when I pawned her brooch –'

'You pawned your aunt's brooch?'

'Yes.'

'And that endeared you to her?'

'I will explain all that later. Meanwhile, let me begin at the beginning. Have you ever run across a man named Joe the Lawyer?'

'No.'

'Stout fellow with a face like a haggis.'

'I've never met him.'

'Endeavour not to do so, Corky. I hate to speak ill of my fellow-man, but Joe the Lawyer is not honest.'

'What does he do? Pawn people's brooches?'

Ukridge adjusted the ginger-beer wire that held his pince-nez to his flapping ears and looked wounded.

'This is scarcely the tone I like to hear in an old friend, Corky. When I reach that point in my story, you will see that my pawning of Aunt Julia's brooch was a perfectly normal, straightforward matter of business. How else could I have bought half the dog?'

'Half what dog?'

'Didn't I tell you about the dog?'

'No.'

'I must have done. It's the nub of the whole affair.'

'Well, you didn't.'

'I'm getting this story all wrong,' said Ukridge. 'I'm confusing you. Let me begin right at the beginning.'

This bloke, Joe the Lawyer (said Ukridge), is a bookmaker with whom I have had transactions from time to time, but until the afternoon when this story starts we had never become in any way intimate. Occasionally I would win a couple of quid off him and he would send me a cheque, or he would win a couple of quid off me and I would go round to his office to ask him to wait till Wednesday week; but we had never mingled socially, as you might say, until this afternoon I'm speaking of, when I happened to look in at the Bedford Street Bodega and found him there, and he asked me to have a glass of the old tawny.

Well, laddie, you know as well as I do that there are

moments when a glass of the old tawny makes all the difference ; so I assented with a good deal of heartiness.

'Fine day,' I said.

'Yes,' said this bloke. 'Do you want to make a large fortune?'

'Yes.'

'Then listen,' said this bloke. 'You know the Waterloo Cup. Listen. I've taken over as a bad debt from a client the dog that's going to win the Waterloo Cup. This dog has been kept dark, but you can take it from me it's going to win the Waterloo Cup. And then what? Well, then it's going to fetch something. It's going to be valuable. It's going to have a price. It's going to be worth money. Listen. How would you like to buy a half-share in that dog?'

'Very much.'

'Then it's yours.'

'But I haven't any money.'

'You mean to say you can't raise fifty quid?'

'I can't raise five.'

'Gawblimey!' said the bloke.

And looking at me in a despairing sort of way, like a father whose favourite son has hurt his finest feelings, he finished his old tawny and pushed out into Bedford Street. And I went home.

Well, as you may imagine, I brooded not a little on my way back to Wimbledon. The only thing nobody can say of me, Corky, is that I lack the spacious outlook that wins to wealth. I know a good thing when I see one. This was a good thing, and I recognized it as such. But how to acquire the necessary capital was the point. Always my stumbling-block, that has been. I wish I had a shilling for every time I've failed to become a millionaire through lack of the necessary capital.

What sources of revenue had I, I asked myself. George Tupper, if tactfully approached, is generally good for a fiver ; and you, no doubt, had it been a matter of a few shillings or half a sovereign, would gladly have leaped into the breach. But fifty quid! A large sum, laddie. It wanted thinking over, and I devoted the whole force of my intelligence to the problem.

Oddly enough, the one source of supply that had never presented itself to me was my Aunt Julia. As you know, she has warped and peculiar ideas about money. For some reason or other she will never give me a cent. And yet it was my Aunt Julia who solved my problem. There is a destiny in these matters, Corky, a sort of fate.

When I got back to Wimbledon, I found her looking after her packing; for she was off next morning on one of those lecture tours she goes in for.

'Stanley,' she said to me, 'I nearly forgot. I want you to look in at Murgatroyd's in Bond Street, tomorrow and get my diamond brooch. They are re-setting it. Bring it back and put it in my bureau drawer. Here is the key. Lock the drawer and send the key to me by registered post.'

And so, you see, everything was most satisfactorily settled. Long before my aunt came back the Waterloo Cup would be run for, and I should have acquired vast affluence. All I had to do was to have a duplicate key made, so that I could put the brooch in the drawer when I had redeemed it. I could see no flaw in the scheme of things. I saw her off at Euston, sauntered round to Murgatroyd's, collected the brooch, sauntered off to the pawnbroker's, put the brooch up the spout, and walked out, for the first time in many weeks in a sound financial position. I rang up Joe the Lawyer on the phone, closed the deal about the dog, and there I was, with my foot on the ladder of Fortune.

But in this world, Corky, you never know. That is the thing I always try to impress on every young fellow starting out in life – that you never know. It was about two days later that the butler came to me in the garden and said a gentleman wished to speak to me on the phone.

I shall always remember that moment. It was a lovely, still evening, and I was sitting in the garden under a leafy tree, thinking beautiful thoughts. The sun was setting in a blaze of gold and crimson; the little birds were chirping their heads off; and I was half-way through the whisky and soda of a lifetime. I recollect that, an instant before Baxter came out to fetch me, I had just been thinking how peaceful and wonderful and perfect the world was.

I went to the phone.

'Hullo!' said a voice.

It was Joe the Lawyer. And Baxter had said it was a gentle-man.

'Are you there?' said this bloke Joe.

'Yes.'

'Listen.'

'What?'

'Listen. You know that dog I said was going to win the Waterloo Cup?'

'Yes.'

'Well, he isn't.'

'Why not?'

'Because he's dead.'

I don't mind telling you, Corky, that I reeled. Yes, your old friend reeled.

'Dead!'

'Dead.'

'You don't mean dead?'

'Yes.'

'Then what about my fifty pounds?'

'I keep that.'

'What!'

'Of course I keep it. Once a sale s gone through, it's gone through. I know my law. That's why the boys call me Joe the Lawyer. But I'll tell you what I'll do. You send me a letter, re-leasing all rights in that dog, and I'll give you a fiver. I'll be robbing myself, but I'm like that. . . . Big-hearted Joe, I am, and that's all there is about it.'

'What did the dog die of?'

'Pewmonia.'

'I don't believe he's dead at all.'

'You don't believe my word?'

'No.'

'Well, you come round to my stable and see for yourself.'

So I went round and viewed the remains. There was no doubt about it, the dog had handed in his dinner-pail. So I wrote the letter, got my fiver, and came back to Wimbledon to try and rebuild my shattered life. Because you can readily see, Corky, that I was up against it in no uncertain manner. Aunt Julia would be back before long, and would want to see her brooch; and though I'm her own flesh and blood, and I shouldn't be surprised if she had dandled me on her knee when I was a child, I couldn't picture her bearing with anything like Christian fortitude the news that I had pawned it in order to buy a half-share in a dead dog.

And the very next morning in blew Miss Angelica Vining, the poetess.

She was a gaunt sort of toothy female who had come to lunch once or twice while I had been staying in my aunt's house. A great pal of my aunt's.

'Good morning,' said this disease, beaming. 'What a heavenly day! One could almost fancy oneself out in the country, couldn't one? Even at so short a distance from the heart of the City one seems to sense in the air a freshness which one cannot get in London, can one? I've come for your aunt's brooch.'

I braced myself up with a hand on the piano.

'You've what?' I said.

'Tonight is the dance of the Pen and Ink Club, and I wired to your aunt to ask if I might borrow her brooch, and she has written to say that I may. It's in her bureau.'

'Which is, most unfortunately, locked.'

'Your aunt sent me the key. I have it in my bag.'

She opened her bag, Corky, and at this moment my guardian angel, who had been lying down on his job pretty considerably for the last week or so, showed a sudden flash of speed. The door was open, and through it at this ·juncture there trickled one of my aunt's Pekes. You will recollect my aunt's Pekes. I pinched them once, to start a Dog College.

This animal gazed at the female, and the female went off like a soda-water bottle.

'Oh, the sweet thing!' she bubbled.

She put the bag down and swooped on the dog. He tried to side-step, but she had him.

'Oh, the tweetums!' she cried.

And, her back being turned, Corky, I nipped to the bag, found the key, trousered it, and back to position one.

Presently she came to the surface again.

'Now, I really must hurry away,' she said. 'I will just get the

205

brooch and scurry.' She fumbled in her bag. 'Oh, dear! I've lost the key.'

'Too bad,' I said. 'Still,' I went on, thinking it might be all for the best, 'what does a girl need jewellery for? The greatest jewel a girl can possess is her youth, her beauty.'

It went well, but not quite well enough.

'No,' she said, 'I must have the brooch. I've set my heart on it. We must break the lock.'

'I couldn't dream of such a thing,' I said firmly. 'I am in a position of trust. I cannot break up my aunt's furniture.'

'Oh, but– '

'No.'

Well, laddie, there ensued a pretty painful scene. Hell hath no fury like a woman scorned, and not many like a woman who wants a brooch and isn't allowed to get it. The atmosphere, when we parted, was full of strain.

'I shall write to Miss Ukridge and tell her exactly what has happened,' said the poetess, pausing at the front door.

She then shoved off, leaving me limp and agitated. These things take it out of a fellow.

Something, I perceived, had got to be done, and done swiftly. From some source I had to raise fifty quid. But where could I turn? My credit, Corky – and I tell you this frankly, as an old friend – is not good. No, it is not good. In all the world there seemed to be but one man who might be induced to let me have fifty quid at a pinch, and that was Joe the Lawyer. I don't say I was relying on him, mind you. But it seemed to me that, if there was a spark of human feeling in his bosom, he might, after a good deal of eloquence, be persuaded to help an old business colleague out of a very tight place.

At any rate, he was the only relief in sight, so I rang up his office, and, finding that he would be at the Lewes Races next day, I took an early train there.

Well, Corky, I might have known. It stands to reason that, if a man has a spark of human feeling in his bosom, he does not become a bookie. I stood beside this bloke, Joe the Lawyer from the start of the two o'clock race to the finish of the four-thirty, watching him rake in huge sums from mugs of every description until his satchel was simply bursting with cash ; but when I asked him for the loan of a measly fifty pounds he didn't even begin to look like parting.

You cannot fathom the psychology of these blighters, Corky. If you will believe me, the chief reason why he would not lend me this paltry sum appeared to be a fear of what people would say if they heard about it.

'Lend you fifty quid?' he said, in a sort of stunned way. 'Who, me? Silly I'd look, wouldn't I, lending you fifty quid!'

'But you don't mind looking silly.'

'Having all the boys saying I was a soft-hearted fool.'

'A man of your stamp doesn't care what fellows like that say,' I urged. 'You're too big. You can afford to despise them.'

'Well, I can't afford to lend any fifty quids. I'd never hear the last of it.'

I simply can't understand this terror of public opinion. Morbid, I call it. I told him I would keep the thing a dead secret – and, if he thought it safer, not even give him a line in writing to acknowledge the debt; but no, there was no tempting him.

'I'll tell you what I will do,' he said.

'Twenty quid?'

'No, not twenty quid. Nor ten quid, either. Nor five quid. Nor one quid. But I'll give you a lift back as far as Sandown in my car tomorrow, that's what I'll do.'

From the way he spoke, you would have thought he was doing me the best turn one man had ever done another. I was strongly inclined to reject his offer with contempt. The only thing that decided me to accept was the thought that, if he had as good a day at Sandown as he had had at Lewes, his better nature might after all assert itself even at the eleventh hour. I mean to say, even a bookie must have a melting mood occasionally; and if one came to Joe the Lawyer, I wanted to be on the spot.

'Start from here at eleven, sharp. If you aren't ready, I'll go without you.'

This conversation, Corky, had taken place in the saloon bar of the Coach and Horses at Lewes; and, having said these few words, the bloke Joe popped off. I stayed on to have one more, feeling the need of it after the breakdown of the business negotiations ; and the fellow behind the bar got chatty.

'That was Joe the Lawyer just went out, wasn't it?' he said. He chuckled. 'He's wide, that man is.'

I wasn't much in the mood to pass the time discussing a fellow who wouldn't let an old business friend have an insignificant sum like fifty quid, so I just nodded.

'Heard the latest about him?'

'No.'

'He's wide, Joe is. He had a dog that was entered for the Waterloo Cup, and it died.'

'I know.'

'Well, I bet you don't know what he did. Some of the lads were in here just now, talking about it. He raffled that dog.'

'How do you mean, raffled it?'

'Put it up for a raffle at twenty pounds a ticket.'

'But it was dead.'

'Certainly it was dead. But he didn't tell them that. That's where he was wide.'

'But how could he raffle a dead dog?'

'Why couldn't he raffle a dead dog? Nobody knew it was dead.'

'How about the man who drew the winning ticket?'

'Ah! Well, he had to tell him, of course. He just handed him his money back. And there he was, a couple of hundred quid in hand. He's wide, Joe is.'

Have you ever experienced, Corky, that horrible sensation of having all your ideals totter and melt away, leaving you in a world of hideous blackness where it seems impossible to trust your fellow man an inch? What do you mean, my aunt must often have felt that way? I resent these slurs, Corky. Whenever I have had occasion to pinch anything from my aunt, it has always been with the most scrupulous motives, with the object of collecting a little ready cash in order to lay the foundations of a vast fortune.

This was an entirely different matter. This fiend in human shape had had no thought but of self. Not content with getting fifty quid out of me and sticking to it like glue, he had deliberately tricked me into accepting five pounds for all rights in a

208

dead dog which he knew was shortly about to bring him in a couple of hundred. Was it fair? Was it just?

And the terrible part of the whole thing was that there seemed nothing that I could do about it. I couldn't even reproach him. At least, I could – but a fat lot of help that would have been. All I could do was to save my train-fare home by accepting a lift in his car.

I am bound to say, Corky – and this will show you how a man's moral outlook may deteriorate through contact with fellows of this stamp – I am bound to say that there were moments during the night when I toyed with the thought of taking a dip into that satchel of his, should the opportunity occur during the journey. But I dismissed the plan as unworthy of me. Whatever the injuries I had sustained, my hands at least, please heaven, should be clean. Besides, it seemed very improbable that an opportunity would occur.

And, sure enough, I noticed next morning, when we started out, that he kept the satchel wedged in between him and the side of the car, entirely out of my reach. He was that sort of man.

How strange it is, Corky, that in this world we seem fated never to be able to enjoy life to the full! No doubt it is all for a purpose, and is intended to make us more spiritual and fit us for the life to come ; but it is a nuisance. Take my case. I am particularly fond of motoring; and circumstances have so ordered themselves that it is only occasionally that I am able to get a ride. And here I was, bowling along the high road on an ideal motoring day, and totally unable to enjoy the experience.

For there are certain conditions, laddie, under which the heart cannot rejoice. How could I revel in the present when the past was an agony to contemplate and the future as black as ink? Every time I tried not to let my mind dwell on the way this man beside me had done me down, it skidded off into the future and dwelt on the interview which must so soon take place between me and my aunt. So that fact that it was a lovely day and that I was getting a ride for nothing practically escaped me.

We buzzed on through the pleasant countryside. The sun shone in the sky: birds tootled in the hedgerows: the engine of the two-seater hummed smoothly.

And then, fairly suddenly, I became aware that the engine was not humming so smoothly. It had begun to knock. And then there was a sizzling noise, and steam began to creep out of the top of the radiator-cap.

Joe made one or two remarks concerning the man at the hotel who had forgotten to put water in the radiator.

'You can get some at that cottage,' I said.

There was a cottage down the road, standing by itself in a lot of trees. Joe pulled up the car and got down.

'I'll stay here and look after your satchel,' I said. There was no sense in not being civil and obliging.

'No, you won't. I'll take it with me.'

'It will hamper you if you're going to carry a pail of water.'

'I'd look silly leaving my satchel with you, wouldn't I?'

I don't know which distressed me the more, his sickening want of ordinary trust or his absurd respect for appearances.

The man seemed to go through the world in a restless fear lest some action of his might make him look silly.

And he couldn't possibly have looked sillier than he did about two minutes later.

This cottage, Corky, was separated from the road by iron railings with a gate in them. The bloke Joe shoved this gate open and went into the front garden. And he was just starting to move round in the direction of the back door when round the corner of the house there suddenly came trotting a dog.

Joe stopped, and the dog stopped. They stood there for a moment, drinking each other in.

'Ger-r-r!' said Joe.

Now mind you, there was absolutely nothing about this dog to inspire alarm. Certainly it was on the large side and had rather a rolling eye; but I could see at a glance that it was just one of those friendly mongrels which your man of the world greets with a cheerful chirrup and prods in the ribs without a second thought. But Joe seemed ill at ease.

The dog came a step closer. I think he wanted to smell Joe, though I could have told him, as a friend, that there was neither profit nor pleasure to be derived from such a course.

'Gerroutofit!' said Joe.

The dog edged forward. Then, in a tentative sort of way he

barked. And Joe seemed to lose his head completely. Instead of trying to conciliate the animal, he picked up a stone and threw it.

Well, you simply can't do that sort of thing to a dog you don't know in his own garden.

It was the satchel that saved Joe. It shows the lengths to which fear will drive a man, Corky; and if I hadn't seen it with my own eyes I wouldn't have believed it. But it's the truth that as that dog came leaping up in a business-like way that it did me good to watch, Joe the Lawyer, having given one look over his shoulder at the gate and decided that he couldn't make it, uttered a piercing cry and flung considerably over two hundred quid in bank-notes at the animal. The satchel took him low down on the chest, got entangled in his legs, and held him up. And while he was trying to unscramble himself, Joe nipped to the gate and slammed it behind him.

It was only then that he seemed to realize what a perfect chump he had made of himself.

'Gawblimey!' said Joe.

The dog left the satchel and came to the gate. He shoved his nose as far through the bars as he could manage, and made a noise like a saxophone.

'Now you've done it,' I said.

And so he had, and I was glad, Corky. It pleased me sincerely to find a man who prided himself on his acumen capable of such perfectly cloth-headed behaviour. Here was this blighter, admired by all – provided they didn't have business dealings with him – for his wideness, breaking down lamentably in the first crisis where he was called upon to show a little ordinary intelligence. He had allowed himself to be outgeneralled by a humble unit of the animal kingdom, and I had no sympathy for him.

However, I didn't say so. One must be diplomatic. I had not altogether given up hope of floating that loan, and anything in the nature of frivolous comment would, I felt, have the worst effect on the negotiations.

'What'll I do?' said Joe, after a few general remarks.

'Better shout,' I suggested.

So he shouted. But nothing happened. The fact is, these

bookies are never in very good voice after a day at the races, and he was handicapped by a certain roopiness. Besides, the owner of the cottage was evidently one of those blokes who plough the fields and scatter the good seed o'er the land, and he seemed to be out somewhere ploughing and scattering now.

Joe began to get emotional

'Gawblimey!' he said, with tears in his voice. 'This is a nice thing! Here I am, late already, and if I don't get to Sandown in time for the first race it's going to mean hundreds of pounds out of my pocket.'

You will scarcely credit it, Corky, but this was the first moment that that aspect of the affair had presented itself to me. His words opened up an entirely new train of thought. Naturally, I now perceived, mugs being what they are, every race a bookie misses means so much dead loss to him. Sandown was crowded with potential losers, all waiting to hand their money over to Joe ; and, if he was not there, what would happen? They had to give their money to someone, so they would hand it over to one of his trade rivals. I felt as if a sudden bright light had flashed upon me.

'Look here,' I said, 'if you will lend me fifty quid, I'll go in and get that satchel for you. I'm not afraid of a dog.'

He did not answer. He cocked an eye at me ; then he cocked an eye at the satchel. I could see he was weighing the proposition. But at this moment the luck went against me. The dog, getting a bit bored, gave a sniff and trotted back round the corner of the house. And no sooner had he disappeared than Joe, feeling that now was the time, popped through the gate and galloped for the satchel.

Well, Corky, you know me. Alert. Resourceful. There was a stick lying in the road, and a leap for it and grab it was with me the work of a moment. I rattled it energetically along the railings. And back came old Colonel Dog as if I had pulled him at the end of a rope. It was an occasion when Joe had to move quick, and he did so. He had perhaps a foot to spare, or it may have been eight inches.

He was a good deal annoyed, and for a while spoke freely of this and that.

'Fifty quid,' I said, when there was a lull.

He looked at me. Then he nodded. I don't say he nodded genially, but he nodded. And I opened the gate and went in.

The dog bounded at me, barking; but I knew that was all swank, and I told him so. I bent down and slapped his tummy, and the dog shoved his paws on my shoulders and licked my face. Then I took his head and waggled it sideways once or twice, and he took my hand in his mouth and gnawed it slightly. Then I rolled him over and began punching his chest; and then, when these civilities were finished, I got up and looked round for the satchel.

It was gone. And there was that blot on the human race, Joe the Lawyer, standing outside, fondling it as if it were a baby. Not that a man like that would fondle a baby, of course. Much more likely to kick it in the face and break open its money-box. But what I mean is, he'd dashed in when my back was turned and collared the satchel.

I had a grim foreboding that our little deal was off, but I displayed a cheerful exterior.

'In large notes,' I said.

'Eh?' said the bloke Joe.

'I'd rather have my fifty quid in large notes. They take up less room in the pocket.'

'What fifty quid?'

'The fifty quid you were going to give me for getting the satchel.'

He gaped.

'Well I'll be blowed!' he said. 'I like that! Who got the satchel, you or me?'

'I soothed the dog.'

'If you like to waste your time playing with dogs, that's your business. I'd look silly, wouldn't I, giving you fifty quid for playing with dogs? But, if you like doing it, you go on playing with him while I step down the road and get some water from one of those other cottages.'

Black-hearted. That, Corky, is the only adjective. It seemed to me at that moment as though this bloke Joe had allowed me to peer into his soul; and it was like looking into a dark cellar on a moonless night.

'Here, I say –' I began, but he had gone.

How long I stood there I don't know. But, though it seemed a lifetime, it couldn't really have been long, for Joe didn't come back with the water ; and a faint hope began to steal over me that he had found another dog at one of the other cottages and was now being bitten to the bone. And then I heard footsteps.

I looked round. A cove was approaching.

'Is this your cottage?' I asked.

He was a rural-looking sort of cove, with a full beard and corduroy trousers with string tied round the knees. He came up and stood gazing at the car. Then he looked at me, and then at the car again.

'Ah?' he said. A bit deaf he seemed to be.

'Is this your cottage?'

'Ah.'

'We stopped here to get some water.'

He said he hadn't got a daughter. I said I never said he had.

'Water!'

'Ah.'

'But there was nobody in. So the man with me went down the road.'

'Ah,' said the cove.

'He was frightened by your dog.'

'Ah?'

'By your dog.'

'Buy my dog?'

'Yes.'

'You can have him for five shillings.'

Now, as I said before, Corky, you know me. You know that the reason why one of these days I shall make an enormous fortune and retire to spend the evening of my life in affluence is that I have that strange knack, which is given to so few men, of seizing opportunity when it calls. An ordinary mutton-headed fellow like you – I use the expression without any intention of offence – would, undoubtedly, at this juncture, have raised his voice a trifle and explained to this bearded cove that the intricacies of the English language had led him into a pardonable error.

But did I? No, I did not. For, even as he spoke an idea exploded in my brain like a bomb.

'Done!' I cried.

'Ah?'

'Here's your five bob. Whistle to the dog.'

He whistled, and the dog came running up. And, having massaged his ribs a while, I picked him up and shoved him inside the car and banged the door. And then I saw Joe the Lawyer plodding up the road slopping water from a big pail.

'I got it,' he said.

He went round and unscrewed the cap of the radiator and was starting to pour the water in, when the dog barked. Joe looked up, saw him, and dropped the pail – happily over his trousers.

'Who put that dog in the car?' he said.

'I did. I've bought him.'

'Then you can damn' well take him out.'

'But I'm bringing him home with me.'

'Not in my car.'

'Well, then,' I said, 'I'll sell him to you, and you can do what you like about him.'

He exhibited a good deal of impatience.

'I don't want to buy any dogs.'

'Nor did I, till you talked me into it. And I don't see what you have to complain of. This dog's alive. The one you sold me was dead.'

'What do you want for him?'

'A hundred pounds.'

He staggered somewhat. 'A hundred pounds?'

'That's all. Don't let the boys hear of it, or they'll think me silly.'

He spoke for a while.

'A hundred and fifty,' I said. 'The market's rising.'

'Now, listen, listen, listen!' said the bloke Joe.

'I'll tell you what I'll do,' I said. 'And this is a firm offer. One hundred pounds, if paid within the·minute. After that the price will go up.'

Corky, old horse, I have in my time extracted various sums of money from various people, and some of them have given cheerfully of their abundance and others have unbelted in a manner that you might call wry. But never in the whole of my career have I beheld a fellow human being cough up in quite the spirit that this bloke Joe the Lawyer did. He was a short-necked man, and there was one moment when I thought his blood-pressure was going to be too much for him. He turned a rather vivid shade of maroon, and his lips trembled as if he were praying. But in the end he dipped into the satchel and counted out the money.

'Thanks,' I said. 'Well, good-bye.'

He seemed to be waiting for something.

'Good-bye,' I said again. 'I don't want to hurt your feelings, laddie, but I must decline to continue in your society. We are nearing civilization now, and at any moment some friend of mine might see me in your car, which would jeopardize my social prestige. I will walk to the nearest railway station.'

'But, gawblimey –'

'Now what?'

'Aren't you going to take that dog out of the car?' he said, specifying what sort of a dog it was in his opinion. He also added a few remarks in a derogatory spirit about myself.

'Me?' I said. 'Why? I simply sold him to you. My part in the transaction is ended.'

'But how'm I going to get to Sandown if I can't get into my car?'

'Why do you want to get to Sandown?'

'If I'm late, it means hundreds of pounds out of my pocket.'

'Ah?' I said. 'Then, of course, you'll be willing to pay large sums to anyone who helps you to get there. I don't mind lending you a hand, if it's made worth my while. Removing dogs from cars is highly specialized work, and I'll have to insist on specialist's prices. Shall we say fifty quid for the job?'

He yammered a good deal, but I cut him short.

'Take it or leave it,' I said. 'It's all the same to me.'

Whereupon he produced the stipulated sum, and I opened the door and hauled the dog out. And Joe got in without a word and drove off. And that, Corky, is the last I have seen of the man. Nor do I wish to see him again. He is slippery, Corky. Not honest. A man to avoid.

I took the dog back to the cottage, and bellowed for the bearded cove.

'I sha'n't want this, after all,' I said. 'You can have him.'

'Ah?'

'I don't want this dog.'

'Ah! Well, you won't get your five shillings back.'

'God bless you, my merry peasant,' I said, slapping the cove genially abaft the collar-stud. 'Keep it with my blessing. I toss such sums to the birds.'

And he said 'Ah' and pushed off; and I toddled along to see if I could find a station. And I sang, Corky, old boy. Yes, laddie, your old friend, as he strode through those country lanes, trilled like a bally linnet.

Next day I looked in at the pawnbroker's, shelled out the requisite cash, recovered the brooch, and bunged it back into the bureau drawer.

And on the following morning my aunt turned up in a taxi and, having paid it its legal fare, backed me into the library and fixed me with a burning eye.

'Stanley,' she said.

'Say on, Aunt Julia,' I said.

'Stanley, Miss Vining tells me you refused to allow her to obtain my diamond brooch.'

'Quite right, Aunt Julia. She wanted to break open your bureau drawer, but I would have none of it.'

'Shall I tell you why?'

'It was because she had lost the key.'

'I am not referring to that, as you know very well. Shall I tell you why you would not let her break open the drawer?'

'Because I respected your property too much.'

'Indeed? I incline to think that it was because you knew the brooch was not there.'

'I don't understand.'

'I, on the contrary, did – the moment I received Miss Vining's letter. I saw it all. You pawned that brooch, Stanley! I know you so well.'

I drew myself up.

'You cannot know me very well, Aunt Julia,' I said coldly, 'if you think that of me. And allow me to say, while on this subject, that your suspicions are unworthy of an aunt.'

'Never mind what they're unworthy of. Open that drawer.'

'Break it open?'

'Break it open.'

'With a poker?'

'With anything you please. But opened it shall be, now, and in my presence.'

I gazed at her haughtily.

'Aunt Julia,' I said, 'let us get this thing straight. You wish me to take a poker or some other blunt instrument and smash that bureau?'

'I do.'

'Think well.'

'I have done all the thinking necessary.'

'So be it!' I said.

So I took the poker, and I set about that bureau as probably no bureau has ever been set about since carpentry first began. And there, gleaming in the ruins, was the brooch.

'Aunt Julia,' I said, 'a little trust, a little confidence, a little faith, and this might have been avoided.'

She gulped pretty freely.

'Stanley,' she said at last, 'I wronged you.'

'You did.'

'I – I – well, I'm sorry.'

'You may well be, Aunt Julia,' I said.

And, pursuing my advantage, I ground the woman into apologetic pulp beneath what practically amounted to an iron heel. And in that condition, Corky, she still remains. How long it will last one cannot say, but for the time being I am the blue-eyed boy and I have only to give utterance to my lightest whim to have her jump six feet to fulfil it. So, when I said I wanted to ask you to dinner here tonight, she practically smiled. Let us go into the library, old horse, and trifle with the cigars. They are some special ones I had sent up from that place in Piccadilly.

READ MORE IN PENGUIN

In every corner of the world, on every subject under the sun, Penguin represents quality and variety – the very best in publishing today.

For complete information about books available from Penguin – including Puffins, Penguin Classics and Arkana – and how to order them, write to us at the appropriate address below. Please note that for copyright reasons the selection of books varies from country to country.

In the United Kingdom: Please write to *Dept. EP, Penguin Books Ltd, Bath Road, Harmondsworth, West Drayton, Middlesex UB7 ODA*

In the United States: Please write to *Consumer Sales, Penguin USA, P.O. Box 999, Dept. 17109, Bergenfield, New Jersey 07621-0120.* VISA and MasterCard holders call 1-800-253-6476 to order Penguin titles

In Canada: Please write to *Penguin Books Canada Ltd, 10 Alcorn Avenue, Suite 300, Toronto, Ontario M4V 3B2*

In Australia: Please write to *Penguin Books Australia Ltd, P.O. Box 257, Ringwood, Victoria 3134*

In New Zealand: Please write to *Penguin Books (NZ) Ltd, Private Bag 102902, North Shore Mail Centre, Auckland 10*

In India: Please write to *Penguin Books India Pvt Ltd, 706 Eros Apartments, 56 Nehru Place, New Delhi 110 019*

In the Netherlands: Please write to *Penguin Books Netherlands bv, Postbus 3507, NL-1001 AH Amsterdam*

In Germany: Please write to *Penguin Books Deutschland GmbH, Metzlerstrasse 26, 60594 Frankfurt am Main*

In Spain: Please write to *Penguin Books S. A., Bravo Murillo 19, 1° B, 28015 Madrid*

In Italy: Please write to *Penguin Italia s.r.l., Via Felice Casati 20, I–20124 Milano*

In France: Please write to *Penguin France S. A., 17 rue Lejeune, F–31000 Toulouse*

In Japan: Please write to *Penguin Books Japan, Ishikiribashi Building, 2–5–4, Suido, Bunkyo-ku, Tokyo 112*

In Greece: Please write to *Penguin Hellas Ltd, Dimocritou 3, GR–106 71 Athens*

In South Africa: Please write to *Longman Penguin Southern Africa (Pty) Ltd, Private Bag X08, Bertsham 2013*

BY THE SAME AUTHOR

The Adventures of Sally

Pretty, impecunious Sally never dreamed a fortune could be a disadvantage until she became an heiress. Life in New York became complicated enough, but a trip to England seemed only to make matters worse.

Bachelors Anonymous

Their methods were borrowed from Alcoholics Anonymous: whenever a member felt the urge to take a woman out to dinner, he relied on the others to reason with him until the madness passed. But even the most hardened bachelor can occasionally fall by the wayside . . .

Cocktail Time

Uncle Fred, off the leash and into the Drones Club, cannot resist firing a well-aimed Brazil nut at the hat of Beefy Bastable. From this incident springs the injured barrister's mistaken exposé of the misdeeds of the younger generation, in a novel which causes only trouble for its hapless author.

also published

Big Money   Company for Henry
A Damsel in Distress   Do Butlers Burgle Banks?
Doctor Sally   French Leave   A Gentleman of Leisure
The Girl in Blue   Hot Water   If I Were You
The Indiscretions of Archie   Laughing Gas   The Little Nugget
The Luck of the Bodkins   Money in the Bank   Money for Nothing
Pearls, Girls and Monty Bodkin   Piccadilly Jim
Quick Service   Sam the Sudden   The Small Bachelor
Spring Fever   Summer Moonshine   Ukridge
Uncle Fred: An Omnibus   Uncle Dynamite
Uneasy Money   Young Men in Spats

BY THE SAME AUTHOR

LIFE AT BLANDINGS

'For Wodehouse there has been no fall of Man ... the gardens of Blandings Castle are the original gardens from which we are all exiled' – Evelyn Waugh

The tranquil idyll of life at Blandings is once again shattered by scrapes and skulduggery, mishaps and mix-ups in:

Galahad at Blandings

A major mix-up at the Castle, in which Gally introduces yet another impostor to Lord Emsworth's residence, and the Empress of Blandings somehow gets drunk in her sty.

Heavy Weather

Forced to seek alternative employment when his editorials for *Tiny Tots* magazine become too adult, Monty Bodkin has been engaged as Lord Emsworth's personal secretary.

also published

Full Moon
Pigs Have Wings
Something Fresh
Sunset at Blandings
A Pelican at Blandings
Service with a Smile
Summer Lightning
Uncle Fred in the Springtime

and the omnibus editions

Life at Blandings
Lord Emsworth Acts for the Best
Imperial Blandings

BY THE SAME AUTHOR

SHORT STORIES BY P. G. WODEHOUSE

Blandings Castle

'A collection of short snorts between the solid orgies' was how P. G. Wodehouse regarded these stories, which range from the Blandings of Lord Emsworth to the Hollywood of the Mulliners.

Eggs, Beans and Crumpets

Dine out on this feast of stories. They include the antics of Bingo Little, as told in the haven of the Drones Club, further episodes from the life of Ukridge and, of course, the romantic encounters of Mr Mulliner's young relatives.

The Man with Two Left Feet

Twelve vintage cases of decent chaps entangled in the snares of love, and helped or hindered by dogs, cats and even the incoming tide.

The Gold Bat and Other School Stories
The Pothunters and Other School Stories

Wodehouse won the first of his many laurels with these school stories where, in the daily round of prefects, fags, dorms and cricket, he creates a gloriously absurd and immortal world which never palls.

and

The Man Upstairs and Other Stories

The Mike and Psmith Books
Mike at Wrykyn   Mike and Psmith
Leave it to Psmith   Psmith in the City   Psmith, Journalist

and the omnibus
The World of Psmith

and

Wodehouse on Wodehouse
Yours, Plum